Praise for Abida

"In addition to writing short stories and novels, Abidah is nationally renowned as a poet who writes strong religious verse. The flavor of her poetic language has greatly influenced her fiction. It is not going too far to say that she is one of the best novelists in Indonesia today—her novels could even be considered to be the height of Islamic literature."

—*Harian Republika*

"Abidah is noted as a female poet in the Sufi tradition who explores aesthetic experience and the freedom of religious humanism. She expresses the awareness of love for The Creator, the search for conscience, empathy for humanity, faith, and honesty."

—*Koran Sindo*

Nirzona

Nirzona
A Love Story

ABIDAH EL KHALIEQY
TRANSLATED BY ANNIE TUCKER

amazoncrossing

Previously published as *Nirzona* by LKiS in Indonesia in 2008. Translated from the Indonesian by Annie Tucker. First published in English by AmazonCrossing in 2016.

Published by AmazonCrossing, Seattle

www.apub.com

Amazon, the Amazon logo, and AmazonCrossing are trademarks of Amazon.com, Inc., or its affiliates.

ISBN-13: 9781503938366
ISBN-10: 1503938360

Cover design by Shasti O'Leary Soudant

Printed in the United States of America

Chapter 1:
Sulamtaque

Dead of night. The dim light of a five-watt crescent moon. Labored breathing. April Fools' Day coming in with the chill. No sound except the horn of a military truck, like a dragon's blood-spewing cough. Red. Sidan pulled his jacket tighter, bowing his head against the underlying stillness. Cringing. A few more steps and he stopped in front of the food stall. Before sitting down on a chair, he looked up. He saw a sky the color of soot, and its darkness scattered down like ash falling across his soul, penetrating to the innermost core.

The ticktock of his heartbeat gave off a wary rhythm. This was the wilderness. You could be finished off with just one pounce from behind. The only law here was the law of the jungle, a judge's gavel frail in comparison.

How old are you? How good are you at dodging fate? And as for fate, everything comes down to the tip of a bullet.

Sidan was melancholy. He was unable to rouse any hope in this gray village and was dreaming of a grieving city that had somehow been carried away across the sky, snatched up by a vulture with a thousand talons.

"A hot tea, please."

"Sweet, warm filtered tea, as clear and brown as a pair of eyes peeking out from behind a burka?"

"Exactly! And *burukiek* curry if you've got any."

"*Burukiek* only fly over Seulawah Mountain. Something else?"

"How about *cane Punjab*?"

"Ah, *paratha* bread . . . your taste never changes. Usually young kids like to experiment."

Experiment? Like an experiment in the field of nuclear technology or genetic engineering? Or like experimenting with amateur terrorism right under Mother's nose and then raping her like a gang of soldiers? Or like a thought experiment about a land above the boundless clouds and wind, about an independent country, complete and whole, the owner of a peaceful body and soul, its own essence and nature, its past and its future?

Words with double meanings, like the word that had just slid out of the old man's mouth, made Sidan uncomfortable.

He stammered out his order. "I'd like to experime—*burukiek*—eh, *cane*."

Two soldiers, wearing camouflage and buzz cuts, passed by on Sidan's left and then sat right across from him, staring him down with cagey smiles. For a moment Sidan was unnerved, but not for long. By now he was good at telling when two black dots didn't have much brain behind them, when the creatures were really nothing but claws, like the lobsters in the Simeulue Sea. He knew how to outsmart them—Sidan just had to smile back calmly and hold his ground.

"You new here?" asked the first buzz cut, pointing right at Sidan's nose, like a commander suspicious of his men.

"No, I've been here for a long time. Quite a long time, in fact," Sidan said, smiling widely, equally cryptic.

"First time I've seen you," the second buzz cut chimed in.

"Oh! Him, he's a regular customer, has been for a long time, Sergeant. Maybe this is your first visit here? It seems that this is the first time I've seen you," the old man interjected.

He balled up some dough and then pressed it out, widening and flattening it into a disc, swung it aloft like a fisherman's net, folded it into four, and then put it onto the fire. The smell of cooking *paratha* bread spread. Mmm!

What did this guy even mean, asking about new people and old people? This is our country. You all come with your weapons and shoot us, bang on our doors in the middle of the night and drag away our fathers, treat our mothers rudely and leer at our younger sisters. It's you all who come and go in waves, seeking your fortune on our land full of natural gas and oil reserves and forests and glittering gold and then divvying up the profits.

It's you all who just arrived, learning how to pull your triggers in Serambi Makkah. We call it Banda Aceh Serambi Makkah, or Mecca's Veranda, because it is a holy place, the place where Islam first arrived in Indonesia, the point of the archipelago closest to Mecca, and even today, the point of departure for pilgrims leaving on the hajj. *But you all come into our mosques on Friday covering your heads with the* meukeutop, *carrying your holy books and prayer rugs with your revolvers still at your hip. We go to the mosque then too, supplicating with reverent spirits. And you? You start sniffing during the* Takbir *recitation that God is great, wondering which one of us could possibly be eliminated. You bow down while feeling for your weapon, thinking who might be gotten rid of. You prostrate yourselves, all the while demeaning us and our dignity. At the moment of* tahiyat, *the prayer of greeting, it is well understood that your trigger finger itches to shoot us once the sermon is finished.*

"Where are you from?"

"Oh, I live in the barracks, keeping the peace."

"I mean before the tsunami."

"A house in a village. Two hundred meters from the Malacca Strait."

"How many of your relatives are living in the barracks?"

Such an interrogation! Sidan was nearly fed up. But he had the patience to deal with a mere high school graduate—what's more, one who liked to put on airs like this.

"It's just me. There are no others. I'm by myself."

"You're not lonely?"

"I was very lonely. So I went looking for friends. The barracks are close to one another and we have established a brotherhood there—because in fact we truly are brothers."

Sidan began to gaze eagerly at the *cane Punjab*, piping hot and steaming on a transparent glass plate, as enticing as a lovesick angel. One gulp of warm, sweet tea was enough to whet his appetite for that savory, delicious treat, a small plate of *canai* bread with a bowl of duck curry. The pleasure of a feast enjoyed in a peaceful place is like the singing eyes of a virgin who is punch-drunk with love. This was a night full of contrasts, of darkness and brightness, full of challenges.

"Pardon me, but I'll eat first. You arrived after me."

"It's fine. Go ahead. I'll have white rice with fried duck, please—is there any?"

"Of course. And you, Sergeant? Would you like duck as well?"

"Just *bueluekat* sticky rice and strong coffee."

With a casual expression, Sidan hid his smile of victory at the bottom of a cave that had been silent for a century. Only this food stall, Sulamtaque, made dreams a reality and turned the world upside down; winners and losers sat beside each other here, and whoever came first was the first to enjoy its delights. Whether you were a deer general like in the trickster legend—small and clever—or a sergeant major, if you came later, you were invited to wait your turn. The old-man proprietor was the judge, deciding who won and who lost.

Sulamtaque was peaceful and quiet, even though it wasn't far from the military headquarters. The food stall had been built after the tsunami, and the name stamped on the blue banner hanging out front came from the words *suara-dalam-tenggorok*, which meant a sound in your throat, a sound of knotted pain. And who was in pain?

This entire land is a giant sick ward where thousands of patients are waiting for the hands of a doctor who is stuffed to the gills after a big meal and dozing off in a rocking chair. We have suffered injury on top of injury. Our bodies are battered and bruised. Our spirits are laid out flat, dying. It's strange how well the doctors can sleep, gently rocked by dreams day and night.

"Shit!" Sidan cried out, jumping up from his chair, lost in thought, as if walking and talking in his sleep.

The first sergeant was startled. The duck meat caught at the base of his throat—it didn't go down but it didn't come back out either. It was lodged right in the middle of his windpipe. His buddy, the *bueluekat* eater, immediately struck the nape of his neck and the duck went flying out in a choked gasp. *Ack, ack, ack!* The partially chewed meat landed right on Polem's chest just as he arrived at the food stall.

"Hey! What the hell is this? You're spitting on me?"

"Sorry, I didn't do it on purpose. I didn't mean to spit on you, it's just that he almost killed me! What are you doing, shouting out 'shit'?" Sergeant One demanded, pointing right at Sidan's face.

"Wait, no—"

"Don't bother coming up with excuses! If you feel like cursing at a soldier, then you can do it at headquarters tomorrow. Or we can head over there right now if you want!"

"Forgive me! I was saying that *this* guy was shit, not you." Sidan said, pointing at Polem's meat-smeared chest.

Polem's eyes bugged out and Sidan stared back at him with two black dots that were sharp with warning and insinuation. Polem immediately understood and instead of resisting, he swiftly shifted his role like an amateur actor.

"So, even here you curse me? Even after our last fight, you *still* haven't had enough?"

"Why else do you keep following me, if not to continue what we started?" Sidan replied, improvising the sophisticated scene.

The old man stepped in. "That's enough, you kids. This fight ends here. Shake hands and apologize to one another. No matter how good a quarrel is, a handshake is truly a thing of beauty."

The two sergeants blinked, completely fooled. Sidan's bitter laughter echoed silently, smoothing out the scars on his heart. *One–nothing*, he thought. That's how easy it was to outwit them. He tapped his index finger on the table. Gotcha!

"Alright, then! Sit down. Let's eat together. Please forgive both of us, old man."

The two friends, Sidan and Polem, sat facing the two sergeants. Nauseated. Night wind sighed mischievously. Moonlight shimmered. Then a deafening *brumm . . . ppssstt!* shred everyone's ears as the air brakes of the army trucks shook the dark forest. In its wake, an even deeper silence settled over the miserable setting.

"Asei paleih!" Sidan once again spontaneously exclaimed in distress, startling even himself.

The two dumbfounded sergeants didn't understand what he had said. Maybe they were Javanese or Sundanese, or maybe they were from Sumatra and didn't understand Acehnese. They could only guess from his tone—his loud voice and his face contorted with pure hate—that surely it must have been an insult or a curse.

"What did you say?" demanded Sergeant One.

Sidan went mute and so did Polem. The old man stayed mum. The tense silence reached out and snatched up all their feelings, yoking them together and translating them into just one word: pain! Even the crickets forgot to sing. Even the stray cats, who usually knew no shame with their howling, fell silent. It was as if they were waiting out one of the aftershocks that often came on nights like this. But whether he wanted to or not, Sidan finally had to open his mouth—if something bad was bound to happen, it was better to start a fire than to slowly get choked to death by a boa constrictor.

"I said '*asei paleih*.'"

"What does that mean?"

"Mangy dog."

"Who's a dog?"

"A dog is a dog. There are lots of them roaming around by the barracks, in the villages, at the street corners, and in the crossroads. They sniff and they howl."

"Yeah, I get it. But *who* were you calling a dog?"

"I just told you, I was calling a dog a dog."

Sergeant One whispered into Sergeant Two's ear and then they both nodded their heads. Whispered some more and nodded some more. They fingered the butts of their guns at their hips. Sidan sputtered. Polem trembled. The old man went limp and almost fainted. An owl hooted on a branch.

"So a dog is a dog? Has anyone ever told you that in fact *you* were the dog?"

"Yes, you just did," Sidan said.

Under the table, Polem punched his friend's knee. The old man anxiously massaged his chest. A raven croaked on top of a mango tree. Then a few more faces appeared at the food stall. They were members of Sidan's performance troupe—Nangi, Sawang, Leubei, and Sani. If there was a fight, two against six wouldn't be manly, but Polem calmed down a bit, while Sidan kept cool, waiting for whatever was going to happen next.

"The way you are talking, you sound pretty sure of yourself."

"I tell it like it is," Sidan said.

"Well, if that's the case, then show me where all these dogs are roaming around."

Sidan said nothing. Of course, those dogs were just an image Sidan had of the figures who barked and sniffed at corpses, who howled at night frightening babies and making them cry as their trembling mothers pressed against the flimsy wooden walls of the barracks and their fathers and sons escaped, going as far away as they could get—climbing mountains, creeping into the dark forest, not even hoping to ever see their friends again. They hid for days, for weeks, for months, for years, without enough food or clothing, keeping their distance from those sniffing dogs with bullets for eyes and weapons for cocks. They disappeared, swallowed by the jungle wilderness, holing up perched on cliffs. They became *orang gunung*, mountain men, separatist rebels, anxiously shouldering rifles far from their families and the rest of humankind, far from peace and happiness. They became a people who were purifying themselves from all human cravings with no end to their sacrifice in sight. They wandered in the mountains, climbing ever higher and getting ever closer to the embrace of the Almighty.

"Answer me!"

"They are clearly visible wherever they are roaming about. There's no way you haven't seen them."

"I've never seen one."

"Are you sure? You're not just saying that?"

The two sergeants' faces turned scarlet, seething. Blood rushed to their heads. Their fists pounded the tabletop. *Bam!* Standing up straight, the first sergeant leveled his gun at Sidan's forehead.

"Hey, you ugly longhair!" snorted the sergeant. "Don't even think about disrespecting us!"

As he spoke he sputtered out hot spit, which stung Sidan's face. Sidan blew up.

"Hey, you mangy dog! Don't you even think about trying to conquer our land!"

Sidan pointed threateningly back at the soldier's face, his finger landing right in the middle of those two black dots that bugged out, indignant at the unexpected defiance. Just as soon as Sidan's words were out of his mouth, the other sergeant whipped out his AK-47, pointing it right at Sidan's chest.

The night became a blue haze. The mood darkened. The fireflies stopped dancing. A mouse squeaked, stranded and looking for a place to hide. But right then, a small three-point earthquake rattled them. *Boom!*

Sidan shouted out in pain as the soldiers grabbed him and held him down. They lunged at his chest, pounding him, as if they were afraid he would resist.

Overcome with panic and confusion and not knowing what he should do, the old man fainted even before Sidan fell, smeared with red.

Polem lifted his friend, and together the five members of the performance troupe carried him back to the wretched barracks, through the doorway with its sign that read "Papa's House." At first, silence blanketed all the pain, but it was soon broken by sobs and the arriving neighbors. Sidan was unconscious.

Practiced hands administered medicine, sincere souls enveloped him in rising prayer. Together they gazed upward to the heavens to ask for his recovery. With grief-stricken tears and quivering lips, they recited words of supplication to the All Compassionate, the Almighty, and the All Knowing. Fruits were sent from Suak Seumaseh village, most of which had been destroyed in the tsunami. There were cookies left over from an aid package sent by a television station and some warm beef kebabs from an old Turkish relative.

The people exchanged glances. Here everything was understood—there might still be looming questions, but everything was quickly understood. Because here everything was like a cycle—it had all happened before and for the same reasons. Death by death, loss by loss, everything was easily understood, but at the same time so difficult to truly comprehend. They were caught between terror and death, between weapons and disaster, actual earthquakes and the earthquakes of rumbling cannons. Their misfortunes overlapped, coming one after another in quick succession.

So here people used the language of silence to communicate. Words had already lost their meaning—only weapons had power. Silence was a blessing sent from the All Powerful to fight those in control. The people were silent amidst the thunder in their chests. They were silent amidst smarting wounds. They were silent, bearing all the scars on their bodies and all the thrashing of their souls. They were experts at maintaining a truly charged and resounding silence.

"Oh, oooh, Allah . . . I'm thirsty!"

Polem hurried with a glass of cool water as all the eyes around Sidan cooled down with smiles of joy. He was offered food and fruits, but Sidan wanted his phone.

"My cell, Lem. Help me! Where's my phone?"

"Eat this first," Polem urged.

"You know I'm full. I just want to text her and get this off my chest . . . Oof . . . Where's my phone?"

Lying on a pillow donated by the World Health Organization, disregarding the pain that reigned over his body like a king, Sidan began to type on his keypad with trembling fingers.

Sidan: My left chest is burning with a hot stabbing pain, like I'm being gored by wooden beams and iron rods. Boiling with sweat, bitterness in my throat, I'm gasping for breath. Maybe I caught the flu . . . but it's nothing to worry about!

Firdaus: Am I reading literal or metaphorical words?

The response made Sidan scratch his head. He replied:

Sidan: Every syllable is set on fire and they all
melt together until they share one meaning.
There is no literal and there is no
metaphorical, eternity has exhausted fact
and fiction. Here, everything is united for
all time. Ow! This sucks! My chest is on
fire!

Firdaus: Oh Gentle One! Oh All Forgiving One!
Send an abundance of peace, a renewed
heart and mind. You are the Keeper of
All and I entrust Sidan to Your Abode of
Tranquility. Amen.

Sidan: I am grateful for the caring souls who came
to greet me and handled me with kindness.
I feel that we are one.

He sent the final message, but it didn't go through. How could
it still be pending? His phone connection was working fine. Had she
turned off her phone? What's up, Firdaus? Sidan went limp, languish-
ing, feeling alone and abandoned. He wanted a friend, but not Polem
or Sawang or Sani. He yearned for some tenderness amidst the burning
coals. He needed a little heaven in the middle of this big pit of hell. He
had hoped Firdaus would sing him one of her love ballads, reach out
her gentle hands to caress his spirit. But where did you go, Firda? You
have left me when I am wounded like this? You, who more than anyone
knows how I feel? Firda. Oh, Firda.

Archangel Michael laughed to hear Sidan's moans and immediately
reported back to God on his throne.

"He's suffering so much, isn't he, Lord?"

"Yes, I can see that, Michael. What are you waiting for? Give him what he wants!"

Firdaus: I will always remember your name in my
prayers. Be patient and try to stay
upright and strong. The wide expanse is
not enough to separate us. We are still
united. My soul is with you.

"Ha! Then which of the favors of your Lord would you deny?" Sidan cried out.

He forgot how many people were sitting around him. His friends and neighbors had not yet moved to go, still surrounding him with their hearts pounding. Sidan came back to his senses, and brought his phone to his lips as if it were a fragrant rose blossom. Then his eyes scrutinized every single word on the screen. Oh, Firda. My Firdaus!

Sidan: If only it wasn't just your soul! I also
want your alabaster fingers to comb through
the tangles in my hair, to put out the
embers burning in my chest.

Firdaus: I want that too. But circumstances will it
otherwise. Sleep and get plenty of rest.
We will meet in dreams.

Sidan: Yes. I really, really want that. But it's
not circumstances but weapons that will
it otherwise, so that even our dreams are
censored. Is there any garden left for
longing, Firda?

Firdaus: A   garden   of   cell   signals   that   you
            keep sending me. An ocean of longing,
            turbulent with waves. If I look out into
            the distance, the wide expanse of blue
            welcomes our poetry. Just this is already
            heaven enough for me.

Sidan sighed.

Yes. Just this is already heaven.

You are my heaven, Firdaus. A heaven that makes my body and soul convulse in agony. The heaven of a beautiful fast that never ends. A heaven of love so high above me that I can never reach it. I walk so far and wait so long, but I'm not even sure what I am waiting for. To wait is to imagine something that hasn't yet happened. So forgive me! Maybe my imagination is running too wild. Maybe I take you too boldly in my fantasies. I would like to carry you away, go anywhere with you, wander in a jungle of dreams.

Do you know, Firdaus? Every morning I have to take a bath to cleanse myself of impure thoughts after coming home from heaven, searching for you, who are wild and satin. I meet seventy-two virgins and hand out copies of The Ultimate Desire *by Mathori A. Elwa. Then I wake suddenly and plummet. Then I ask, what is a great height for, if above it there is nothing but emptiness and below it there is only downfall? So I prefer to play in a low valley that is comfortable and safe—not elevated, not lost in an illusion, but prostrating myself, with my head on the level of feet and dust.*

It's true what you say. Just this is already heaven enough for me.

Sidan smiled to himself. He was like the legendary lovesick Majnun, tired from a night's journey wandering across the wilderness, reciting love poems and obsessively thinking of nothing but his beloved Layla, whom he could never have. Sidan's neighbors understood and quickly took their leave. Guard your health, don't forget to take your medicine, and, most importantly, watch yourself. We only appear to be defeated. Solitary. Orphans. With no mother or father. Alone. But it's better to temporarily lose in the moment in order to ultimately win than to give in to your passion and unleash your hatred. Know who we are and who they are. That is the advice of our wise brothers. Sidan nodded politely.

Then he slipped back out of consciousness, attempting to flee into the heaven of dreams, but he was intercepted by the enemy. With bulging eyes and cudgel fists, they once again tortured Sidan with all their might.

"You think you are the only one who is civilized?" they demanded, with clenched fists and roaring rifles.

"You think you are the only one who has power? You think you are the only one who can destroy the nation? If I were a legislator or a cleric, I would fatwa you all, condemn you to an excruciating death in the abyss!"

Sidan was in agony, but his mouth kept moving, answering their challenges with curses.

"It seems like you'd rather die than live!" they bellowed.

They choked Sidan and kicked his stomach dozens of times. Heartburn and nausea. Fat, rough fingers squeezed his guts, twisting them left and right. It felt like the earth was shaking, but Sidan held on.

"You all think you own death! You steal what rightfully belongs to God and you think you've won? You are nothing but heartless killing machines!"

"Shut up or we'll send you to hell!"

They yanked out his eyeballs and bit off his earlobes, and, still not satisfied, they grabbed fistfuls of his hair and slammed his head against a telephone pole, again and again. Blood poured out. The main road turned red. Like Sarajevo.

"Hell does not deign to receive me. But it roars with laughter to swallow you whole, all of you, greedily, leaving no trace! You filthy sinners!"

A ruthless horde of them smothered Sidan's mouth until he fainted. He tried to get back up and kept on trying, but he couldn't. The whole world went dark. There were only wasps buzzing, piercing his eardrums. Still Sidan held on, moaning and moaning without cease until he broke through the veil of his dreams.

"*Astaghfirullah*, Allah forgive me. They keep coming, even in my dreams!" he hoarsely lamented.

He reached for his phone and texted Firdaus.

Sidan: They came again to attack me in my dreams. Like the Dutch, they stand arrogantly on the corner with their legs spread and their arms folded, they intercept me by the roadside. Who do these executioners pray to, Firda?

He didn't care that time had quietly passed and it was now after two o'clock in the morning. He didn't care that rain was pouring down out in the yard. He didn't care about the gaping wounds in his chest. What did he care if the electricity went out? There was nothing to see but the hands of ghosts lining up to grab his throat, fighting over it in their thirst to suck his blood. Wanting nothing but blood and blood, like Dracula waking up from a thousand years of immortal sleep. Thirsty and thirstyyy! Never satisfied. So Sidan didn't care. The important thing was that everything had to be reported back. This entire story had to be told so that Firdaus could feel that she was still close to him.

Firdaus: That's a hallucination. Stay calm, Sidan! You will keep on having nightmares if you don't stay calm. Okay, so let's get ready for bed with some jokes and cheerful conversation.

Sidan: Thank you. It's just that suddenly I felt
all alone. A night like this is so quiet.
No one can heal these wounds except you,
Firda, nothing but the caress of your spirit
and loving care will do. Your prayers help
me awaken and arise again. But forgive me,
that so early in the morning I am squawking
at you like a seagull.

Firdaus: Oh, my precious seagull from across the
ocean! Every second of my life belongs
to you. But are you still fasting? Still
forbidding yourself to come see me?

Sidan: Oh, Firda . . . this fast seems to be never-
ending. I so want to see you, but I don't
know when I can come. When will the clock
strike to announce our reunion on the holy
plain of Arafat, like Adam and Eve? Or
where shall we meet, Firda?

Firdaus: In the land above the clouds and wind,
my love . . . at the zero hour, when
everything begins, the starting point of
an impossible journey.

Impossible? How absurd is it if a wish comes true? Life is a field of
ongoing holy battle, and we will plow it until death comes to ambush
us. But whatever the case, Firda, we keep moving forward. From the
nadir toward the culmination in the plain of Arafat, where Adam and
Eve reunited after being cast from Eden, and where the best lovers drink
from the purest spring, an ocean of love. I would travel to the ends of

the earth in order to inhale your aroma, to stand at your altar and with my quivering lips, kiss your Black Stone, your holy essence, to calm this magma exploding inside my chest.

Then, *knock knock!*

A knock on the door this early in the morning? At Papa's House, which is little more than a muddy ruin? This village is an archive of bad dreams for me—for thirty years I was suffocated by war, deceived by the treacherous. They have been trying to kill me ever since I was in the womb, but they can't kill me. What, are there some remaining jewels that you want to steal? Are there untouched coffers of treasure that have lured you here? Even with my chest injured like this, please launch another attack if you haven't yet had enough of brutalizing me!

"*Salamu'alaikum!* I'm sorry, Dan! But if you can get up, open the door!"

Sidan recognized Polem's voice, his closest friend and his neighbor from the barracks next door, also left an orphan after the sea touched the land. Staggering through the pain, Sidan moved toward the door. As soon as he opened it, Polem collapsed inside as if there were a ghost at his heels.

"What are you doing up at two in the morning?"

"It's your phone—silence it unless you want them to get even more suspicious! A truck just arrived at the post and its nose immediately sniffed out the sound of your ring!" Polem whispered frantically.

"Oh really? Well, they always come and they keep coming, hunting me, whether I am awake or asleep. I want nothing more than to plug my nose so that I don't have to smell those foul worms anymore. I need to seek refuge in heaven, and you know where my heaven is."

"I know. But this time, your heaven will harvest hell. So cut it out, just for tonight."

"No, tonight is actually the ultimate heaven. She is such an angel that she makes me forget that I was just plunged into hell. Oh, Lem, do you know the taste of pure honey, born from the essence of a rose?"

"You're delirious! You live your whole life in a delirium. Look, Dan! Look at this barracks that is your 'palace.' We are surrounded by great suffering, grievous wounds. We are living in a coma."

"If so, then what's wrong with rising up to heaven, when compared to this coma?"

"It's definitely wrong if the stairs taking you up there are suddenly demolished by soldiers. You could fall and bang your head, fall down into the depths of hell! And only then will you feel the pain!"

Polem was really angry, and Sidan realized the danger. Even though he wasn't fully willing to emerge from heaven yet, and his soul was still adrift in its serenity, as he eased back into bed he placed his phone on the pillow beside him. Who knows, maybe his angel didn't even need the phone to come stroke his hair and caress his soul with love songs. Ah yes . . . Peace until dawn!

This is my country. Its eyes are shrouded in melancholy. Every breath that comes out of its body smells like ash. And how could it be otherwise? It's not just the speeches and Friday sermons—even our dreams are censored, so of course our thoughts have reached a dead end. But what about our fantasies? Everything must proceed according to the will of those in power, those with coercive hands. Even ants are forced to confess that they are separatists. Indeed, many "ants" live in the mountains, cutting themselves off from their friends in the fields and rice paddies. The ants rise to become elite rebels; that's a choice, and maybe also a necessity for survival, but most certainly a human right. People must have the right to determine the course of their own lives, whatever country they live in. Whether they want to be in the valley, on the mountainside, or atop a mountain range, who has the right to forbid them?

But all the background noise of military action has become a tool of oppression—it keeps ringing in our ears, keeping us forever on edge and polluting our daily lives. Ask the women how much time they spend trembling after hearing the sound of an approaching military truck. Ask the innocent little babies about the long river of tears they cry, caught in waves of catastrophe. The young men have given up—when they try to move forward they are struck, when they retreat they are struck. But don't ask how many young girls have been traumatized by the hooligans who forced them to have sex at gunpoint.

This is my country. For sixty years deceived by a famous magician. Even before the Javanized regime took power, we had already fallen for the ruse of those agitator crybabies who shed crocodile tears and refused to eat their breakfasts until they were given Seulawah Mountain. Their cries were so piteous and pleading that our mothers were willing to give up their fortunes, donating them to a giant bird, big brother Garuda. Then came the time when the leaders went wild. Even though they like to go to Istiqlal Mosque in Jakarta for Friday prayers, they are not devout in worship; they are more like a Brutus who likes to reap the rewards but never helps to sow. They dredge our land until it is full of sinkholes, leaving us nothing but dregs. We die and are swallowed up by earthquakes while they saunter around talking about prosperity and receiving commendations from the United Nations.

That is how extraordinary the luster of power is in the hands of these Pinocchios, and the liars' noses are so long they stretch out like a highway built by bosses and their minions. We see sweat on their foreheads, their thrones towering on top of the hill. The pity is we are only left with misery, abandoned out on the far end of the country where they throw out their junk. Their powerful hand is like Pharaoh. Like Baal.

Then Sidan vomited.

"Now, there you go," Polem exclaimed happily. "Throwing up is much better than climbing up to heaven!"

"Why is that?"

"If you throw up, they will think you're contacting the doctor because you have dengue fever."

"Dengue fever, my ass! I'm feverish with longing. But I threw up because I am super disgusted with their behavior. It's true what you say—on a night like this it seems like the best thing to do is vomit as much as possible," Sidan said as he laughed and retched again.

"And now you are laughing too?"

"Should I be crying?"

Hahaha . . . pssst! Don't you hear the crow, cawing out its song in the orange jasmine tree? Don't you realize how close the soldiers' guard post is to the barracks? The blue dawn is coming, but here there is no dawn. There's no more dazzling orange sunrise. Either dawn has already come and gone, or it is staying far away in the jungle, buried in lies. There is only dusk here. Everything has the face of afternoon: dark and dim. Children play with falling leaves. Lam yakunish-shubhi huna. Goh shuboh hino. *In Arabic, or Acehnese, or however you want to say it, there's no more dawn here.*

There is no sun rising on the coast. It must have been defeated. We need a conqueror, a great leader, to change our history. But—and there is always a but—here there is no Messiah. There is no long-awaited Imam Mahdi, no redeemer of Islam who will rule before Judgment Day and rid the world of evil. Here we are just sitting, waiting our turn, which is not as He has commanded it. We are in the middle of a holy pilgrimage. If I look up, there is heaven, love, and death. Morning is indeed beautiful and bright for other people, but I have tried for four months, and I haven't been able to feel that way.

Another ring resounded throughout the barracks. Who comes to break the silence? Sidan measured his breathing, looking left and right.

"There's no one else except us two and your phone that keeps chirping. I told you to turn it off," Polem fretted.

"My angel is voicing her longing."

"Turn it off! Care a little bit about your life, brother!"

"My body is ready to collapse, but it's my natural disposition to reply to greetings. It's *fardhu ain*, my personal spiritual obligation."

"You're full of it! What do you mean *fardhu ain*? Staying alive is *fardhu ain*; responding to a greeting is *fardhu kifayah*, it's a communal obligation! It doesn't always have to be you who is fulfilling it."

"Shh! Just let me embrace my rose blossom first."

"You're just like Majnun."

"Yes, I am. Majnun was prepared to die in Layla's lap."

Lovesick, Sidan reached for his phone and began to read the text message. His eyes widened in disbelief at the violent words that he saw.

Unknown: *Hey, you ugly filthy longhair! You'll have to comb your hair a thousand times if you want to be more like us—neat and sharp and always strategic!*

Who could be so crazy this early in the morning? Sidan felt like his chest was exploding. He imagined those two bug-eyed sergeants ramming his guts with the butt of their weapons in the dim Sulamtaque light. It couldn't be anyone else—they had to be the ones texting him from that blocked number. But their faces were not a secret to him, and their actions showed their hand, no matter how they tried to cover it up. Polem saw Sidan grow anxious and grew even more worried himself.

"Lem, it's not just my body and dreams—now they have also stolen my phone number. What do you have to say?"

"I've got nothing to say. Turn off your phone and go to sleep. That would be safer."

"In whose opinion?" Sidan said. "You can sleep here if you want. You can also call Sawang, Sani, and the others."

"Just admit that finally you are afraid too, friend."

"You're wrong. I just want you all as witnesses in case something happens to me."

"You think it will go that far?"

"Read this crazy text. They think they can threaten me. They don't know that the royal blood of Aceh flows in my veins. My ancestors, bright people from Serambi, built this land, a civilized country. But soldiers, those goddamn smiling thugs, completely flattened it."

"Aye, aye, Commander! I'm ready to carry out my duty."

"Come, call your friends to *sahur*, to eat their last satisfying meal before we begin a fast that will never end."

"Roger! I will run and chase after your dreams, Commander!"

"You're all talk."

"Roger! I . . ."

"'The thing is, I'm afraid of the dark night, Commander!'" Sidan taunted his friend before pushing him out the door.

Polem was immediately drenched in cold sweat. His legs, which usually stepped on the ground firm and strong, now wobbled. When his eyes came to rest on the soldiers' guardhouse that was only a few yards from the barracks, his entire body shook. As soon as he saw a figure coming out of the guards' shack, Polem darted back inside and collided with Sidan's wounded chest.

"*Ilahi Rabbi,*" Sidan swore. "You have created this sissy creature before my eyes. Only You know all the secrets of creation."

"Forgive me, that was an accident, but they came outside. I hope they didn't see me!"

"I hope they did."

"Don't joke around. I've been having a bad sense of foreboding."

"Your fearful premonitions don't live up to your name, *Commander!*"

The sound of Sidan's phone startled them both. Sidan froze, wondering whether this next message would be the justification for Polem's feeling of foreboding.

"It must be them again," Polem wailed. "We're dead men!"

Firdaus: You're not answering, hon? Well, thank God you can rest some more without being captured by the bad guys. So sleep, folded in the arms of a Firdaus symphony, and may your blood flow toward the sea of health. I will say the bedtime prayer:

Oh Allah, I die with your name and I am born with your name. Bye!

"Ah, Lem. My angel is going beddie-bye. She's leaving me again, going up to heaven."

Sidan: Sleep has not touched me yet, Firda. There are too many rainbow mosquitoes here. So sleep, let me man the security post, the nights of fasting until Judgment Day, haha. I'll sing you an Acehnese lullaby, dodaidi . . .

Without another look at Polem, Sidan wrapped himself in a blanket donated by the WHO, collapsed beside the phone that was still glowing, and closed his eyes. Firdaus was his life, a spirit living in an intangible, faraway realm, one that he had not yet been able to go retrieve. Maybe tomorrow they would meet, but still only as two cell phone signals, dancing together while the world was sleeping peacefully. That was when Sidan's spirit came back to life, reignited by his soulmate in the heaven of Yogyakarta. How could he turn off his phone?

He was already so weary. If that blocked number appeared again, all he had to do was delete it with one press of a finger, and it would be done—he would have wiped away the rancid black dust so that it would scatter and fall back into the jet-black mud. But what about his Eve? If even one message from her slipped through his fingers, Sidan would suffer a supreme loss.

She is the fragrance that I must inhale. She is the jasmine flower that I must pluck from the Garden of Eden. She is the morning star that lights the way of my dark path. She is the blue flame that stokes the furnace of my life.

Sidan's thoughts began to dive underneath the sea of his warm blanket, swimming to and fro, approaching the shells of memory buried in the deep. Yogya was a passionate memory that returned every week, woven into the golden braid of his longing. It ripped through him, pounded in his chest, made his body and soul convulse. Because there had been a particular kind of clarity to those sane days when he saw the sun in Firdaus's eyes, warm and penetrating into the very marrow of his bones. But all that sanity had been just one rush of breath. One blink of an eye.

Meanwhile the crazy days, when the memories of the past became stab wounds that riddled his body, were days made up of a quintal of suffering, a bathtub of tears pressing down on his back, making him old and gray with misery. He ran and tried to get away from the giant dragon's coil, but there was always something that held him back. He imagined speaking to Ma Tsu Po in China, unburdening his heart to the old man.

"Read *Empire of Heaven*. On page eight, you will find strength," said the old man from the Gold Orchid Guild. And indeed on page eight, Sidan read:

Art lets everything pass. They who master it are able to bear a thrashing by centering themselves in the liminal spaces between the waves of suffering, entering into the transition until they are able to stab themselves without pain. Pain indeed must be confined, all the doors to it closed except the one leading to that transitory space which is being passed through.

"That's the only way to overcome the feelings of emptiness, after oceans of departure and loss. Life is paranoia," Sidan said.

He hadn't felt strong enough to do anything ever since he had been attacked.

Sidan: It's like there is only half of my life left, but it's nothing. Don't worry!

Firdaus: What happened, Sidan? Did they hurt you again?

Sidan: This time nobody did anything. It's just
that every once in a while, thirty bloody
full moons rise from the depths of my
subconscious and enter my awareness and then
everything tightens up, from my hamstrings
to the crown of my head. Dead hands, gaping
mouth, crystal breaking in my chest.

Firdaus: Crystal breaking in your chest, what does
that mean?

Sidan: Haha, Firda . . . Firda! It's no use. I
mean that this body is like a volcano.
White lava bubbles under the craters of
my skin and then boom! It erupts in my
chest . . . My teeth clench tightly, as if
I had tetanus. Ha!

Firdaus: Studying and thinking too much will make
you suffer, Sidan. You need to take a
break. Don't just keep reading all the
time, you'll make yourself sick.

Sidan: You're right, Firda. Poison is already
working in the secret chambers of my heart.
Ma Tsu Po says it's because long ago I
left something behind, something that
makes people grow old. So I have forgotten
something, but I stay young forever . . .

Firdaus: If I might guess, I think you forgot
to break your fast, and maybe you need

to eat something, haha. Come to Yogya,
there's plenty of restaurants—Mbok Berek,
Mama Suharti's, Texas, or KFC, all you
have to do is choose which one you want,
haha . . . You'll certainly stay young
that way!

Sidan: There are only two things I want, Firda. To
act and to make love! The climax of human
paranoia is reached when you're in the limbo
of an identity crisis, between heaven-
hell, heading toward a universalism . . .
Romantics never get old. They all die young!

Firdaus: Is that true? I heard a song on the TV,
"Now you are the one who I miss. Now your
name is the name that I call." Have you
heard that one?

Sidan: Yeah. Just two things. Act and make love.
"Now you are the one that I want. Now and
forever you are the one that I love." Have
you heard that one?

Firdaus: No. Now I'm sleepy! All I want is a bedtime
mantra!

Sidan: Oh yeah? Tomorrow to be continued. Don't be
afraid: maine pyar pagel helized tilmiz,
bapa biyung kakang kawah, muchos gracias,
mille la partiza, lun fatih deniz dinergi
kizilay. Sweet dreams!

Archangel Michael was touched. He smiled and granted the couple a lakeful of blue dreams. The clouds hung low, like a canopy guarding the streets the two walked along. The wind rustled, soft and delicate. Wrens warbled and gazelles frolicked. Walking through a garden of purple bougainvillea, Sidan never stopped teasing Firdaus, showering her with tears and happy laughter.

"The fate of casanovaism falls to the end of the island," he said. "Sorry, I cannot refuse the owner of heaven. And I don't want to. He wholeheartedly submits to three miraculous little words—*je t'aime . . . wo aini.*"

"Oh my God, who is 'he'? You're delirious!" Firdaus chided.

"If the bridge connects, then the two crazies will meet. But let us be delirious. We are proven conquerors, ever since Princess Pahang was brought here from her kingdom in Malaysia to the secret tunnel under the castle. It's no thanks to heaven, but we are real men!"

"Aaa-aaaa-*choooooo!*"

"What's wrong? You have a cold?"

"Flu epidemic. Crocodile Dundee. Oh, Conqueror of Love!"

"Do you have a fever?"

"I have Layla fever, and it's getting worse as Majnun's body temperature rises."

Haha . . .

Hiya, Conqueror of the Future!

Chapter 2:
A Silent Place

Civilization is for those who have the strength to live, so I am slamming the door on defeat, Sidan said to himself. He was speeding on his motorbike toward Suak Timah, a fishermen's village on the coast. Ocean wind. Wet grass. A flickering low-wattage lamp from a generator turned off exactly at 11:00 p.m., thanks to the rising price of gasoline. Encroaching darkness. Puffy tents. Drizzle typing out tomorrow's fate on the roof. Sidan recited prayers as he rode into the isolated region of lonely rebels.

He'd left the bare-board barracks, shoddily built by the Agency for the Rehabilitation and Reconstruction of Aceh. Living there was like waiting at a bus stop—it felt temporary but indefinite: it was overcrowded and chaotic; one wants a cigarette, the other is allergic to smoke; one likes to pray and the other's hobby is singing; one tries to read quietly until the other's kids start jumping around.

How fetid and cramped the wide world had become, with the powerful barons and brokers and their minions chasing out the well-intentioned foreigners trying to develop Aceh. Let this good project be kept "in the family."

"We are not strong enough to resist," Sidan smarted. "Even our vocal cords have been cut by those who keep mangy dogs."

Look at the land barons working under the Serambi Balkan Reconstruction logo, constantly divvying up the plentiful spoils, ever since '45, really, growing ever more greedy and ravenous. They rezoned the land however they pleased and there was no sense of comfort after that, no place called home, just houses disconnected from their villages and communities. *Nirkota*: nowhere cities. Like a body without a head. The government had promised to build more houses, but after almost ten months these had still not materialized. There were nothing but empty promises from the NGOs who came to collect data as a way to facilitate transactions with their donors. Then after waiting for months, some wood beams and bricks arrived. The survival rations for the people in the barracks, ninety-three thousand rupiah a month per person, about ten dollars, were only paid out for two months and then got held up.

It was said that the world's donations to us were "redirected" to cover the national debt. We were proud that even in our time of suffering, we could still help save our country.

All the aid intended for Aceh was processed via Jakarta and then became absorbed into the national budget. Haha. Which of the favors of your Lord will you deny? We were hungry and thirsty. Alone at the farthest corner of a silent barracks. Then we took whatever work we could find. We cleaned up the neighborhood for thirty-five thousand rupiah a day, paid out every two days. We were forced to become chameleons—one day petty slaves, the next day actors, the next day athletes. We went shopping early in the morning for eggs and carrots and cheese. Then we puked and got the runs. Blackouts, dead engines, diarrhea, and sleeping in. Ten packets of Oralit drunk down with one hundred poems. That was how to endure pain and sickness. Barf!

Sidan the romantic didn't eat breakfast. He just drank one liter of plain water upon waking, then rinsed out his mouth. His stomach had to be cleansed so that the words that came forth were pure because his tongue had been broken by the military horn that sounded like a cobra's cough. Only once a week, on Sundays, did he eat his long-awaited breakfast at Sulamtaque: white sticky rice mixed with mung beans and a little liquid palm sugar. Every once in a while he ate *cane Punjab* and *burukiek* curry from Tangse, in northwest Aceh, but only if he had money. His daily agenda was mostly filled with empty pockets and a rumbling stomach. He kept track of his debt, writing it down at the food stall. As the holy book says, if there are those among you who have debt, make a note of it. Sweet, right? But then all the stalls went bankrupt because all the customers were eating on credit and Sidan was left to chew on his fingers.

So he was going to the western coast, to Meulaboh, city of the delicious fried *keukarah* cake. The scent of salt blowing in dark Portuguese faces. The beach kids who were left stunned by the tsunami. It rained all the time, endless needling drops. The fishermen's village was hemmed by silver sap trees. They had been hit by the wave and were only now starting to turn green again at the tips. Fasting teaches resilience, even though it is difficult. Here the wave had come rushing in to greet the sky, and as it receded it had uprooted all the trees. All orphans are family.

Sidan sat quietly in the tent of Mr. Kerani, the village secretary who was now a widower. His wife and children had been taken by the tsunami. Suak Timah village had lost six hundred people out of its fifteen hundred inhabitants. Kerani's face looked desiccated, as if all his tears had already been shed, enough to fill a lake. The children were cradled in the embrace of the marsh, the ocean, and the hot sand. They were jet black and smelled of fish. They laughed. In Suak, no one was traumatized by the ocean, but instead felt their abiding love for it grow. Yet Sidan looked into their eyes and he saw the loss. *We are one,* their eyes said.

"So what's left, sir?" Sidan asked, trembling.

"The ocean and everything in it."

The secretary's tears, somehow still surfacing from his arid face, melted and flowed to the farthest reaches of the heavens.

"Yes. The ocean and everything in it, and the One who holds dominion over all."

"There was no escape, son. Our only road out goes along the beach."

In the next tent over, a lake of tears had been dredged up by the sea. Every night in the silence of nighttime prayers, that lake water churned as if it was being boiled on a stove, and smoke billowed out of it in a sorrowful saga of souls torn apart by bitter melancholy.

"I know."

"Before, when the military came after us in pursuit, they would chase us to the water's edge and our escape would be blocked by the sea. So we disappeared slowly, one by one, in chase after chase. But this time we all disappeared in an instant, and this time we were chased and taken by the sea."

Sidan knew. The army headquarters had also been pounded by the wave, but many of the soldiers had survived. To this remote village, a huge portion of its population decimated and washed away, those soldiers were like an eight-legged parasite bred by the New Order in the community's orchards. Now it felt like practically the only people left were soldiers, since the mountain rebels didn't want to fight anymore. Last week they beat ex-rebel elites. They asked to be given respect, not treated with scorn. But that was the fruit to be harvested after thirty years of planting guns in Serambi. They were first greeted with kindness, but responded with weapons and turned the locals into the grandchildren of martyrs—yet still they asked to be respected. "We have nothing, just guns," they said. "We don't even have any brains." Imagine, how are you supposed to react to zombies without brains?

Sidan began to feel nauseous, forever nauseous. He looked at Kerani's face, and the man's tears sparked a flame of rebellion in him. In a spirit that is young and forever young, bitterness becomes a ship to ride the waves, plunging into the ocean, bringing even the sharks to heel. Almost unable to control his urge to vomit, Sidan pressed the keypad of his phone and it lit up.

Sidan: Soldiers never die, Firda. They think they
       are victorious and they don't feel ashamed,
       their clamor never stops. The mountain
       weapons are destroyed and they mistake
       that for surrender. But they forget, the
       Acehnese people never surrender.

"If I may ask, who are you contacting so late at night, young man?"

"A friend in a faraway city. I have no one else left, sir."

"Praise God you still have a friend to ease your loneliness. You don't feel like an orphan if you have a friend, no matter who it is or where they are."

Sidan grew melancholy. The drizzle kept hammering out its gray tone in the vicious cold. He remembered Firdaus's big eyes, which made her look like a gazelle on the summit of Kaliurang Mountain.

Here there is silence and the rustle of the coastal wind—what are you doing where you are, Firda? Isn't this a purple Saturday night, like the ones we shared long ago? Such a long time ago. At some point in this existence, who knows when, a day will come and it will be all blue, with both of us in the lap of a blue flame. Flying and diving, rising and falling in an ocean of love. Merging in serenity, feeling it all the way to the crowns of our heads, overcome. In our own corner of twilight, Firda.

"You should stay in Yogya. What's the point of going to wait for death at home?" Firdaus had said cuttingly.

"My mother is all alone there, Firda. Once I tried to take her with me far from home and she immediately came down with an incurable illness. She was homesick."

"A real man doesn't leave his village during times of war. But a real romantic ventures forth to capture his lost love."

"So if I go home, does that necessarily mean that I will lose you, my love?"

"That's the law during wartime. And it's not just my love that could be lost, but also your heart, your young passionate soul. The pull of a trigger could end it all, for nothing."

Sidan was shaken. For a long time now his thoughts of home and war had been raging, filling the quiet nights in his rented room. The homesickness for his village had been building up in him for years, but his mother had kept on forbidding him to return. Not because she didn't miss her beloved child, but because the odor of weapons and gunpowder still lingered in the air. What mother would let her son follow his father into martyrdom, covered in red in the courtyard of an old mosque, slayed by the weapons of the soulless?

His mother knew best how smart Sidan was, had helped him rise through the ranks in competition after competition, starting in elementary school all the way until university. Sidan was one out of thousands, a potential future leader of the country who needed protecting from the life-stealers who violate God's commandments. Like all the mothers in Aceh, Sidan's mother carried a mountain of worry in her heart. To be a young man in Aceh was to forever be a fugitive: if you left the house you were confronted with weapons, but if you stayed inside, those weapons would still come to hunt you down.

Who knows what they had done wrong? Their one most glaring sin was simply that they existed. The young men of Aceh were a generation that made those in power—the soldiers and the gangs of corruptors—tremble, because they saw that in the eyes of these youth there were red coats, an eternal testimony to their history. Those youths had saved the old clothes stained with the blood of their fathers and their uncles, of their sisters and their women, all of those who had vanished into unmarked graves, thousands upon thousands of them, tens of thousands. This was something that could not be forgiven and forgotten.

For now, soldiers were building their careers in Aceh, so to be a young man there was to be part of a group that only had two choices: rebel or feign loyalty. If you chose to rebel, then you had to go into the mountains, and if you feigned loyalty, you would continue your education for as long as you could, in order to develop an eloquent tongue that could speak the word: *independence.* Sidan chose the second way. His mother completely supported him, and so one July she put Sidan on the first flight out to Yogyakarta.

She had her own reasons for sending Sidan away from Serambi. First, Yogyakarta's royal landmarks were precious history for the Acehnese, because their own palace had been burned down by the Dutch. Sidan liked to visit the Imogiri Cemetery, where the royalty from the Yogyakarta sultanate were buried. There were four urns there, and one of these was a souvenir that Sultan Mughayat Syah, the first sultan of Aceh, had given to the sultan of Yogyakarta in the sixteenth century. It was placed next to the other urns that had been sent as love tokens from Siam and Turkey. The blood that flowed in Sidan's veins was the blood of chiefs. Blue *bantasyam* blood.

But there was another reason. It was clearly safer for Sidan to grow up and prepare for his future outside Serambi. Yogyakarta was out of harm's way, a breath of fresh air. Time moved so slowly there—seconds passed away in the dim morning and then squirmed back to life in the warmth of the sunshine. As Sidan became increasingly involved in student movements, which fostered his hearty passion for revolution, he did not finish his studies quickly. He had turned into an eternal student.

"It's already been more than seven years, Firda, and I've only gone home once, four years ago."

"I know you miss your mother. But I'm worried about you, just like she is."

"Why? I'll just go home for a little while and then at some point I'll come get you."

"At some point? You don't sound so sure about it. And anyway, you won't simply 'come get me,' because I won't go just anywhere with you, especially not to a country that's basically a war zone!"

Sidan laughed. He understood where Firdaus was coming from and similar thoughts had crossed his mind. But Firdaus's proposal that he stay in Yogyakarta was unsettling. Sidan felt torn between love and patriotism, but he really was homesick for his village and he missed his mother. He wanted to see her so he could discuss his plans to marry and ask for her blessing face-to-face. He didn't have to settle down in his village permanently. He could contribute to the struggle from wherever he was, as long as his dedication was sincere. Being a wanderer, to him every place was temporary. But what about his homeland? His roots? The Prophet Muhammad had needed to reclaim Mecca, even though he was buried in Medina. Sidan imagined all the important events of his village happening without him, and that caused an excruciating melancholy deep in his soul.

"No, Firda. I am positive. I'm only going home for a little while. Trust me."

"I know I can't forbid you, because the more I forbid you the more desperately you will want to go. So go home, but don't bother looking back over your shoulder. You don't have to think about us anymore! Just think about your future in your village."

"Why do you keep being so cynical? If you keep acting like this, how can I possibly go home?"

"I've already told you how. So now it's up to you to make your choice."

Then Firdaus left Sidan alone in a daze.

What he needed was moral support, but she had only added to his burden, making his thoughts even more chaotic. There was no way he would go home with his face bruised by Firdaus's fury, so Sidan only went as far as Jakarta, to finish a documentary he had been working on with a number of other young filmmakers. But he vowed to himself that he would approach Firda and bring up his plans to go home again, perhaps once his financial situation had improved a bit. In the meantime, he would wait for her heart to soften.

The weeks sped by, as if time was impatient. And then came the December day that shook the entire world: the day of the tsunami. All of a sudden, one drizzly morning, after an earthquake with a Richter-scale magnitude over nine, black waves rose from the sea bed. Three tall spears came at breakneck speed, in rolling coils that moved a mile a minute, snatching up whatever lay in their path. The ocean devoured the land. The mouth of the monster wave broke over front yards, crumpling up the region, knocking over its villages and cities and all of the civilization they contained.

Sidan sat agape in front of the television. His entire being was consumed, haunted. His thoughts immediately flew to his house, so close to the Malacca Strait. *Mother. Mother. Mother.* For a moment, Sidan collapsed. Everything had gone dark. Then he realized there was no time left to wait.

Sidan: *Firdaus, my darling! I have to go home! There is no other choice!*

Firdaus: *Yes, go! Send my greetings to your mother. My prayers enfold you.*

In his haste, he forgot to comb his hair or put on proper shoes and wore only flip-flops for the entire journey from Jakarta all the way back to Banda Aceh. Beside himself, Sidan could only sit there stunned and powerless. But that day, everyone understood and forgave his condition. The entire world was full of apologies and tears. He was granted kindness after kindness along his journey, amidst the onslaught of this mighty disaster.

Getting off the airplane was like falling from a rented Eden. The smell of corpses attacked his nose and rubbed his nerves raw, sending him into a nightmare of apocalypse that had now become only too real. Sidan could only stare mutely at the dead, who lined the road from the airport all the way to his village. He was unable to touch them until the third day. His mother had also been swallowed by the wave. The memory of her face pounded Sidan's heart until it was broken.

A tsunami on top of the tsunami.

The jumbled wreckage of houses, mosques, barns, markets, rice paddies and fields, libraries; corpses hanging from trees, impaled on truck hoods that had broken off and been carried away, or wedged in between the splintered debris of buildings—all so tragic! The smell of black mud mixed with the stench of death and destruction. It was worse than he could have ever imagined. Endless questions assaulted his soul.

Sidan felt he had awoken in a strange realm, as if he were on the planet Mercury. He had lost all familiar landmarks. Where was Lingkhe, Manyak Payet? Where was Jeuram? Where was Glumpang Minyeuk? Where? There were no addresses left for him to visit. There were no faces left for him to recognize. There were no mouths left for him to talk to. There were no answers for his questions. Nature now wore the face of a great ruin. The expression of the earth was one of crazy sorrow. The universe was nothing but rubble and debris. *Allahu Akbar!* Sobs broke out. Tears flowed to the farthest corners of heaven.

His second morning there, Sidan awoke under the roof of a blue tent. There was a pillow and a blanket donated by the WHO. Then he saw a mass of tents, like a row of giant mushrooms, stretching out in a contorted row. Giant black clouds of smoke billowed through the air. There were children's shrieks and a line of lonely faces. The refugees looked like temporary guests on earth, come back from the underworld, worried about a future that looked dark and grim. Sidan joined the back of the line and then stood in it for hours, until he was dripping with sweat.

He touched foreign rice and filled his mouth with molten tears.

His soul was hollow.

"May I sit here and join you, friend?" a man asked.

"I'm not a friend. I'm family. Be my guest, brother."

He looked at the two black dots before him. Then Sidan forgot his manners, staring. Those eyes were so hollow. They looked empty, as if the soul within them had gone somewhere else. Sidan recognized his own eyes in the eyes of his new brother.

"Do you have family in the tent?"

"I'm alone," Sidan said.

"They were all swept away? You're the only one who survived?"

"I survived because I was out of the city. I arrived here one day after the disaster. But if I could have chosen, I would have wanted to join them."

"Don't say that, brother. We are alone, but we're not truly alone. Look at all of us. We have all become family. We have many friends. Don't feel alone."

"How many did you lose?"

"About twenty-seven. There are a few we are still looking for. We don't know yet where they are or what became of them."

Sidan was aghast. Twenty-seven? How easily the man had said it. But the next day he realized there were those who had lost forty, those who had lost forty-five, and others who had lost even more. Maybe whole clans had disappeared in an instant. Out of three hundred people in one village, there were only thirty who survived. In another village that used to number fifteen hundred, now there were only eighty left. The survivors emerging from the piles of debris were like scattered broken pieces with nothing left but the deepest silence, which held the secret of nature's dreadful power.

Finally the rice on his plate was finished too. The funeral banquet was over. And then Sidan had diarrhea and kept on having diarrhea! Then he got the flu and started vomiting. He had a fever. In the silent night, his mother's face beckoned him from the door of heaven. His poor mother, who had been all alone when the tsunami snatched her from him.

When she was alive, his mother had never spoken of her love for him, even though Sidan felt it abiding in every one of the kisses she gave him on his forehead every time he went out or arrived home. The silence became a mirror that showed Sidan his younger self, when he had been a baby in his mother's arms.

Now he had been denied the chance to say the words he had planned to say—so Firdaus's name had not yet been mentioned in his mother's prayers; she had not yet received his mother's blessing, nor the love and affection of a mother for her future daughter-in-law. And Sidan had not yet had the chance to dutifully repay his mother for all her hard work, to show her that he had in fact become successful. Sidan was still at the beginning, on the very first step.

He was so anxious thinking about the land, the water, the village, the houses, and the future. During the quiet nights in the tent, he would feel like he was alone in the middle of the jungle, black and miserable. Then the earthquakes would come, one after another. The tents would rattle and everyone would be forced to evacuate, becoming refugees once again.

On the days when the weather was good, Sidan began to go visiting from tent to tent, getting anyone willing to talk with him to share their feelings of grief. Full of empathy, he listened to all the lamentations and he witnessed all the tears. He began to check in on the orphaned children, with their trembling souls, and every night he cried for them. Every time he looked into their eyes it felt like his chest was being barraged by a thousand bullets, stabbed by the blade of a knife. He invited the children to play, climb atop his shoulders and go around the refugee camp. He laughed and cried with them.

"*Mak ho ka,* Uncle? Where's my mother? Where?"

What could Sidan say? Every question that emerged from those tiny lips set Sidan swimming, looking for the best answer at the bottom of a dark ocean. But he couldn't find it. The children kept asking, and it destroyed his soul every time.

"Where's my older brother? Where's my little brother Sani?"

On a morning without earthquakes, Sidan went out and ran into Polem. His friend was carrying a bundle of children's toys, heading toward the camp. He was with a Frenchman who didn't understand Indonesian, so Sidan volunteered to serve as an interpreter. He whispered to Polem that he should express concern for the fate of children who had nothing, sympathy for their pitch-black futures.

Then Polem, who liked to play music, joined up with Sidan, who liked acting, and they both went wandering around, looking for friends to recruit among the scattered tents. After gathering eleven friends, seven men and four women, they formed a performance troupe. They went around from one refugee camp to another, telling stories and performing in an effort to provide some spiritual medicine, to allow the people to heal. They held prayer recitations and theater events, trying to tell new stories that might help the children envision their future. They carried a big *rebana* tambourine, with its distinctive Acehnese sound. This was accompanied by a *grimfeng,* a small drum stretched across a pair of thin perforated metal strips. Its sound, *crik-crik pheng,* became a mooring for lost and empty eyes.

At first the troupe played at night in the dim illumination of four generator-powered neon lights set up at the corners of the stage; but after fighting broke out again between the separatists and the soldiers, the nighttime seemed too dangerous and the troupe played during the day. The children still crowded around them cheerfully. The adolescents and adults were calmer. When prayers were recited over the microphone in Arabic and Acehnese before the performance began, the children solemnly joined in and the adults began to weep, remembering all the family no longer with them.

Then Sidan took a microphone and introduced the musicians beside him. Leubei took out the *gambus*, a stringed instrument typical of the desert, and began to softly pluck in the *tirando* style, creating a desert rhythm the way Andrés Segovia did when he played the classic Spanish composition "Capricho Árabe." Occasionally he used the rounder *apoyando* style to accentuate certain notes. Nangi accompanied him on the *rapai*, an Acehnese percussion instrument that was not very different from the small Javanese *ketipung* drum. Sawang lifted his trumpet and blew into it, playing in harmony, and then Meutia, Dena, Yeti, and Zubaedah joined in, and the children joined in too, because it was a familiar Acehnese folk song that had been sung for generations.

Apa Ma'e folk tales came next—comedic stories about Apa Ma'e, a hapless local trying to get by during the military occupation, the tsunami tragedy, and the subsequent arrival of the volunteers and foreign soldiers to the land of Serambi Makkah. The stories riveted the audience. Laughter reverberated, breaking the silence of the frail night.

"For humanity, for the people of Aceh . . . my religion is for me, your religion is for you, don't be afraid!" This was Apa Ma'e's message. "Aceh was formed from a number of nations, so we have ties to America, Japan, India, Pakistan, Saudi Arabia. So we were not alone when the tsunami came," Apa Ma'e declared and was answered by festive cheers.

Sidan always invited the refugees to perform too. Some sang *nadham*, devotional music. Some recited verses about the twenty-five prophets and other prayers, legends, and tales. Then the metal rings lining the curved sides of the *grimfeng* drum began to clang, and the performance of *dabus*, which the Acehnese also sometimes called *top daboh*, began. Fingers slapped the percussion in unison, like flames, until heads swayed back and forth in ecstasy. As the music played, molded iron spikes were brought out, heated in the fire, and then used to pierce the mouths, arms, thighs, chests, necks, and backs of the performers. Pain climbed toward its climax, but before it became an unendurable reflex, it was resisted! The performers recited prayers and mantras so that they felt nothing and emerged unscathed. The fire of the pounding drums seemed to burn the barracks porches. The refugee children standing there brooded, looking up at the sky, knowing that on their own, those on earth were powerless.

Sidan took the troupe all the way to the most remote regions, including the Tamiang district and the island of Simeulue. Wherever they went, they spread the same message, which was that despite the tsunami, the people of Aceh should not allow themselves to collapse. The troupe's tour also became an early witness to the hegemonic fate that was afflicting the people in every city and village, and they felt their artistic offering was a way to reintroduce the traditional arts of Aceh to the younger generation. For Sidan, being in the troupe was one way to give meaning to life amidst suffering. These were days of performance, days of love.

Sidan: It's clear this morning, but it's humid because it rains every night. There are only one or two souls here at the airport. If you have an atlas, Firda, look for an island north of Nias, it's called Simeulue. I'm going there in a helicopter.

Firdaus: You're touring to Simeulue? I've seen that island above the coral, it's on television a lot. That's great!

Sidan: Yeah, we are performing to help the children develop new positive narratives about their future. Oh, the UN heli is whirring! Wish me safe travels! I will return with some good stories!

Firdaus: Safe travels, my love . . . you are in
my prayers. Take care of yourself! Guard
the wealth of the future! Good luck!

The words of Firdaus's text, sent from the new morning in Yogyakarta, were like a breath of fresh air in Sidan's heart, giving rise to a longing that floated above the helicopter and the clouds. His secretive smile caught Polem's attention.

"It must be a cup of warm milk coffee from Yogya. And all he does is smile as he drinks it down. It must be delicious!"

"You know-it-all," Sidan said. "People smile during prayer. They don't have to drink a cup of milk coffee."

"They smile secretive, mysterious smiles like that when they're praying?"

"There are many angels and *jinn* all around us. What's wrong with smiling at them?"

"Oh my God! Since when are you friends with *jinn* and angels?"

"Ever since I was born. They have been my companions morning, noon, and night, from the beginning of days until the end of time."

"So they're the ones who just texted you, making you smile at the crack of dawn?"

"They are the stokers of the fire, but who texted me was a blue flame . . . but this blue flame stokes my spirit."

"Aha, so finally he admits it. The point is, morning, noon, and night your soul is on fire."

With such jokes, the time passed quickly. They soon descended into a quiet village that had nothing except the call to prayer and a peddler selling *kuini*, a local mango-like fruit. This was life on a remote island. There was nothing but the sea and its pungent smell of lobster and seashells. All they saw along the road were vacant stares and closed lips, dry like parched fields. Unsmiling young women with their heads covered peeked out from behind wooden-roofed houses. Mothers searched among the fronds, look-ing for kindling. No electricity, no television, no radio. There was no news whatsoever, except when the wind brought news of a coming storm.

Of course, Sidan's phone didn't work here. This far-flung land was always falling behind. Like how the morning newspaper arrives in the afternoon at the far end of the peninsula in Ule Seuneuleuh. Like how the broadcast of the Independence Proclamation of August 17, 1945, didn't arrive until September. After the price of gasoline rose and rose again, the islanders boiled Jatropha seeds—ten kilos of these seeds, boiled and squeezed, produced three and a half liters of biodiesel. They used to plant Jatropha trees in a row in front of their houses as a fence, now they used it to stoke their kitchen fires. This was Aceh, which since before the time of the Proclamation had been dubbed a resource-rich region, useful for stoking the fires of the Republic of Indonesia, even as it was kept impoverished and isolated from the resulting progress.

Sidan was sad and anxious. He was saddened by the sight of the decrepit village. Even the prison was made from nothing but wood walls with an iron-sheet roof that was susceptible to the weather. He was anxious because his communication was cut off by the dumb, unreli-able cell reception. It would take four days to travel around Simeulue, and for that time, black night would be haunted by a hovering ghostly specter of longing. Thankfully he could still eat Indian biryani rice with *keumamah*, also known as *ikan kayu*, fish that had been chopped up into small pieces and preserved with chili and herbs, then left out in the hot sun for days, like the *haji* who liked to eat their biryani with tamarind curry and starfruit that had been dried out in the sun. That biryani was filling enough to last you two days in the forest.

They didn't need to worry about attacks from the burning interior. The only threat came from troublemaking outsiders. Local Portuguese. The real Portuguese had gone back home centuries ago, afraid of being turned into satay meat by Admiral Keumalahayati, the woman who had led the famous band of *inong balee*, fierce female warriors who sank the Portuguese in Malacca. But those Portuguese had gone back home only to leave an even wilder group of local Portuguese, who carried cannons and made hearts tremble.

But what if, Firda, what if in this war zone, on this battlefield, it wasn't just revolvers that had the right to bark—but love also had the right to make some noise?

Here, amidst an ocean of loss and death, the only thing that could save your life—the only proof of your legitimate existence—was an identity card. Survivors without an identity card were assumed to be rebels and denied aid, and those who had died without an identity card were buried unceremoniously in unmarked graves. The Dutch East Indies Army brought two cannons into the city, just like they did in the Battle of Surabaya in '45 during the fight for Indonesian independence. A dream of war realized in broad daylight: kill or be killed! Just like the song about morning coffee in Cilangkap, soldiers were sent to Aceh from the Cilangkap army headquarters in Jakarta. When the people asked, they said it was just a war exercise.

But in the middle of the city? When shells fell on the barracks, it was the ultimate suffering! We are busy with logistics but terrorized by trauma. And that's without even mentioning the refugees they robbed. As long as the army corps is fed, what do they care about the people? The myth that the military exists to serve the people is just bullshit the state dishes out!

Firdaus: And what happened with the barracks? What about the people who live there?

Sidan: Oh, Firda! They ran and ran, as far away as they could (even a young widow who had just miscarried could suddenly run for two kilometers straight) . . . an unimaginable mystery.

Firdaus: And did you run away too, with the rest?
And were the barracks destroyed?

Sidan: Oh, my love! Don't ever leave the barracks!
Don't ever leave the quiet! Don't ever leave
my infinite enduring grief! Don't . . . if you
do I'll be taken! I'll certainly disappear!
Representatives from private organizations
were roaming the barracks, carrying a bag
full of money. They called over two kids,
told them to hold the money while they took
a picture, and then they left with the bag
still full. They took it back with them!
All the disaster for us, all the profit for
you . . . We choose silence!

"Hey! You're daydreaming! What's going on? You're not getting any sweet little texts?"

"The operator is snoring. Maybe he ate too much fruit and fell asleep, and so the phone reception went out."

They were lying down on the front porch of the house belonging to the village chief, waiting to go home. The children came and greeted them, carrying *kuini* that tasted sour, sweet, and tart all at once. It was good for making Acehnese-style *rujak*, a raw fruit salad made spicy and tangy by red chili and sago palm. If you didn't like that, it could also be used to make *kuini* juice, which was fresh and fragrant.

"This is all we can give you, older brother. We don't have anything else. Once you're back home, don't forget us. We're happy that you came."

The polite, straightforward words of the nation's next generation.

Sidan wiped away his tears. He forgot for a moment that now he himself didn't have anything either—these children, they still could give him something, with light and pure hearts. So he couldn't stop his tears; they flowed all the way to the end of time. Until Judgment Day.

The performance troupe walked carefully, stepping on the wet dirt with their heads bowed. They knew that there used to be gold mines under this earth, but these had been dredged by Jakarta and used to build Monas, the national monument, a torch as tall as a skyscraper with a gold-plated flame on top. Everything in this land ultimately ended up belonging to Jakarta, while the rightful owners were simply shot. If the people complained, then foreign aid would be sent to help Aceh, but somehow Jakarta would be in charge of it. What a cleptocracy!

So please, people from every corner of the nation should come to Aceh. There's money here, to make the engine of the economy turn on pain and suffering. All the disaster for us, all the profit for you. We were never fully humanized, just despised and tricked, bullshitted! So it's fitting that those who came from abroad rubbed our bowed heads as if we were children. But those who came from the Dutch East Indies were in collusion with one another. Want to get rich? Come to Aceh! If you're looking for money, go to Aceh. And if you're looking for Aceh, you don't need to go anywhere. It only exists inside our hearts; it was killed by myths born from a long history of misunderstanding about an as-yet unfinished project of building a Great Nation, but crucified by the sacred nails of those who didn't have any brains, let alone hearts.

History lies in the hands of the demons from Jakarta!

When will the Dutch East Indies do more than make Aceh empty promises? Sukarno lied because he thought that compared to the rest of the country, the people of Aceh only knew how to pray and sin. Aceh didn't know Lady Justice, didn't know the Messiah; all it had were martyrs and dark eschatological dreams. The Dutch East Indies raped its mother, and so Aceh unsheathed its blazing dagger. But when a mother forgives wrongs, her children should realize what they have done, then educate and correct themselves. Not try to assert their power with acts and symbols that are repeated over and over—necro-nationalism, the flag, the national anthem, and Pancasila, *the five moral principles of the nation. Why must Aceh be*

*forced to do this or that when not even those in power go to the presidential
palace on Independence Day every August 17?*

Sidan's head throbbed. His wild thoughts drifted far behind the
clouds, to the end of the world, as far as the eye could see. His fists
clenched and collided with the empty air. Oh, fragile universe, Republic
that loves the world.

Then he thought wryly, *If Aceh became an independent country, then
all the workers from the Dutch East Indies would become illegal foreign
workers. But we would not be arrogant, because we would know that they
had no other choice in a bankrupt country of corruptors.*

Firdaus: Oh, where has my soul mate wandered to?
        Why is there no news? Your phone just
        keeps saying pending!

Sidan was surprised. He had been waiting for even a short message
from Firdaus, and he enthusiastically replied, forgetting all thoughts of
smarting wounds and a zombie republic.

Sidan: When I was coming home in the UN heli, I
       saw villages far below the sky, like a lush
       green carpet in a mosque that has been worn
       thin from use and the prostration of the
       black wave that came that Sunday.

Firdaus: Thank goodness you're safe! Are you doing
        well? I hope your troupe has continued
        success! I'm waiting for stories from the
        land above the coral.

Sidan: I'm healthy, wrapped in your prayers and
       passionate love. But at night I am blanketed

in a cold that I can hardly bear. The wind
brings no sweetness with it, Firda. But the
show must go on . . . Until tonight! My
warmest greetings!

"Hey, hey, hey! You just got home and you've already been welcomed with a glass of orange juice. Wow, it must taste fresh, man," Polem teased.

"It's not orange juice, but sherbet with . . . This is what I've been waiting for!"

"Now I'm curious. What does your angel look like?"

"She looks like an angel . . . she's gentle and beautiful, she's smart and doesn't like to be outsmarted. She makes me suffer too, though."

"But why would you suffer? Doesn't your smile appear whenever she sends you a message, wherever you are?"

"How could I not suffer? She's so far away in Yogyakarta, at a distance of thousands of kilometers that can only be crossed by a cell phone signal. Imagine, in a mortally wounded country, Majnun's memories keep smoldering, and then on top of that, the reception is uncooperative. It's terrible."

"Don't you also chat a lot on the Internet?"

"The Internet is full of spies, don't you know? Letters get sniffed out too. Maybe only a fraction of a smile and one strand of hair can reach its destination safely."

"So maybe you shouldn't stay so far away from your sweetheart."

"Absence makes the heart grow fonder. Longing can also be quite enjoyable, as long as you are not too lonely and your phone has good reception. On the fragrant evenings that we talk, I forget that Azrael is lurking everywhere."

They went home from the airport on a *labi-labi*, a small pickup truck with a makeshift roof covering the twelve passengers. They skirted the edge of the city that still stank, covered in dust and dry mud, scarred at the corners. All that was left of the old city was a sliver in the moon's eye. The rebuilt city had grown along two kilometers of road leading to the barracks, but Sidan didn't like to go into the city and he didn't like to read the newspaper much anymore. To him, there was nothing true left in the papers. The journalists were hyperrealists. But he still occasionally read the Sunday paper because he still liked to follow the literary world. All of the books he had amassed during his studies had been swept away by the great water, and Sidan couldn't do anything about it, although he had loved them so much.

Sidan liked quiet. When the people from the other barracks gathered to drink coffee and eat Acehnese noodles together, Sidan didn't join in—all of the traditional rituals had been erased from his mind and memory. He only wanted to spend time with his phone, sending its signal dancing to his Layla, his beloved, his Firdaus in Yogyakarta.

"Please drink some coffee, Sidan. Don't just drink in the news," said a neighbor from the barracks. "You have a sweetheart in a faraway land?"

"Thank you, it's just that I prefer to drink warm tea. And the latest news is my snack. My tuna fish sandwich."

"What? It looks like you are sending news to your sweetheart. Where is she?"

"Maybe she's somewhere above the sky—but sometimes she feels so intimately near, pressed so close to me. It's like she's here, in this warm cup."

"You're starting to sound crazy."

"Pleasure is crazy and beauty endures."

His fellow wanderers began to get fed up, turning away their faces from him and exchanging glances. Sidan didn't care; he didn't worry about it. His fingers got pins and needles when they couldn't play with his phone. Whatever he did, whatever thoughts and feelings he was bottling up, he reported to Firdaus. That was the only way he could feel calm and not alone, knowing that there was someone with him, waiting for him. There was a faraway angel who loved him faithfully.

In the breezy morning, when the sun had just awoken, he began sending his signals of love and affection. He had memorized the rhythm of Firdaus's life, what she was doing every hour of her day. There was no time difference between Aceh and Yogyakarta, but the sun set one hour later in Aceh. Even though he himself liked to sleep in, Sidan faithfully woke with the alarm around the time Firdaus left for school to send her a text. And when she ate and took a nap and went to sleep at the end of the day, the text messages housed the lovers under one roof.

But out of all the hours of love, Sidan preferred the dead of night. Like tonight, when all of Suak Timah village was silent. Once it stopped drizzling, he went to drink coffee in the Bombay coffee shop. As he sat there he thought that he was now at peace with the eyes of the innocent kids he had seen playing on the raft in the water nearby. There was no grief in them, even though all of their houses had been destroyed, all their brothers and sisters had disappeared without a trace. They looked just how the village secretary had looked. They were strong people. Their whole families had vanished, but every day they worked for a new life. They weren't afraid of the sea. They loved Suak, which was the river near the bay—they cheerfully went swimming and fishing right where the river kissed the ocean. Sidan had recorded it all, the whole thing. He had immortalized the strength in their eyes on the memory card of his digital camera. He was finishing up his newest film. It would be called *Suak Timah*!

The village secretary, Mr. Kerani, had to make his rounds through the village once a day, even though there wasn't much that he could accomplish. He was trying to find a wife and child to replace the ones he had lost to the tsunami. He went around the neighborhood to monitor the situation according to his duties, while clearing land for his future home. Village secretaries everywhere frequently criticized the independent organizations in the region that had broken their promises to redevelop Suak Timah. The secretaries had a map of the village and a blueprint for self-guided development. They had refused the assistance of the Ministry of National Development Planning, which didn't understand Aceh or Suak village. Three months post-tsunami, they also shook off the Agency for Rehabilitation and Reconstruction.

Because of Sidan's immense feelings of love and care for the children who had been orphaned, either by the tsunami or the soldiers, he held on and invited them to play in the front yard of the old mosque or in abandoned boats. He would tell them bedtime stories in tents that were becoming increasingly worn out as the days went by. After they had fallen asleep, Sidan would get up and look out at the encampment, which briefly seemed like a tiny army of desert travelers, sleeping for the night so they could get up again the next day, their flaming daggers ready. Whenever a large vessel arrived in the glorious dawn, with a catch of cheap and big fresh fish, it would dock in the bay and Sidan would be waiting at the pier.

Sidan: Hey, Yogyakarta night . . . if you're not asleep yet, this is Aceh, ready with a chat about full moon nights. But if dreams have already taken you wandering, I will chase thee with the bedtime prayer, Oh Allah, I die with your name and I am born with your name. Ma'a salama!

Firdaus: Hello to Aceh . . . you still comfortable in Suak? Or are you making plans to move back to a barracks by the seashore? What's new?

Sidan: I'm still in my other village—Suak is kind of like my alter-ego, where the rain attacks and the waves are fierce . . . but this time it's not a true-love match, I'll go back home tomorrow, teaching compassion in the hopes of breeding a new generation *of romantic visionaries that will arise to fight someday. Freedom!*

Firdaus: Have you heard about the "rebel flags fluttering" on top of electricity poles? Getting found with one of those flags was once punishable by death. I saw it on television earlier this afternoon.

Sidan: Those electricity poles are witnesses to the horror of a tense cease-fire . . . The Republic of Indonesia can't yet be trusted, but as the supposed known and innocent party, they are free to do what they want and then accuse the unknown element, the guerillas. But when will the divine wisdom of the Republic of Indonesia descend to earth? Is it really so sacred?

Firdaus: Well, there's the Aceh Monitoring Mission. That is a neutral, outside team that can conduct its own investigation to prove who the culprits are. But do the orang gunung trust them?

Sidan: The Aceh Monitoring Mission is a bridge, so the two sides it is connecting have to trust them. The Republic doesn't have to be secretive. And the orang gunung don't have to worry if the soldiers are pulled out. But in this case, as the unknown element, they are more suspicious of the known party . . . because they were deceived by them for sixty years.

Firdaus: Okay then! I have to go to sleep now for school tomorrow. I hope the Suak waves calm down. Have a nice night!

Sidan: Are you sleepy? Then don't try to stay up, it's bad for you. I'm already used to it, it purifies my soul. But you have to sleep! Fatih terekurler, lutfen oturun turk-ogretman icin selam sogle bismikallah! Sweet dreams!

Firdaus: What's that? It doesn't make any sense. I want something funky.

Sidan: Walaya'uk buhana engkot wataramah santan watapeugot timphanik! Fatih Kizilay wa fuadi saidy. Fatih syukria lekulekling! Ciao!

Firdaus: Ahaha, what the heck are you saying? Whatever you say, I don't care, I'm just so sleepy.

Sidan: It's just a mantra for hugging your pillow! Okay, enough already, I thought you were ready to go to bed, but here you are awake and chatting up a storm! Who's the crazy one and who's the sleepy one here, kid . . . Okay, go in the Lord's name!

Chapter 3:
Memories of the Past

"Do you know the difference between Imru' al-Qais and Tarafah?" Firdaus quizzed her friend Adib Bahalwan. They were studying the Mu'allaqat poets, the most well-known pre-Islamic poets from the sixth century.

"Imru' al-Qais is a little bit like our classmate Sidan. Do you know him?" Adib asked.

"Not well," Firdaus said. "I've just seen him around campus."

She knew Sidan was a guy from Aceh who liked to recite traditional *pantun* love poetry and epics, but to her he didn't seem so different from all the other Acehnese students milling about, except for the fact that he recited them in the Sunan Kalijaga State Islamic University auditorium in front of hundreds of students, crowds of applauding friends. Firdaus had happened to hear him read some of his writing, which in her opinion was not as beautiful as the sixth-century poets she had been studying.

She knew that he was an actor in a number of campus theater troupes, and had even founded his own group in his department. She had also seen him a few times at antigovernment protests. "From what I know about him, he doesn't strike me as being like Imru' al-Qais," she said. "He's more like Qais Majnun, the character in the legend. They called him Qais the Crazy One, who was so obsessed with his beloved, Layla, that her father forbid their union and he went insane and did nothing but wander in the wilderness, reciting love poetry."

"You're right that he's like Majnun, but it's not because he's drunk on his beloved Layla—he's drunk on war!" Adib said. "He's taken an oath to fast from worldly pleasures and keep fighting until he has won. It pulses like the blood in his veins. It's like a dagger he carries with him wherever he goes."

"Wait a minute, he carries a dagger with him wherever he goes?"

"No, of course not, not a real one. He just carries it in his spirit, which is always on fire. It keeps flaring up!"

Then, like the rain that is eagerly anticipated during the dry season will fall, or ears that are perked up will tend to hear some news, right at that moment Sidan sauntered by in front of them. Firdaus stared in disbelief—now she could get a better look and wonder: Who was this Sidan? A Majnun from what planet?

"As handsome as that, and he wants to be a soldier?" Firdaus whispered to Adib. Had he ever been captured by the police because of his protests or his activist poetry? Firdaus didn't know. But when she looked at him now, she felt like there was no way that the owner of such beautiful eyes could ever do anything illegal or violent. "Maybe he really is insane!"

"Who said he wants to be a soldier? More like he wants to be a martyr."

"A martyr for who? His lover? His homeland? That's absurd!"

"Chat with him sometime, and you'll see how militant he is."

"Why should I? What do I care about him?"

"Of course! What do we care? Why are we even talking about Sidan? We were talking about Tarafah."

But then Firdaus went to go hear Sidan at his next reading, and his poetry reminded her of Zuhair bin Abi Sulma, that wise poet of the battlefield.

The seagull's song will cause a storm on the ocean
Daggers will crowd onto the crest of a wave
Refusing the grave before crashing on the sand

That sounded like poetry written by a seafarer. It must be because Sidan was from a maritime world, living close to the waves, lulled by sea breezes. Then Firdaus learned that he had been born in Lingkhe, only two kilometers from the Malacca Strait. When he was a child, Lhoknga Beach and Lampuuk had been his playground. Then she learned how devoted Sidan was to the revolutionary cause and she tried to find out more. He cared deeply about his homeland, which in his opinion was being unjustly occupied by its own brother, the nation of Indonesia. Nanggroe Aceh Darussalam—it was known as Aceh, the Abode of Peace, a name chosen to pay tribute to the land's rich past.

Yet he knew only too well that there was currently no peace in Nanggroe Aceh. That name was a hollow symbol, ever since everything had been forbidden, ever since the most recent emergency, ever since the people no longer had peace in their own country, subject to arrest after arrest. Ever since blood had been spilled in an unholy manner, scorching the village earth. Ever since the disappearance of the clerics and the intellectuals.

Finally Firdaus figured it out. Apparently Sidan was basically blind; he only opened his eyes when the world was talking about War and Death. He never went anywhere, just flitted back and forth between War and Death. He could fly across the firmament for hours, dive down to the bottom of the ocean and explore continents, lost in thought about War and Death. He went to class and circulated among the campus libraries, devouring any number of tomes. He was fluent in multiple foreign languages, had achieved soaring intellectual accomplishments, and was cosmopolitan and localist at the same time. He was friends with all kinds of people, from Eastern and Western countries: Portugal, Cuba, Senegal, Morocco, China, Libya, Hungary, Spain, Turkey, and more. He discussed and debated with his professors and friends and enemies.

He wrote poetry because of the War. He acted because of the War. Like most people from Aceh he was smart, even brilliant (maybe because of all the salmon they ate, packed with omega-threes, caught fresh from the ocean right in their backyard). The Serambi people were known for their distinctive love of knowledge. They had passed down high culture from their ancestors, ever since the thirteenth century when the old port states of Pidie and Pasai were international trading centers. Ever since the Portuguese had occupied Malacca in the sixteenth century and driven out the local Muslim merchants, pushing them to unite in a new sultanate, the kingdom of Aceh.

Sidan's eyes would open wide and come alive when talking about the problematic fact that Aceh had been declared a "military operational area" by the Indonesian government. This counterinsurgency campaign against the Free Aceh independence movement had no regard for human rights. For nine years the mothers of Aceh had been forced to witness 8,344 souls cut down, their blood spilling all over the land of Serambi; 875 people disappeared indefinitely into the jungle; 1,465 people widowed; 4,670 orphaned; 34 virgins brutally raped and wounded; and 298 souls disabled for life. And that wasn't even yet accounting for the property that had been destroyed: 809 houses, 667 of them burned and 112 demolished.

After the "military operational area" designation was lifted, then came Operation Task Force Authority 99, which was also run by the military and also turned out to have many so-called technical problems, like the capture and beating of civilians by armed elements and the riots in Pusong, Kandang, Lhok Nibong, and Simpang Ulin that resulted in at least twenty-nine fatalities and the loss of about 500 billion rupiah worth of property.

Sidan's mouth hung open. His eyes were wide and shining. Thrashing souls burned, their fists pounding, God is Great!

Hot nights drove him out of his rented room and brought him to campus and to café tables to meet friends—Mr. Musa, Nizar and Fikar, or Brother Sitompul and Brother Andi from Medan. He spoke with fiery eyes—his chest was blazing but there was snow in his head. He yelled, stomped his feet, his face streaked with tears. He was a visionary romantic who stayed out day and night, and when he finally returned home again, he brought all these worldly problems to bed.

"I'm sorry, I'm a busy man. I'm always working, even in my sleep. The world has many answers that still must be questioned."

That was how he always answered his friends when they asked him to attend various events. Now Firdaus was really intrigued, and her nagging question mark grew even bigger—because who else didn't like to go to parties, who constantly refused invitations?

"How about a feminist poetry reading?" she had once tried asking him herself.

"I'm sorry, that's not really my thing. I have something else going on."

Firdaus was taken aback by how stuck-up he seemed, but she also felt slighted. It was so weird. Did Sidan behave like that with others too? Even if he didn't care about anyone or anything except his cause, Firdaus still couldn't accept such treatment. She was fed up.

"I'm going to turn Sidan's head," she declared.

So she researched the thoughts that churned in Sidan's brain, tried to find out about his life. Completely fascinated, she found many peculiarities, many imbalances in his character. She edited her research, she revised, checked, and rechecked. Then, one quiet evening, she came face-to-face with that poetic figure. He was so beautiful, he called her back to him again and again, in vision of partnership and togetherness.

Firdaus opened the classic novel *Layla-Majnun* right under Sidan's nose. It turned out they both were familiar with the Indonesian version of the Persian legend, where Majnun wanders the desert praying and reciting devotional love poems until he hears of Layla's death and goes to weep on her grave, until he himself dies there. Then she asked him a flurry of questions, one right after another, without stopping to take a breath: Did the story of Majnun really just end in the grave? What was the world without his crazy howl? Would the poet Nizami, who first wrote the story, still have become such a legend if Layla had lived? And what about the Sufi interpretation of the tale? Did Sidan agree that most people lived their lives as if asleep, not knowing their true purpose, and only realized life's true meaning once they died and came face-to-face with God? And if that was true, wasn't Majnun, on his quest for divine love, actually saner than everyone else?

Sidan was hypnotized. It was as if Firdaus wasn't talking about Majnun, but about himself. He felt like she was exposing him, sizing him up, and that she was the only one who really knew his worth.

"Yes. Perhaps Majnun was more sane than everyone else," Sidan echoed.

"So much of our lives are lived in a kind of coma. Have you ever felt like that?"

His throat was dry. He was thirsty. He gulped down the last dregs of warm sweet tea from his glass.

"Um . . . I've never felt like that. But that's my life. Uh . . . I mean, that's the life I'm leading. Yeah, something like that, more or less!"

Firdaus secretly gloated seeing Sidan nervous. It was a monumental moment worthy of being recorded on a digital camera, but the only camera was in Firdaus's memory. The red light was on.

"Oh really? In what way?"

Sidan seemed to get even more nervous. He wasn't used to this. He searched for something in Firdaus's eyes, deep underneath the layers of everything she had seen, everyone she had known—her essence. But the window to her heart was opaque. He could only reach out for her tentatively, or maybe he didn't know her at all. He was a blind man, emerging from an absurd cave. A cave that had been silent and untouched for a hundred years. A thousand years.

"There is orange juice. Would you like some?"

She was just giving this new approach a try. Firdaus went to bring him a glass of juice and a small plate of croquettes. It was near the end of break, and the student cafeteria wasn't very crowded. Firdaus could focus and open Sidan's eyes so that he could look deeper.

"Oh. Thank you! But why do you have to go to all this trouble?"

"It's no trouble. You're not in a rush, are you? Go on, tell me more. What has happened, so that now some people have to live their lives in a coma?"

"Um . . . yeah. Maybe it's the nightmare—there is a colossal nightmare that is being acted out by many in this country, and it's being performed at gunpoint."

"And you are one of the players in that performance?"

"Yes."

"How far will you go to live up to your role?"

"Until I myself am in a coma!"

"When did you realize that this nightmare performance was going on?"

"Ever since I realized there was a script, which I read, and became disillusioned. I vomited and kept on vomiting. I had a headache. I was dizzy, agitated, and then my fever rose until I was in a fever dream. I became a blind sleepwalker. It was so dark that I couldn't see anything except the most terrifying nightmares."

Firdaus gasped. It seemed that the path toward achieving her goal was quite smooth, but this thrilled her, making her tremble. She looked into Sidan's eyes. A ghostly round sun behind two lucid black windows. She felt a rising desire that demanded to be satisfied, a desire to touch

Sidan and give him a heartfelt caress in thanks for his honesty—and for those limpid eyes, which Firdaus wanted to swim in until she sank.

"I can see the wounds in your eyes," Firdaus said empathetically. "Deep wounds. I have sympathy for you, Sidan."

Sidan's hand spontaneously reached for Firdaus's hand, and she reached for him. Sidan was dumbstruck. Firdaus was stunned. They were bound together in a warm sensation of affection and friendship. Then the sun appeared from behind the clouds in Sidan's eyes and his eyes were opened and he awakened into the present, saw that there was another world right before him that had commanded his attention and turned his head to truly look at it. He could see that there was something else besides a coma. There was a whole other life outside of War and Death.

That morning was the beginning of Sidan's life, and Firdaus felt the same way too. Yogyakarta greeted them with gentle breezes and genuine warmth as their story began. Now that they were together, the warm campus, with its chirping birds and fragrant roses, seemed to bubble over with enchantment. As they walked along romantic streets and alleyways, the days passed in love's embrace. Poetry fluttered and roared.

There were no more weary jaded eras or histories speeding out of control. There were no more crazy-making dreams. There was no long-suffering soul sickness or fallen past. A stone thrown into the mud finally reappeared, rescued from a gaping epidemic. Crazy Majnun went home again and became a sane man. Sidan, who had been so blind, was finally awakened to the fullness of the universe. He looked at Firdaus through a new lens that was so much brighter than the lens of War and Death.

Sidan: The stars above my pathway home are like your eyes watching over me. Did you know I was about to arrive? How did you guess . . . or did I already tell you I would come home at dusk?

Firdaus: The sun is still low in the sky, Sidan. Morning has just begun. But the seagull flies out to sea and comes home at dusk . . . Enjoy it! Enjoy entering the world of rainbows.

Sidan: Yes. In between rain and light, there in the middle, the two meet and create a reflection in the water as the rays entwine to form a colorful spectrum. Life must be better in this rainbow of colors.

Firdaus: Well, at least it feels richer, more meaningful. Do you still remember the legendary Majnun?

Sidan: After he howls to seven layers of heaven, now he falls quiet for . . . happiness? Or maybe he just wants to rest for a moment!

Firdaus: Why do you feel unsure about being happy?

Sidan: Majnun can never be happy. He has a problematic past. Hopefully in heaven everyone speaks Acehnese, haha!

Firdaus: If they do, then you can be my private tutor. Teach me how to see heaven.

Sidan: But if we go to hell, well, we are both already fluent in Indo-Jakartanese . . . so we'll be safe! Haha. Oh, Conqueror of the Dawn!

The days seemed to grow shorter, that was how fast the minutes flew by. When they were together, it was as if their steps floated above the clouds, in a weightless cotton world that drifted along without any cares. Only jokes could climb the rainbow bridge to that world. There was an angel there, and mysterious divine beings, the *wildan mukhalladin*, each carrying trays of silver and gold. *I'll sing and you dance. We are like two orchids in the garden of life.*

For a moment Sidan forgot his old self—maybe he had purposefully forgotten, or maybe he was just temporarily putting aside the black memories of the early military emergency, when the media was crowded with news of death and the tragedies in Aceh. Anyway, the news was really only tired statistics, not to be wept over but to be laughed at. The incredible becomes banal. Then everything falls silent and dies silently, like a television soap opera series is canceled so that it will get good ratings. TV is like opium. Capitalism only likes the first look, the sensation of the new.

Now that he was feeling good, he tried to complete his thesis, which up until this point had been limping along. He needed the fists of Firdaus's love to beat him into shape. He was happy with her critical mouth, which was never silent, but nagged him day and night in a new kind of symphony that he had never enjoyed during his dark periods. He had never known that such a beautiful and fragrant rose existed. Even when—or, *especially* when—she insulted him and threatened to wave good-bye, he realized more than ever that God had created her just for him.

Her essence came to him at night without warning, squeezing in through his pores, taking up residence in his bones and in his raving thoughts, becoming a wave in the ocean of his heart. In the morning, the Timoho neighborhood was truly beautiful, blanketed in fog, its face shaded and full of love. Then Sidan grew cold and went running to look for the sun in Firdaus's eyes. She who was wild and satin. She who was never docile, cutting through space with her confident strides.

She with eyes the color of Roro Jonggrang's well. Yes, she was like Roro Jonggrang, the fierce princess who protected her virginity by insisting her suitor complete impossible tasks, including digging a deep well, and when he managed to succeed, she lured him into that well and buried him in it underneath a pile of rocks.

It had taken him three years to research his thesis, but it only took him three months and three days to write it. His hands and fingers were animated by a mysterious energy. He saw stars. His computer screen froze. He chewed gum. And, of course, he enjoyed it when Firdaus embraced him from behind, surprising him and spiking his adrenaline, warming his entire body. He stayed awake night and day, working as if possessed, because the only grade he could bring home to Aceh was an A. As they said back home, *Nibak singet got meuruwah*, better to fall than to lean, better to fail completely than do a mediocre job. This was the principle of those who left their homeland in order to fight for a better future.

Sidan wrote on the dedication page of his thesis: *To a country whose warriors forge armor, but will nonetheless soon be wiped off the world map. Its pain has inspired me to write about it.*

"Wiped off the map?" Firdaus protested.

"After being in a coma. What else could happen to it, if not disappear?"

"There are always miracles in this life, don't you believe that?"

"A romantic is an optimist who keeps his thoughts to himself in a pessimist wasteland. There is no more hope."

"There must be some. Just eat as many cookies as you can, and then later you will see a change."

"What kind of theory is that?"

Firdaus fed him with her fingers, filling his mouth with handfuls of love. Unable to refuse, Sidan devoured two pieces of pizza and a croissant. He smoked and drank coffee. He also liked to drink warm tea and plain water, every kind of fruit juice, and sherbet. There were a lot of coconut sherbet vendors around his place, and Firdaus bought a cup for him every time she came to visit. Supermarkets and mini-markets surrounded the campus on all sides. Plus there were plenty of restaurants—KFC and Texas Chicken, Padang food, and the Bungong Jeumpa chain serving Acehnese cuisine; all you had to do was choose which one you wanted.

Together they liked to frequent the Acehnese place if they were in the mood for biryani rice, *pli'u* coconut goat curry, banana-leaf-wrapped *timphan* sweet rice cakes made with jackfruit and eggs, *paeh-bileh* steamed fish, or *canai Punjab* with duck curry, Firdaus's favorite. They would go home with four layers of Acehnese-style *martabak*, an omelet with a distinctive taste from the mix of *cane* bread and the *burukiek* layered in the middle. Sidan liked to eat *bueluekat* for breakfast, because he said the sticky rice flavored with fruit—sometimes durian, sometimes jackfruit—and drenched with liquid palm sugar was the food of kings. Delicious!

They often hung out at Bungong Jeumpa, enjoying fried duck and fresh sambal, sweet basil, and slices of fresh cucumber. If he was in a revolt against plants, Sidan consumed *burukiek* curry from Tangse. But if he was in a vegetarian phase, he only ate bread spread with Iranian korma, which could last him for twenty-four hours, and a few cloves of garlic or raw onion washed down with two liters of water. Yuck— Firdaus couldn't stand the aroma and would tease him. Then he would hurry to chew on some candied nutmeg or tamarillo, and that was taken care of!

"So, how about now? Do you feel like there has been any change?"

"No, your theory doesn't hold water, Firda!"

"The problem is that bad dreams are clinging to your brain, darling. Shake them off and then you'll feel better!"

"There's no guarantee that life in the future will be any better! Unless it can be stitched together from the fallen past, cutting ties with the dreams that drive everyone crazy. But it's hard. It's so hard, Firda."

"What's harder, cutting off your curly locks or cutting off a dream?"

"If you love being bald and barren, either one is quite easy to do."

"There you go. So what else?"

Firdaus quickly tried to move away before being swallowed by the tempest. But a hurricane always moves faster, giving its prey no time to rest. Sidan's hands, which were stiff from typing, needed to be limbered up by a little bit of fun—and Firdaus's impertinence demanded just retribution.

"Do you want to fool around?"

Firdaus almost collapsed, held upright only by Sidan's tight embrace.

"Fool around with what? You wouldn't need to hold me so tight if you really were a man!"

"Oh yeah? Don't wild things need to be locked up? Whether I'm a stud or a wimp, this is the law of nature."

"Ow! Yes, fine, you are a real Acehnese man . . . Please let me go. I'm going to pass out!"

The computer was still on. Books were scattered about in a comfortable silence. Two cups of popcorn and a quartz clock ticking to the rhythm of a drunkard's heart. They were both hit by a hurricane of desire. Two souls wandering in the silent night. All that was left was a glass of strawberry juice and a rising thirst.

"Enough, Sidan. Believe me, I like guys with long hair."

"Who doesn't like them?"

"You, who never seem to get your fill!"

"If heaven is like this, then who would want to have their fill, oh, my thirsty one? I'll never get full drinking you in!"

"You must be drunk. Don't you know this is a sin?"

"Once eyes meet, tongues must meet. Now, if a weapon meets a skull, *that* could actually be called a sin. Remember?"

"Yes, I remember. But what if a weapon meets a weapon, shouldn't that be punished?"

"What do you mean?"

"If total war confronts total war, isn't that the way it's supposed to be?"

"And who, pray tell, is practicing total war?"

"There you go, pretending you forgot again. You've aged prematurely, haven't you?"

"If what you mean by total war is a soldier, then he will almost certainly come face-to-face with another soldier. Not an entire militia. That's *makruh*, disapproved of under Islamic law."

"Isn't a guerilla war a manifestation of total war? In fact, the famous war philosopher Clausewitz composed his lectures on Small War based on guerilla uprisings in Germany and Spain. Aha! So then the *orang gunung* separatist rebels can be considered to be manifesting the doctrine of total war because they are carrying out guerilla warfare. In other words, the mountain people actually have formed an occupying regime that is using the invader's strategies: total war."

Sidan was stunned. He released his loving embrace and looked deeply into Firdaus's eyes, trying to understand her ulterior motive. Her question seemed to be in earnest, although she wasn't usually so worked up, like an earthquake in a sleepy season.

"Are you trying to say that what the *orang gunung* are doing is wrong?"

"Have I ever said that what they are doing is right? In fact, they are nothing but a coalition of marijuana sellers, enemies of the New Order, criminals, and bitter men looking for a shortcut, taking up arms, and committing acts of terrorism."

"Firda, what are you saying?"

"I just want a different atmosphere."

"A different atmosphere?"

"Yes!"

"Okay, so do you want me to slap you?"

"What would you slap me for? On what grounds?"

Sidan was shaken by Firdaus's fervor. There was no shadow of fear or retreat in her face. She was really challenging him. Sidan was intrigued—what was really going on? What wind had turned the ship around, sending it back to port? He really did have the urge to slap her, but his eyes fell on those two piercing black dots. He saw that they were already old and deep, buried underneath dozens of memories— maybe hundreds of years old, survivors from when the *inong balee*, the Acehnese warrior women, sank the Portuguese in Malacca. Those were the same two black dots that appeared in the eyes of the famous heroine Cut Nyak Dhien when she realized her husband had fallen and she would have to avenge him on the battlefield. But why were they now in Firdaus's eyes?

"At the very least you know that they are an image of flame, burning in silent suffering, Firda. You also know that I don't profess to be part of any rebel group. Why is your tone so hostile?"

"I already said, I just wanted a different atmosphere. I wanted to see you mad at me for once, not just at all of them!"

"If I have to get mad at you, it will certainly be for a different reason."

"Are they really so different?"

"Yes, just like they differentiate us from all the other citizens of this country."

"How do they do that? Give me an example."

"There are too many examples. Even our identity cards look different. Throughout the whole country we are spied upon, suspected. We are forced to do this and that, conduct the flag ceremony, monitored even when we are going to the bathroom. We are also *forbidden* to do this and that. Living in Serambi is no different than living in prison, despite the fact that we are independent people."

"But the rebels are coercive too. They forbid the people to raise the flag, right?" Firdaus said. "I heard that many police officers have been killed, even though they were also Acehnese, while shopping or taking their kids to school. The rebels also perpetrate ethnic cleansing, chasing out people who are not Acehnese—even killing many of them. Ethnic cleansing is their official policy. Isn't it true what I'm saying? In some villages near Tiro, people even have to be careful about what honorific they use when they greet a man. They have to be careful not to call him *mas* but *abang*, because even though both mean 'older brother,' the word *mas* is thought to have a Javanese feel, and all things Javanese are detested. Just like the separatists forbid the Independence Day celebration on August 17, threatening to attack any household that raised an Indonesian flag, whether they were Acehnese or Javanese. As further proof of their cruelty, even if people from their own tribe supported the Republic, the rebels still stamped them 'Javanese' and slaughtered them."

"It seems like you know more about all this than I do."

"Hey, now you're angry. But I have a point! The Acehnese people are very resistant to outsiders. They even questioned the integrity of their own head of state because he married a white American woman. How could Acehnese people trust someone as a leader, a guardian of the nation, when he had married a foreigner? How could the heirs to the throne be of foreign descent?"

"That's not a big problem," Sidan said. "The queen of Jordan is a white woman, and some prime ministers in India have white wives—that's nothing new. Six hundred years ago we brought in princesses from Malaysia and from the Bugis Kingdom in Makassar; even dark-skinned girls from Bangladesh entered the palace."

"Of course, and some Arabian princes also collected a harem of white women . . . but the white first lady of Aceh? Now that would be news. Or do you yourself also want to go looking for a harem of white women? There are still plenty of blue eyes left over from when the Portuguese were in Lamno. I've heard it said that Acehnese men like collecting harems." Firdaus was quite fired up.

"So? That's not a problem, is it? It's legal."

"Yeah, well . . . it would certainly become a problem if the Acehnese queens were given power. Now I know why rich men shackle their queens," Firdaus declared.

"Why?"

"It's obvious. It's not because of Islamic law, but because they are afraid of the competition—*especially* men in authority, rich men. They know that when women take command, like the four historic female sultanas did when they ruled Aceh in the seventeenth century, they will use their power to shift policies and create new laws. The truth is, men don't want to share their power—what's more be rivaled."

"Maybe they don't want to formally share their power," Sidan acquiesced, "but Eve flows in their blood, swims in their veins, infuses their heartbeat, is incarnate in their souls, and acts through them subconsciously. If that wasn't the case, women would have no power at all."

"But men monopolize power. The strange thing is that every time a ship is about to sink, the captain always shouts: help me, women are the pillars of the nation! It seems they only remember that when they are hanging off the edge of a cliff."

Sidan laughed in agreement before saying, "But we know that men's strength is sown by mothers and then cultivated by girlfriends, harvested by lovers, polished by wives. Probably a formidable ninety-nine percent of men's true capability actually comes from women—maybe just one percent comes from themselves. But then what do they use it for once they gain power? They use it to oppress women. That's a tragedy, isn't it?"

"Completely!"

Firdaus felt strange talking about power with Sidan. On the surface it was as if nothing important was happening, when in fact the ocean kept churning inside her, there was a river of magma that was ready to erupt at any time. Firdaus wanted to know whether it was true that Acehnese men looked down on women. Was the presence of four queens in the golden history of the Acehnese sultanate, and then the prominence of the prototypical female warriors there like Cut Nyak Dhien, truly a sign of men's support for women to appear on the world stage?

No! That's not how it was. If Acehnese women took the political stage or participated in the international arena, it was not thanks to men supporting them, but due to their own independent character and their powerful fighting spirit. They refused to give up. Ever since Aceh had been declared a "military operational area," approximately 900 women had been widowed per year, their husbands dead or disappeared. They were victims who had watched as their husbands and sons were abducted and executed, their blood spilled before their very eyes.

Acehnese women, the most vulnerable, were the hardest hit by the effects of war. At least for the men who died, their problems were over, but not so for the women. They had to carry on with their lives even though their souls had been torn apart, trying to survive as single parents in the middle of an incredibly difficult and hostile situation. The loss of the people they loved, their husbands and children—they might be able to forgive, but it was impossible to forget.

When Sharia law was implemented in Aceh after the tsunami, women bore the brunt of the burden. They had to wear the *jilbab* and cover their hair. Meanwhile all of the decisions about and interpretations of that law were made by men. Out of the twenty-seven clerics who made up the MPU, the *Majlis Permusyawaratan Ulama*, the Consultative Council of Islamic Clerics, none of them were female. That was why men were not required to say their Friday prayers at the mosque.

"There are twenty-seven people in the MPU. How come not one of them is a female? Has Aceh run out of intelligent women?" said Firdaus.

"Certainly not. But even the letters *MPU* come from the word *pere-MPU-an*, which means woman. So why should they actually join it? They are already in a good position. There have been Acehnese queens and admirals and war commanders, and now the New Order supports the Dharma Wanita women's organization, which is huge. Yes or no?"

"No, because accepting that would mean accepting a multicentury regression in Islamic law. Was Teuku Umar, the rebel leader against the Dutch, put to shame by his wife Cut Nyak Dhien, who fought bravely in his place after his death? I'm serious here!"

"Women are seen as weak thinkers in the doctrine of Islamic religious law, despite the fact that equality is the global message of the Qur'an and is a basic human need. That's the fault of the clerics, not of Sharia law itself, not of *sunnatullah* or the rules of the universe as governed by Allah. Those clerics are not following the true religious path. Now are you taking me seriously or not, my lady?"

In the traditional Acehnese concept of the home, women were indeed the heads of their households. But in practice, the highest decision-making power was still held by men, because they were the ones who made the money. The systemized marginalization of Acehnese women was most obvious in three matters: socialization, education, and work. Most women only got as far as elementary school, and more than fifty percent of women ten years and older didn't have an adequate education.

For Acehnese women, oppression was an everyday experience. It was hard for them to imagine themselves participating in civic life because of the limited opportunities they were given, and their subordinate role was only exacerbated by the ongoing conflict between the separatists and the central government. It was risky to be a woman. Wherever there were weapons, wherever an attack was launched, then the dimly lit shops turned into a complex of thugs who would force themselves on women, causing illegitimate pregnancies, and then set the villages on fire when it was time to go. Then the trickster generals would ask for more war funds!

Sidan himself felt nauseous every time he thought of his family in the village. Ever since his father was martyred, shot in the courtyard of the old mosque, it was his mother and his only little sister who had guarded sadness and continued their grievous journey through days filled with terror and trauma—before his little sister, like his little brother before her, got married and moved away. He felt like he wanted to wrap his body in a cloud of smoke and disappear to a distant land, a country that didn't meddle in his private matters, a country where he could laugh freely without having to worry about being written up by spies. He also had thoughts of revenge, but seeking revenge was impossible, because looking for the perpetrator was like looking for a single grain of sand in the Sahara desert. You would go blind before you found the right one.

"This is a miraculous country," Sidan said. "There are victims but there are no perpetrators."

"They are like roaming phantoms. It takes a special strategy to capture them. You need to develop better tactics, be like Mossad or the CIA."

"How can we, Firda? We're starving orphans here, besieged by fear and anxiety night and day. We can't even begin to think about being Hamas."

"Are you really so dejected as all that?"

"Really gloomy. Gray as twilight. You just realized that?"

"Enough! We always get stuck in these tautologies. Let's just change the subject."

"Agreed. Let's find a cooler, more interesting topic."

"Here's one: you still haven't responded to my father's challenge."

"Huh? For real? What challenge?"

"Do you have amnesia or Alzheimer's?"

"Sometimes both at the same time," Sidan said with a laugh, seeing Firdaus was not amused. "Are you angry with me? Okay then, let's be serious since we haven't been serious enough yet so far, have we?"

Firdaus intended to say that she no longer wanted to hear his breathing or inhale the aroma of his body. She was embarrassed to admit it, but she needed fresh air against her face and wind blowing through her curly hair. She wanted positive energy, but Sidan just inched along like a dying snail. Sure, there were some snails that could win when dueling with a deer—even with its slow pace, a snail could detonate a thousand time bombs—but right now he was really getting her down. Feeling annoyed, Firdaus got up to leave.

"Hey, hey! Where are you going, my lady?"

She hurried off, closing her ears and heart against Sidan's pleas. She could not care less. There was a night wind rustling in the row of mahogany trees like a fairy's breath. The Sunan Kalijaga campus was scattered with radiant lights. The campus never died, it just snored and then sputtered awake, delirious. Firdaus went to a mosque in a far corner of campus and washed her lower arms, face, and feet, cleansing herself for prayer.

It wasn't just on the nights of Ramadan; Firdaus often practiced *i'tikaf*, going into seclusion in the mosque to devote herself to Allah or just to hide herself away, brooding in between the columns on the second floor with nothing but a few scraps of white paper, a yearning pen, and a flame in her heart. The holy book is a treatise of love. Can you smell its jasmine aroma, like a breeze that invites you to nestle into its company? Like a green fragrant park, whose pleasures the world so desperately needs. The All-Laudable Qur'an.

Kaaf-ha-ya-ain-sad! Who would claim to understand those strange letters? Perhaps there were experts who truly understood the pearl hidden inside them, but their brilliance was universal. Firdaus liked to recite them over and over, relishing their penetrating essence, their wonder more perfect every time. Only Allah knew what they really meant—they could not be explained; they had to be felt with the soul. *Alif-laam-miim! Yaa-siin!* A mysterious alphabet that echoed the mystery of God and God's creation. When Sidan was excited he would spontaneously exclaim, *fabiayyiala irabbikuma tukadzdziban?* Then which of the Lord's pleasures would you deny?

"Oh, my beautiful! *Fabiayyialaa* . . ."

"What are you doing, following me here? Don't you have anything better to do?"

Firdaus was not surprised to see Sidan waiting on the corner, behind the men lining up to pray. Usually she would discuss his work with him in front of this mosque. They would sit next to each other at a small table, shoulder to shoulder, making notes. Firdaus stayed faithfully by his side as he edited interviews, traced references, discussing each book he read, analyzing newspaper articles.

When they needed a break, every once in a while they would go to the movie theater and watch a film, but between them they had a colossal collection of DVDs too, and they also liked to hike up to the summit of Kaliurang Mountain. But above all, Sidan preferred the majesty of the sea. They would go to Parangtritis Beach on days when it was quiet, free from the crowds that swarmed in on national holidays. Days where the waves crashed in their hearts alone. Firdaus would dance, frolicking on the dunes. Then they would dart around like two arowana fish, chasing each other and getting pounded by waves.

"You should have invited your friends Fazil and Zulidan along."

"Those know-it-alls? What for? They would just annoy us."

"They said that when you were little, you were really annoying too."

"Go on! What else did they say?"

"Lots of stuff . . . but no. You'll get mad."

"I think I know. They must have said that I was naughty, a liar, that I was nervous, that I liked to be alone, and that I was narcissistic."

"Huh, you admit it and you're not even at gunpoint."

Feeling magnanimous, Firdaus wanted to give him a gift in return for his honesty.

"But," she added, "they said that you are a pearl in the hollow of a mussel shell. Your genius has been wasted, buried by guns. You have long curly hair and Alzheimer's."

"Haha, I know that's not true—it's not them but you who said that. So if you already know more about me than they do, then why did you ask?"

"Who said I asked? They just told me."

"Okay, fine. Just keep in mind, nobody really knows who I am. I am an eternal loner. Hell is other people. My reflection is dim in the mirror. The sun has many faces. Yes or no?"

"Yes. So then, more or less, what is the sun's face like when you are looking at it from a dusky beach like this one?"

"It's like the face of a lover who is willing to be betrothed to the waves, hovering above the ocean, its eyes orange, its cheeks blushing red."

"Sidan!"

Firdaus was mesmerized by the beautiful words that slid so easily out of Sidan's mouth. She looked at him with a lingering pleasure and an insistent longing. His eyes were not quite healthy. There was no desire in them. Typical of romantic rebels from across the sea, they were downcast, like a drooping flower or a shy daughter. But his heart was a different story—if you could look inside, you would see it was defiant, full of embers and flames.

"What is it, Firda?"

"Nothing . . . I just like your eyes. They are the strangest I have ever seen."

"What's so strange about them? I'm not cross-eyed, am I? I don't have trachoma or glaucoma. I don't use lenses, minus or plus. I've never even had too much gunk buildup. But they *do* stay wide open, day and night, aroused by your fragrance, swept up into your soft and wild adventure. Anything else you want to know about me?"

Firdaus chuckled at his honesty, so rare in this ultra-deceptive age. There was no other man as honest as Sidan on the face of the earth, truly. This was even more unusual, miraculous really, when combined with the miracle of his two eyes. Honesty was more beautiful than the Taj Mahal in Agra. Honesty was the purchase of love.

"Yes. I just want to know why you are so honest and naive. You are very valuable to me. There's no one else like you in the entire universe."

"How about when compared to a jaguar?"

"You're still more valuable."

"Compared to a bald professor?"

"The most irksome creature."

"How about when compared to Che Guevara?"

"Maybe you two are about the same. Sometimes you resemble him. You have exactly the same eyes."

They went looking for jellyfish, then a voice called out from behind a boulder on the hillside.

"Don't touch that—you could be stung with blue poison!"

They both looked around trying to see who was shouting. They hadn't noticed another person all afternoon and had thought they were alone, but they were mistaken. There was someone behind the mountain rocks, far in the distance. It was as if he was watching over them—or maybe he was meditating? Finally they saw him and his black skin covered in mud. It was said that spiritual seekers meditated in the small caves on the slopes because of the supernatural forces that were said to inhabit the beach and the waters offshore. Years ago a poet, taken with mysticism, had disappeared into one of the caves and vanished without a trace. They still hadn't found him.

"I think he's right," Sidan said.

"Right about what?"

"This animal that looks like an overturned bowl. It is a powerful sea creature. Just look, even though its entire body is only made from two layers of jelly, it has tentacles."

"What is a tentacle?"

"A tentacle? It's a pipe that hangs down and has a little mouth at one end. In between these tentacles there are nerve centers and sense organs. It is these that make jellyfish dangerous."

"Dangerous how?"

"The tentacles stab and pierce the body of its prey. If a jellyfish stings you, you'll feel weak and have trouble breathing. The tip of the tentacle is directly attached to a gland of poison that can weaken or even kill its enemy. Incredible, right?"

"This rubbery thing is able to kill something?"

"That's the puzzle of the All Just!"

"It lives in the pounding waves and doesn't ever break apart? Glory be to Allah!"

"And this is a giant one. Imagine its offspring—tiny, pliant, and rubbery. But a jellyfish is truly powerful. Even though it is small and cute, it challenges the waves, and the ocean submits to it."

"The Creator of All Things!"

Sidan grabbed Firdaus's hand to pull her up and away from the waves charging toward them.

"Looking down at the water makes me dizzy," she cried.

"Don't look down when the waves come in. It creates a natural hallucination. Look far into the distance. There are clouds over here, and there is another stretch of sky covered by clouds."

"Is that the sky in your heart?"

"Yeah . . . something like that. Now, feel its wild pounding!"

Knowing that Firdaus was a bit shaky, unnerved by the hallucinatory waves, Sidan grabbed her from behind. His warm embrace calmed her down, and she felt like her thoughts were now back under control. She hoped that rare embrace—which felt as rare as if it only happened once every thousand years—would last forever. Because Sidan was so concerned with guarding his image that he never yielded to what Firdaus wanted, but always went for whatever was forbidden. His was the character of a rebel for whom resistance was the breath of life. He would certainly turn left in a hurry if Firdaus wanted to turn right.

"Do you feel it?"

"Feel what? All I feel is that now it's hard for me to breathe," Firdaus said, feigning innocence.

"You felt it, didn't you?"

"You're delirious. Let me go!"

"This time I won't."

Sidan tightened his embrace. His hot breath swept across Firdaus's ear. His mustache and sideburns tickled her and drove her crazy. Firdaus couldn't take it. She struggled, trying to free herself, but he came at her again.

"Oh my goodness, get a haircut . . ."

Sidan just pursued her and kept on pursuing her.

Who can feel the quivering vibration of those crashing waves, receive its tickling mist, if not the heart of the ocean? So Firdaus had to become the ocean. Ready or not, her wings needed to spread to welcome Sidan to her. And that was a heady feeling, like savoring an intoxicant, sip by sip, tasting a heavenly wine.

"What do I know? What do I need to know? All I know is . . ."

"What?"

"You!"

"You're telling me that without any weed or some other drug, an Acehnese can get high? What's going on with you?"

"To me, you are the essence of liquor, the essence of pot, the essence of intoxication, the essence of love."

"Oh my, Majnun," Firdaus sighed.

A bullet meeting a skull, that is still forbidden. But eyes meeting eyes, tongues meeting tongues, that is intoxicating. Your tongue is sweet and my tongue is juicy sugarcane as they join. The waves on the beach rise and fall, toss back and forth, like the pounding in our chests. And chest meets chest.

Spirits are greeted by love. The greeting of embraces and kisses belong to the inhabitants of heaven. Then the earth lifts up and rises to the land above the clouds like a kite.

A shore wind blowing. The roaring of the waves creeping into the innermost layers of the soul, sending a sugary sweetness to solidify at the tip of your tongue. Perfumed silence. Your body is Adam, just come home after centuries of wandering, and my longing is still growing more insistent! I want to swim and swim in the pool of your eyes until I faint.

"Ah, you're too sweet, love. Careful, you might get stung by a tentacle," Firdaus cooed.

The history of bitterness disappeared from Sidan's memory and he shook his fist at the sky, ready to conquer the future.

Bad dreams had been left behind, anchored on the southern shore. They went home on a bridge of cotton. Weightless.

The fragrance of your hair still clings to my lips, lips that pressed against the curve of your neck. And I am still consumed with hunger.

On the veranda of the mosque that night, Sidan's hunger relapsed.

"You should go home and stop bothering me."

"This time I'm serious, Firda. I want to talk about your father's challenge."

"Oh yeah?"

Sidan nodded firmly.

"Why now, after all this time?"

"I just think that now is the best time and place for it. Because I'm serious, so there needs to be a little nuance of the sacred. How about it?"

It was a good answer. Firdaus was happy in the quiet evening on the mosque's veranda, where everyone was engrossed in devotional prayer and contemplation. Here everything had a pure face, everything was a clean slate. Anything could begin. Goodness could grow from ash, as the people here prayed, knowing they would return to ash.

"I'm certain," Sidan said. "We'll marry after I pass my exams."

"You're not asking me for my opinion?"

"No, because I am certain that you will agree."

"Well, I don't."

"Wait, what? Really?"

"I don't want to marry a narcissistic man—or an unemployed college student."

"About my narcissism—that was in the past. And as for being unemployed, of course I have to go through a process to overcome that and get a job. I need your support, Firda. I hope you are not playing around."

"And one more thing."

"What?"

"I still don't want to go to Aceh. You can go find another woman who is ready to become one of its infamous woman warriors."

Sidan chuckled. Even though he knew the land of Serambi needed its share of fierce women, they didn't have to live in Serambi. They could go anywhere, and they could still rebuild Serambi and love it from wherever they were. The world was no longer divided by time and space; it was now the era of the global village.

We dream and then awaken, thrown to the ends of the earth. While rubbing our eyes in Canada, our "good morning" is already heard in Indonesia. Our smiles have already reached Africa. Longing and love have become unimaginable. We are the owners of the ninth dimension, the tenth dimension, the celestial and divine dimension.

"I know the suffering in Aceh is like a virus. There is nothing to be seen there, and especially nothing that a tourist would enjoy. Sabang is parched. The eagle has toppled over at Kilometer Nil, the westernmost point of our country. There's nothing but lonely monkeys in bald forests and ancient majestic tamarind trees that have been standing up to the wind and the passage of time for three centuries."

"Who would want to travel to Sabang?" Firdaus said with a laugh. "If I went to Aceh, I'd be interested in seeing the villages of widows where all the men have been killed, the mass graves in Cot Panglima gorge, and the remains of the great sultan Iskandar Muda."

"Yes, I should take you on a bridal procession back to Aceh in the seventeenth century when everything was so pleasing, blanketed in splendor, with celebrations that exuded greatness and a glorified atmosphere, not a long period of mourning, full of coffins, the mass grave at Cot Panglima, the civil war, and the battle in Cumbok."

"Too late, dear. It seems like everything about you is late."

"For example?"

"You're late to graduate. Late to date. Late to marry. And the most tragic of all, it turns out that you were born too late."

"In that, we are both the same—born too late," Sidan said, laughing now.

"Why are you laughing?"

Sidan just shook his head.

A dash of humor can finish off a pinch of anger—and not just that, humor is a trusted medicine that can heal all kinds of spiritual ills. So laugh as hard as you can. Make a concert of laughter as a therapy that erodes stress, chases away pain. Laughter is gold, my lady! The healthiest aerobics. Do you believe it? One minute of laughing is the same as ten minutes of cycling. If insomnia comes, it's best that you quickly open your mouth to chuckle merrily and chase away depression. Just ask the experts. The stress hormone cortisol is conquered by laughter, sent scrambling this way and that.

"Sadness is forbidden. Gloom is banished. So how else should I be?" Sidan asked.

"You can be quiet. You know a quiet retreat of contemplation in the mosque is also good for mental health. The soul needs to be purified during quiet nights."

"But I've already answered all of your questions, right? Have I satisfied your challenge?"

"As long as it's all not just hot air. This means that your thesis has to be finished immediately, brother. Cut out all your sleeping in."

"Oh man, my lady, you also need to ease up just a little bit. Stop being so hard on me."

If only we weren't on the mosque veranda. If only the owls would turn their eyes away. If only there were no other creatures except for us two. If only night would become night-blind and mistake us for two roses. Your lips are like luscious pomegranates. If only, Firda! Then you could not dodge me any longer; your fierce and clever dance would be finished.

"It's late, Firda. Let me take you home."

"Why do you have to take me? Do you think I'm afraid of ghosts now?"

"It's not the graveyard ghosts I'm worried about, but the lady-killing ghosts who haunt the dorms. Come on. Don't act so brave."

"How about you don't act like you're such a hero just because you have balls. That's so old-fashioned!"

"But men have weapons."

"Don't think you're so tough just because you bear arms. That way of thinking is more than old-fashioned, it's ancient."

Sidan's laughter erupted loudly, breaking the contemplative silence on the veranda. A few pairs of eyes looked over at them, their concentration broken, some giving sideways glances of displeasure. But there were no dark-black assumptions. Night and day the students milled about, studying and learning. The heart of campus kept beating, knowing no rest, even for a moment—if it stopped for a rest, it might collapse.

"Fine. Whatever you want, Lady Feminist. So that I'm not mistaken for a colonizer, so that I'm not thought to be exercising my power, so that I'm not accused of marginalizing anyone or subordinating anyone, I won't interfere."

Now Firdaus's laughter disrupted the silence. She got up, packed her books, swept up her bag, and left without saying good-bye. Because he already knew how she was, Sidan calmly followed her at a distance.

Your dance sways, so charming
No matter what rhythm you are humming
But the thirsty soul cannot be satisfied
Two wild ones, dancing inside a flowerbud of quiet
Never finishing, never done . . .

Chapter 4:
A Land above the Wind

Sidan: Forgive me, Firda. I have to go for a little bit . . . August in Aceh makes all civilized people run as far away as they can, after sixty years as part of the(ir) free country! Forgive me, lady of love!

Firdaus: But I thought you said you didn't want to go very far?

Sidan: Not very far, not so that the spark is extinguished, not like Pluto. Maybe the second planet after Mercury, which is still red as an ember: Mars! Khomeini or Horta!

Firdaus: And what kind of bunker do Horta and Khomeini have?

Sidan: None. Just green earth, oak trees, and a
cup of soybeans . . . with paintings of the
ocean, children's eyes, and a sliver of a
desperate heart. I'm leaving. The ship is
setting sail!

Firdaus: Tell me! Where is the ship sailing to,
Sidan?

Sidan: To the Land above the Wind and Clouds,
Firda . . . Don't worry!

And then he was gone. Every time she sent a message, it just said
"pending," and it stayed that way for ten days. Firdaus obsessively
counted the hours of Sidan's absence, then recalculated as the hours
turned into days. In an attempt to distract herself, she stared vacantly
at the television screen, flipping through channel after channel, frustrated. *Where are you, Sidan?* She devoured newspaper after newspaper.
She contacted all of her Acehnese acquaintances and texted back and
forth with them for a long time until she felt drunk and drowsy. She
fell asleep on the sofa and dreamed of being on a faraway red planet.
Smoldering Mars. It turned out Sidan was waiting there after all, sitting
under an oak tree, smiling.

"Hey! I've been going to the ends of the earth looking for you and
it turns out you are just sitting here. What are you doing, Sidan?"

"I'm thinking about the things of mine that have been stolen."

"Who stole what? You are delirious again, dreaming in broad
daylight."

"I'm awake, Firda. Archangel Michael just clocked me upside the
head. He said I should try to count how many trillions have been made
by the Arun Gas Refinery since 1997—and I did it, and I was shocked,
Firda. Come on, let's sit on this neolithic rock."

Firdaus was drawn to the red hunk with a crater in the shape of a bicycle saddle. She tried to enjoy this foreign place, where everything was so strange and magical. There was an apple tree with tempting, low-hanging fruit. A river of red water snaked down the valley, curving through lush red grasses. There were red mountains and an expanse of bulging hills as far as the eye could see. Red geese chasing each other across a red lake.

This was the land of the brave. The land of real heroes. Firdaus had never seen anything like it. There was no color except red, like blood. A smoldering fire.

"The Arun Gas Refinery? How many trillions?"

"I heard that the Arun Gas Refinery makes four products every year, with annual earnings of three hundred and sixteen trillion rupiah. Compare that to Aceh's annual budget, which is only one hundred and two billion, or not even half a percent of the natural resources they yield."

"Tsk, tsk, tsk. Your country is extraordinarily rich, but you are a real pauper far from home, my love."

"That doesn't even include those in the manufacturing industry, like the Iskandar Muda Fertilizer factory, the Asean Aceh Fertilizer factory, or the Aceh pulp factory."

"Go on, go on . . . What else?"

"The Acehnese forest is made up of 4,130,000 hectares that have been divided into lots by those in power in Jakarta, using Natural Forest Management permits, Land Conversion permits, and Industrial Plantation Forest permits, which make about nine hundred billion rupiah a year. Even some uncle, whose only capital is a permit from National Forest Management saying he has the right to 160,000 hectares of pine forest in central Aceh under the name Alas Helau Corporation, already controls twenty-five percent of the stock in the Aceh pulp factory. In 1985, that stock was valued at eighty-five billion rupiah. That's monkey business."

"Exactly, they are just like an old monkey who swallows hundreds of thousands of hectares of forest in one bite. They never get full, do they?"

"You know why I have to count the riches of my country that they have stolen, Firda?"

"How should I know?"

"Let me tell you. If no one had plundered our coffers, right now all the main streets and highways throughout Aceh could be paved with solid gold. You don't believe it? Aceh is rich but bizarre—its people are poor, their lives displaced in evacuation after evacuation. If anyone wants to join in forest management or enter into a contract with ExxonMobil, which controls the natural gas fields in Aceh, they always say that the decision must come from Jakarta. Monkey business," Sidan said. "The centralism implemented by the crazy folks in the central government, who are actually masters at military strategy, has repressed anything that they think might disturb the stability of their national regime. It already controls almost every corner of the Indonesian archipelago, to the point that even if you want to comb your hair and make a ponytail with it, you have to ask Jakarta for permission. It's absurd."

"So I'm lucky that I already pulled back my hair without asking Jakarta about it first. My ponytail can hang however it wants."

"After gold, natural gas, and the forests have been depleted, sucked up by the Jakarta elements, what do we get? Forget being able to sample a diversity of world cultures, even our right to simply live as creatures of God has been buried deep in the killing fields that were created by our own nation. Long ago, the Dutch colonial advisor Christiaan Snouck Hurgronje was able to conquer Aceh with a cultural and religious approach; as a policymaker in this land of a thousand intellectuals, why would you ever have to use violence and ammunition to exterminate a people who have done nothing wrong? And yet, look at the mass graves everywhere, one pit with five corpses inside. It's tragic!"

"Yes, tragic! Continue!"

"Do you want to try this apple, the fruit of wisdom?"

"Whatever you have to give I will certainly want. I'm sure it tastes like milk and honey."

"Let me feed you a piece of apple. Disappointment after disappointment, Firda, finally reached a climax and found its momentum. So the OOG were born."

"What's that?

"*Orang-orang gunung*, the mountain people, the guerilla fighters who want independence from all oppression and occupation. And are they wrong to want it, when Aceh was illegally sold off by the Dutch to become a part of the Great Nation as recently as December 1949?"

"It's perfectly logical, but why did the *orang gunung* take up weapons? Based on the Declaration of the Ulamas throughout Aceh that was made in October 1945, wasn't Aceh declared a part of the Republic of Indonesia? And didn't the people of Aceh ignore their edict and label them traitors?"

Suddenly, Sidan looked quite distressed, as if there was something pressing in on his head. Firdaus no longer dared to continue her rebuttal. Maybe it would be better to chase after the red fowl on the orange lake or pick red grapes from a field whose soil was the color of brick. *This is a country of revolution,* thought Firdaus. Spewing red blood like in Palestine! Like Sarajevo! Iraq!

"Weapons must be fought with weapons. The integration of Aceh was crippled by international law. We were sold out by the Dutch, but we rejected that with a forty-year war. I'm sorry, Firda, but maybe the historians have a problem with Aceh, so the Acehnese historians compromise. They have no plans of going home. Not like our head of state, not like Muhammad during the reclamation of Mecca."

"If that's how it is, then maybe the soldiers aren't wrong to come to learn how to pull the trigger in Serambi?"

"Ha!"

"The *orang gunung* had already begun an occupying regime with their guerilla war while the army was carrying out an antiguerilla operation. It's true that all the inexperienced young soldiers in the ranks mean that there were a lot of transgressions, but try to look at it honestly, rationally, and systematically. Who really started it? Did the army just idly come to Aceh and then cause a disaster?"

Sidan's face was now even more distressed. Dark red like a ripe Fuji apple. Once again, Firdaus's will to continue receded. If she had been facing some Tom, Dick, or Harry, anyone else who was not Sidan, Firdaus would have argued her point until they were finished. But Sidan?

How can I attack my soul mate? What I feel also becomes what you feel, even though our ways of thinking are different.

But it was that difference of opinion that kept inducing Firdaus to go at him.

"And haven't the politicians sold Aceh to American senators, those wolves in sheep's clothing? The *orang gunung* are also carrying out ethnic cleansing," Firdaus continued tentatively, feeling out Sidan's response.

"But isn't that better than being sucked up by the Dutch East India Company, colonial imperialists refashioned into contemporary government officials coming to Aceh fresh from their elite Jakarta neighborhoods? We prefer to wear jeans over our knock-off shoes, even though we are selling bread and war. At first, American aid could be used like in the Iran-Iraq conflict, but we certainly don't want to become terrorists. We don't use Islam or mysticism. And what you are calling 'ethnic cleansing' is actually the karma of transmigrants who refuse to follow local customs."

"Wait, but isn't karma a part of Indian mysticism?"

"Or it's a doll from India, maybe?"

"How could they not be terrorists if five hundred public schools have been burned, the students and teachers terrorized to the point of insanity, churches bombed, prisons opened, drug money used to buy weapons—they are truly like Pablo Escobar, and on top of that they carry out ethnic cleansing. The *orang gunung* wreak havoc in this country so that the Indonesian troops will be pulled and their military wing will be able to wage an open war. Yes or no?"

"Don't be ridiculous, darling. No churches have been bombed. And Aceh was declared a 'military operational area' because the minister of defense and security, Benny Moerdani, wanted to build more churches in front of the Baiturrahman Grand Mosque and was denied. Really, Jakarta? Okay, fine. I guess that's ambiguous karma. But the killers don't pay *diyat* financial compensation to their victims, and they don't get punished, so what should be done, my love? Those schools were burned because they represented the decades-long crusade for Javanese domination that has been carried out ever since the fourteenth century, when Gajah Mada vowed to conquer the entire archipelago, and continuing all the way through the New Order. Their destruction was a sin. But it's not clear who did it. And then the soldiers join in the mix and confuse things even more, making it seem like we are even more in the wrong. Even though the Dutch are long gone, we are still being badmouthed. What else?"

"But even their own people are killed for flying the Indonesian flag."

"Well, the flag just doesn't understand our traditions yet, but Aceh was forced to become part of this Great Nation under its colors. What else?"

"This apple tastes bitter. I only eat the sweet ones."

"Acehnese apples are super bitter, but the people of Lingkhe put sugar on them. I guarantee you'll love it. Here, try some."

The Red Planet was already fed up with war, so here weapons had been destroyed. There were no weapons meeting weapons; there were only eyes meeting eyes and tongues meeting tongues. Lingkhe poured wine on Yogyakarta's lips, so it wouldn't be wrong to say that Firdaus was drunk on the fruit from the land of Aceh. That wine was full of mantras that could tame lies and draw out the truth. Because honesty is more beautiful than songs and those who sing them.

Your starry eyes zero in on me with one piercing glance. Like the beams of light emanating from Mount Sinai or the eyes of the Sufi mystic Hallaj, no one can understand it, but it evokes a gleaming universe. I collapse on your lap, am enfolded by your bosom, melded with your spirit. Your fragrance lifts me to seventh heaven. My exquisite mantra, from a Sahara of silence.

Two crazies dancing in between drops of rain.

Sidan got up and took Firdaus on a tour of the Land above the Wind. They boarded a red propeller plane, Soul Airlines. Like the astronauts Neil Armstrong and Yuri Gagarin, they flew far from the Green Planet and nuclear thunder, far from the foam of oration and the sermons from the Department of Deception in the Land of the White Goat. It was cool to breathe in a zone forbidden to humans, enter the hiding place of the gods who were up all night holding emergency meetings about the apocalypse, which was drawing ever nearer.

"It's strange, isn't it, love? This plane can rise and fall to the rhythm of our heartbeat."

"You are like one of the Seven Sleepers who hides in a cave and falls asleep for years only to wake up and find the world has changed. We just landed on the Red Planet and you already are openmouthed. We haven't even gotten to the Purple Planet yet. None of the treasures of your Earth are valuable here."

"Oh really? Is that how ancient our earthly cave is?"

"It's not ancient but old, dirty, and coughing. The islands are now like mushrooms beneath the ocean, like scattered leaves. The time has come to sink, because our country has not yet found a proper leader with the strength of character to save us from the flood, like Noah with his ark."

"Oh really?"

"Really! So prepare for my proposal, the day after tomorrow. And for our honeymoon on the Blue Planet."

"Oh really?"

"Yes, my lady, my beautiful angel of the South Seas," said Sidan. "Don't tell me you think I'm joking? And don't ever play with me, okay? We both could be thrown from this miraculous plane. We could crash down onto Antarctica, right at the South Pole."

"That's not a problem, is it? I would like to fall from this plane and land in a different pole. One that's far away."

"Like Adam and Eve . . . Are you really that romantic?"

"Of course. Is that really so bad?"

"Where is Adam and where is Eve?"

"Eve and Adam. Adam and Eve. If Adam is without Eve, doesn't he belong in heaven?"

The red airplane suddenly careened down and then rose again pointing up at the sky, and kept on going up and down. Firdaus was struggling, tense and dizzy. Sidan was being tossed about. Without a seatbelt, without a life raft. There wasn't even a pilot, nor were there any flight attendants. They were the only two passengers. And the red engine light went on every time they drew a breath.

"Where's the pilot?" Firdaus yelled.

"Inside your chest!"

"Ah. The truth."

"Ask your heart."

"So?"

"Yes! That's it!"

"Sidan?"

"Yes, dear?"

"Give me peace."

Sidan engulfed her in his gentleness and affection.

"Give me honesty."

Sidan opened his heart, ready to be touched, explored, read, and analyzed.

"Give me faithfulness."

Sidan closed Firdaus's eyes and opened them again. Then she blinked again and found Sidan still in his seat. He hadn't gone anywhere. Whether he was awake or asleep, Sidan was still in his place.

"Why do you give me everything sweet, Sidan?"

"Because your clear eyes are so sweet and juicy, Firda. So everything will return to you. It's not going anywhere. It's the same with me. How could I go to heaven without you?"

"I'm scared of falling after we have climbed so high, my love!"

"Get a hold of yourself! Don't be tentative and weak. Take care of yourself!"

"I'm scared! Look how high we are. There are layers of clouds beneath our feet and still we rise! Stop the plane or turn around, love!"

"How can I do that? As long as we synchronize our breath, we can go wherever we want. Okay?"

"What do I see over there? A red brick house like in Viking country?"

Sidan peered out the window and scanned the view of an expanse of red grass and a basketball court. A five-year-old kid was playing with an Angora cat. A gardener was picking strawberries with a basket at his left hip. There were streets made of red asphalt, smooth like a professor's bald head, without moles or pimples. The sound of Antonio Vivaldi drifted up, accompanying the Angora's meow.

Sidan jumped and shouted, "That house belongs to the head of state. It can't be anyone else."

"Oh yeah? And who are the people at the edge of the court? The ones playing war?"

Sidan turned his head. He saw a group of young men with Indian, Acehnese, Arabic, Chinese, and Indo-Portuguese faces acting out a war. One of them was wearing a black-and-white *keffiyeh* scarf on his head. He was a middle-aged man from a nomadic tribe with dagger eyes and mighty, deliberate strides, ready to challenge the formidable desert sandstorms. A Bedouin from the Libyan Sahara. Sidan kept staring.

"The guerillas are training under a commander. Look, it's Muammar al-Qaddafi!"

"Qaddafi?"

"Who else? The head of state ordered them to train under him, and it worked. They frightened the state military, which led to the military operation, which only stopped once he fell! But from 1989 to 1998, more than ten thousand Acehnese people were killed. Tragic."

"What was actually done during the military operation?"

"Reconnaissance, spying, checkpoints, clandestine activities, house searches, and mass arrests. During those years, many Acehnese houses were ransacked and burned, and many women were taken captive and sexually assaulted."

"Go on, go on."

"In the middle of the 1990s, the soldiers' violent actions grew increasingly rampant. Low discipline, low wages, and unclear policies meant increasing human rights violations, which caused mass defections. Many people escaped to Malaysia."

"What were you doing in your house at that time? What were you thinking about?"

"I wanted to get out of Aceh as fast as I could and look for a safe place to learn. I had to get out before I hit puberty and grew facial hair and was considered a suspicious person."

"It was that dire and oppressive?"

"There were silent nights, eerie and listless. Ghosts roamed about, back from the dead. The days were painful, blistering, full of fear. Days passed in the quiet anxiety built up over a thousand years of silence."

"Is that when your paranoia began?"

"No. It was long before that. Or maybe it's been there ever since I was born."

The plane once again took a nosedive, descending steeply until it was only a few meters off the ground. Then it righted itself. But Firdaus, absorbed in Sidan's nerve-racking tale, wasn't paying attention to the flight.

She slid over to sit close by his side and looked at him. Her soul so longed for him, and there he was, with his unhealthy eyes that were without desire, despite the fact that he consumed plenty of vitamins and nutritious food. Good fortune comes from heaven, from offering up your heart and mind to Him. Many donors reach out to shake the hand of friendly Archangel Michael. Sidan was still there, pristine curls rippling down to his shoulders, blown about by the wind. With the lips of Mark Antony, who loved Cleopatra and held her all night long. Intoxicating her, swallowing her up in a beautiful embrace. From up above there was a snuffling rhythm that sounded like it was coming from a nose leaking with the flu. Melancholy sniffling.

Firdaus shivered with fever. She was in love.

"What's wrong, Firda?"

"I want to marry you, Sidan!"

"Those are sacred words. It's good that you have said them. But let's wait until after we've landed."

"I want to marry you right away, Sidan!"

Sidan was stunned. The airplane swerved, navigated by his wild heart beating out of control, *thump, thump, thump.* That flying saucer vanished, flying to who knows where, with no warning. The entire view was just a glimpse of hazy red shadows, red bubbles, nothing but foam. Flashes of orange rays like the sunset in Serambi Makkah above Seulawah. In the shadow of the waves of Lhoknga Beach. He needed to get his steering back under control so they didn't crash.

"We will soon be married. Of course we will, Firda! You know that very well. Okay?"

"I need proof."

"Proof at a time like this?"

"Tell me what day, what time, and where, Sidan. Before this airplane tumbles out of the sky and we plunge and crash and never get up again!"

"Tomorrow. Tomorrow morning."

"You promise?"

"On all that is good, I promise."

His reassuring eyes and the firm squeeze of his fingers rooted firmly in Firdaus's heart. They had reached the desired equilibrium. The airplane again was stable and now they were flying over Australia. They enjoyed the misty red Twin Falls in Kakadu National Park, its carved walls and red grass, and its springs like two bulging eyes, two showers of blood gushing out the bitterness of Aborigines, emptying to become a waterfall. But there was no smell of putrid blood, just a soft mountain wind caressing the singing swans. The splendor of life was revealed through the ocean, sand, and sky.

Mighty nature. Beams emanating from a ball of fire above a hill sparkle sharply, making you humble yourself and cast away your eyes. Then your eyes search for green branches, but here the leaves and trees are red. Red sand and a red sea. Here nature leads you to the height of anxiety. Even in a eucalyptus forest, the koalas stand guard in their habitat with red fur. Lake Barrine was full of red reeds and piles of stones arranged to dam a river of red Karijini honey.

"Where are we, love?"

"In the gentle, calm, and cozy realm of the heart. Tomorrow we will prepare for our wedding."

"Truly? What will happen if your mother doesn't approve?"

"How could that happen? She only wants success and all good things for me, happiness and joy, so why would she forbid me my heaven?"

"Heaven has many levels."

"No, Firda. There's only one heaven: Yogyakarta."

In an instant Firdaus was filled with memories of the city. Its slow mornings when time froze and you could just enjoy yourself, sleeping in comfortable Kotabaru. And the Timoho neighborhood, full of tree-lined roads and intersections, food stalls and newspaper kiosks. Houses all pressed together, competing for the students looking for rentals.

Small, narrow, winding alleyways swallowing the faces of wanderers. Black skin, white skin, narrow eyes, crinkly black eyes, protruding noses, snub noses—a cornucopia of all kinds of people.

Sunan Kalijaga State Islamic University and the other universities guarded the city's dignity and raised its prestige, as did the theaters and Taman Budaya, the cultural center. The city was enlivened by the newly built plazas and malls, townhouses, housing complexes and apartments and hotels and craft centers, but if you felt saturated and life had begun to seem boring, you could always take a break and hike to the top of Kaliurang Mountain or go play in the waves of Parangtritis.

"I miss our beach, Sidan!"

"Those waves have witnessed our courtship, love."

"Let's go back there now!"

"There is still a lot of poetry we have yet to discover. Wait, if there is something more beautiful than the past, we will stop to see it."

"Where is there more beauty than in your mournful eyes?"

"Don't mock me! We've arrived at Kilometer Nil. Do you see the blue ocean over there? What was blue before has become red here. Look at the peaceful waves, listen to the rustling of the wind and the quiet behind the hills."

"You mean this is the monument of the Indonesian Republic's Kilometer Nil? The westernmost tip of the nation?"

"On top of that monument is the number zero. There is an inscription in black marble that displays the geographic position of this place. This is the very first kilometer of our republic."

"Are we at the beginning of the world?"

"A small world that is in a coma and dying. We are at the tip of the eagle's talon. He's collapsed, powerless."

"Really?"

"Of course, but we shouldn't suffer from bird flu just because we were foolish and picked a bird as our national symbol. So why don't we reserve just a part of our heart for love and peace in bed instead?"

"That's a good suggestion. Later, when kindergarteners sing the national anthem, the lyrics will be different, they'll sing it like this: 'My love, a bed of principles . . . I am your supporter . . . oh patri-archy . . . just take everything I have.' Haha!"

"Hey, you forgot, didn't you? Don't play with words like that, love. When you do, they lose their sacred aspect, you know? Did you forget? Tugu, Freeport, all the national monuments, and all the city gates are guarded by soldiers with Simeulue lobster claws. The city is crowded with stupidity. Life is full of death and forgetfulness."

"You're starting again. Your old sickness is relapsing."

"I'm telling the truth. This is a bad time for the imagination."

The airplane tilted and almost grazed a small wooden boat floating by on the shifting waves. The tip of Pulau Weh was a sheet of heaven planted on the face of the earth by the Creator. It was so beautiful it could make you fall in love. Then Sabang, with its stadium and three-centuries-old row of tamarind trees, and the Sabang to Merauke telephone counter. To the activist poet Dino Umahuk, to Karel Frederik Holle, the Dutch colonial advisor and enthusiast of Acehnese culture, and to the Acehnese locals themselves, "Sabang to Merauke" meant nothing more than that local telephone counter, which the motorized pedicabs parked in front of as they waited for customers to come out of the nearby hostel. Just that. No more, no less. But that name was taken from the lyrics of the children's nationalist song "From Sabang to Merauke," as if there were emotional ties between everyone in Sabang, the westernmost point of Indonesia here in Aceh and everyone in Merauke, so far away in Papua, the easternmost tip of the Dutch East Indies.

But what kind of game was this anyway? If such national unity did exist, then why was there rebellion throughout Aceh? Why did so many Acehnese people want special autonomy or even independence from Jakarta? Why did so many people of Sabang feel bitter about Jakarta's decision to revoke Sabang's status as a free port in 1985? There was no story here, just like the famous poet Chairil Anwar said in his poem

"Twilight at Little Harbor," "No one goes looking for love in an old port town." It was all dried up.

The patter of rain accosted the airplane window with bulging drops of blood. Whose melancholy blood was dripping above the eagle's shield?

"It's starting to rain, Sidan. We're going to get stuck in a haze of red clouds. Let's retreat, return to the base."

"What base, Firda? You're delirious."

"The airplane base, what else? Birds return to their nests. Children return to their mothers' laps. Airplanes return to their bases. You're the one who's delirious!"

"Aye, aye! I found the base. Let's turn around and head there."

Because this plane is just a vehicle to steer our lives, taking us on a journey to visit the graves of all that has passed away. But still, the river of life flows in our veins and the height of human glory permeates our pores. Seventeenth-century Aceh was a glistening, shining star in the constellation of the country. To visit it, even if only for a moment to be amidst the banquets and the refreshment of exercise, the supernatural atmosphere that radiated from the sultan's throne—that would erase a little of Sidan's thirst.

Firdaus awoke from her dream of flight, her head still full of her never-ending conversations with Sidan about Aceh and its tragic history, its powerful lure for both of them.

Not all of Aceh's majesty had disappeared beneath the onslaught of time; there was some beauty that still remained. Look at the most beautiful marble tomb of Queen Nahrasiyah in Pasai, with Cordoban calligraphy and decorations, or the ancient Javanese script and the Arabic calligraphy on the gravestone of Queen Nur Ilah. There was an intimate link between the greatness of the Majapahit and the Pasai Kingdom, and this gravestone was only one small piece of evidence among many. Firdaus wondered how it was possible the Acehnese head of state could have such antipathy for Indonesia, the modern-day Majapahit. Was it just because Gajah Mada, the *mahapatih* or prime minister of the Javanese Majapahit Kingdom in the fourteenth century, had taken the Palapa Oath, swearing he would fast until the entire archipelago was under his dominion?

Still feeling groggy, Firdaus remembered another conversation:

"We reject the whole Gajah Mada complex," Sidan had said.

"You mean Indonesia?"

"Based on their different historical backgrounds, cultures, philosophy, and their right to determine their own fate, every people living off the island of Java should be independent from the country of Indonesia."

"That's also known as disintegration," Firdaus said with a laugh. "But that kind of self-determining independence can only be achieved *through* the nation of Indonesia, isn't that so? We already decided that, right?"

"The integration of Aceh was crippled by international law. We were sold out by the Dutch. So we rebelled with a forty-year war, Firda."

"The whole world agrees that Indonesia, from Sabang to Merauke, is a sovereign nation, official and legitimate. And for that, we don't need to look any further for a historical justification than August 17, 1945, Sidan. According to international law and custom, after the global recognition of our sovereignty, the former Dutch colonies no longer define Indonesia. Indonesia is whatever the Indonesian people themselves believe their country to be. Yes or no?"

"Oh really? So the cosmopolitan is conquered by a domestic king. That's not fair."

"Fair or not, the princess of Pasai becomes the empress of the Majapahit Kingdom, the conqueror of thirty-five nations, from Banten to Jambi, Palembang, Makassar, Bali, Riau, Pahang, Pattani to Campa," Firdaus answered teasingly.

Her mocking tone infuriated Sidan, but he had to admit that those were the historical facts. The Majapahit had reached the height of its greatness in the middle of the fourteenth century. In his eulogy to the king, Mpu Prapanca said that it was thanks to the leadership of Mahapatih Gajah Mada that Samudra Pasai was one out of the thirty-five nations to be conquered by the Majapahit Kingdom. Aceh reached the height of its power in the seventeenth century, during the government of Sultan Iskandar Muda and his daughter, Sultana Taj-ul Alam Safiatuddin Syah.

After that, Aceh had a series of four sultanas, women who were famous in all of the world's Muslim countries. But then the clerics, who weren't proper authorities in matters of Islamic law, broke the golden chains of the sultanas, and Aceh returned to being led by male sultans. At that time, the Sultan Badi'ul Alam was from the Habaib people, followed by Mahmud Al-Rasyid Perkasa Alam, Jamal Al-Alam Badr Al-Munir, Alauddin Jauhar ul-Alam Syah, and Syamsul Alam. But Acehnese women were still Acehnese women. Even if they no longer became sultanas, they still rose to become war commanders and admirals. And if they didn't do that, at a time when other women were still willing to laugh, gathering in state-sponsored Dharma Wanita ladies' clubs and concerning themselves with inconsequential affairs, Acehnese women were willing to fight in the ranks of the *inong balee*, the female faction of the *orang gunung*. It was fitting that even the Dutch colonial advisor Snouck Hurgronje finally fell in love and married an indigenous woman. Before he died, Snouck acknowledged that Acehnese Islam was different from other sects and was not easy to subdue. So he didn't regret converting to Islam, taking the name Abdul Gaffar, in order to marry his local wife. He loved his woman and he couldn't deceive himself, or others, in matters of the heart. Snouck understood that these matters had nothing to do with Dutch Indies politics and could only be understood between individuals.

Life and dreams and history were all swirling together for Firdaus in the mystical cauldron of Sidan. Has she been dreaming all of this? Had they had this conversation before or was she imagining it now? Firdaus could no longer tell as she opened her phone and read the texts stored there.

Firdaus: Wait! So before Snouck was an asshole but now he's not, love?

Sidan: It's the same difference, Firda. Acehnese people see his face in the mirror, and what's more on TV, and they're still traumatized by something, even in times of peace. But the mirror is embarrassed to be split in two, that's history for the generations.

Firdaus: Why aren't you broadcasting tonight?

Sidan: I'm too lazy. Radio people do whatever they want. Do you know how what a lovely poet I have asked to dinner, to temporarily replace my angel? Her name is Harum Sabnaranti Majdi. So, why would I broadcast? That would be boring!

Firdaus: Oh, my dear, you just get more and more attractive.

Sidan: Maybe this lady poet will be more fun. She has a biryani rice food stall. It's crazy, girl! But my "yang" is still safe, not swayed by worldly pleasures!

Firdaus: You have an extraordinary natural talent
for making up stories. But you're still
an amateur. Continue shoveling the shit
and after a while you'll be famous!
Haha . . . do you know what jancing is?

Sidan: I used to know. But I forgot. What?

Firdaus: If a bride and groom take to the marital
bed . . . Eyes meet eyes, tongues meet
tongues, the penis enters the vagina.

Sidan: Haha, cool! Then lighting strikes and
releases all its power . . . I sing a chant
of longing! Or an Acehnese lullaby.

Firdaus: I sing a chant of love for Allah! Ma'assalam
ya ahlan-niyam. Ma'alliqa' fi hilwatil
ahlam! I send a parade of greetings to
you, my sleeping beauty. Until we meet
again, in sweet dreams.

Firdaus closed her eyes and once again fell asleep. This time, she slept as soundly as a babe in arms.

Meanwhile, Sidan was floating in the silence of a foreign barracks without a friend. He tried to reach out for Firdaus in the black shadow of night. Longing had him in its grip; he could hardly bear its wild agitation. Lying on his back, his clenched fists swung left and right. *Where am I? I have no village, I have no city, I have no independent country. Who am I? A lonely wanderer who has collapsed in the mud, riddled with maladies and gaping wounds. Crazy. But who are they, who steal everything, leaving nothing behind but a worthless tomorrow? Who are they, Firda?*

Archangel Michael arrived in the midst of Firdaus's dreaming bliss with a bouquet of fragrant poetry picked from the garden of Eden.

"An offering from Sidan. Plucked from his bloody hand in a garden of paradise."

"He's already in heaven and he's still so romantic?" Firdaus asked with amusement.

"He didn't ask for seventy-two virgins. For him, one is as good as seventy-two. Seventy-two in just one."

"Are you sure? Tell the truth. Night and day he prayed for martyrs on the battlefield. Seventy-two virgins were the eschatological deposit that he was waiting to cash in on, Brother Mike."

"Seventy-two in one!"

"I know. But nobody sells energy drinks there, so their chorus might leave him breathless."

"In fact he is a real man from Aceh, he doesn't need an energy drink."

She liked to chant the legend of Prang Sabi, the Acehnese epic about the nineteenth-century war against the Dutch:

> *Come I will give you repose,*
> *come I will sing of a spring of life,*
> *like the overflowing Kautsar River of paradise*
> *that brings generous pleasures,*
> *those who drink the water of the spring of life*
> *are only those who make holy war.*
> *Serve Allah, marvel at the Prophets,*
> *for those who kill infidels will certainly fill heaven.*

Then, in her dreams, she recited a parable from Surah Al Baqarah, verse 261, with a special resonance: "Those who invest in Allah are like a single seed that grows into seven stalks, with one hundred more seeds growing on each and every shoot. Allah multiplies the reward to whomever He chooses. Allah the Infinite, the Bountiful, the Omniscient."

These tears welling up in my clear eyes, Brother Michael, show how my heartsick longing is building. I want to see him as soon as possible. Seventy-two virgins in one castle. But I ask, who is lined up in the castle of the martyrs? Are there seventy-two virgins waiting there?

Michael's smile grew quietly secretive and he gave a wink that was hard to interpret. Would seventy-two *wildan mukhalladun*, those mysterious divine servants, greet the martyrs? If war in Allah's name is each and every person's individual responsibility, then every martyr should get the same reward. So says the Saga of the Holy War:

> *Whether woman or man*
> *Everyone, old and young*
> *Adults and little children*
> *Join in according to consensus*
> *Virtuous, wicked, pious, innocent,*
> *Everyone must play their role*
> *Kings, commoners, hereditary chiefs*
> *Must make war as equals*
> *The infidels who threaten our nation*
> *Must be quickly fought*
> *It is sinful to run, required to fight*
> *It is our spiritual obligation,*
> *Each and every one of us*

It was not surprising that martyrs had eagerly flocked to the Battle of Penosan. Dozens fell with a smile in the Battle of Tampeng. And hundreds more in Kuta Reh and in Kute Lengat Baru. The Acehnese people had had the concept of a holy war against the infidels since the Portuguese attacked the kingdom of Aceh Darussalam in the fifteenth century, long before the poet Tengku Chik Pante Kulu was born and wrote the verses to his incredible *Epic of Prang Sabi*. A saga more than 1,100 verses long that ignited the spirit for jihad against the Dutch that lasted thirty years.

The Archangel Michael didn't need to open his mouth. Firdaus already knew the answer. She knew because Sidan was her other half. She began to worry that of those seventy-two, not one of them was her. But how could that be possible? Sidan was truly blind! He had only opened his eyes to see Firdaus appear, to make her part of him. Plus, Acehnese men were terrible liars. They were only good at diplomacy and negotiation. That was their inheritance from the majesty of the sixteenth century, when Aceh was one of the world's five great Islamic nations.

Firdaus calmed down, swimming in a river of dreams that almost swept her away. But what were dreams? It was as if everything in them were real, perceived by her flesh and bones. Dreams were just condensed and contained awareness, a spirit in a coma adventuring in another world that was much safer than this one, and full of possibility. A Land above the Wind. She brandished the accomplishments of her dreams like a champion raising a trophy. When she woke up, she jumped for joy to find her chest beating out words of love.

If dreams were their only place of refuge, that was alright. At least there was a veil of secrecy over both their faces. A place where they could order their longing and sharpen their weapons against hunks of great sorrow.

Firdaus rose from the sofa to look at the clock, which was chiming and dislodging the crown of silence. Night had gone and morning was greeting the breeze through the window shutters, dawn spreading like the sunrise of a new world.

Chapter 5:
The Refugee Barracks

Sidan returned from the distant islands. His homesickness had been like a fire of longing, an incurable illness. He immediately contacted Firdaus, sending a hello to his darling from Arundhati Roy, Aung San Suu Kyi, Jhumpa Lahiri, Siti Zainon Ismail, and all the strong women in the Land above the Wind. He was claustrophobic and his coma was getting worse as he imagined his angel returned to him.

Firdaus was busy preparing for the next day's seminar, typing her paper and racing toward the deadline for the publication of a collection of her essays. She was avoiding contact with everyone and didn't care that her phone was chirping away. Power was rushing through her and her mind was only focused on the letters that came to life on the page, dancing and demanding that the words be completed.

What's more, ten days had passed and she wasn't even sure whether Sidan had returned home yet, descending from the Land above the Wind. Who could know whether he would be gone for ten or one hundred or one thousand days? Sidan was always a puzzle. Firdaus had grown tired of waiting and had succeeded in filling her days, spurred on by big dreams. Still, in those quiet days of waiting, a discordant inner voice sometimes nagged at her.

What if Sidan has disappeared forever? And even if he does return, when will the day come when we can sit together and enjoy a morning meal at the same table, reaffirming our hopes and dreams?

Firdaus truly did not understand why there had to be war and death. Why humans killed each other when they were really brothers. Ever since Cain had murdered Abel, there had been no peace on earth, and as the centuries passed, the joys of life remained elusive. Wealth and crown. Women and power. Children and love. All of it could become ammunition and explode. The atomic bomb was nothing but a weapon made in a factory—the real weapon of mass destruction was hatred that lodged in the chest like an infection. The real execution machine wasn't Kamen Rider Black, but a heart full of soot, encrusted with virus and disease.

Sidan: Why aren't you texting me? Are you busy watching soap operas? Sorry! I'm sick and exhausted. I can barely stand missing you so much . . . but I'm still tied to the world by my memories of you, your last caress didn't completely destroy me . . . Haha, I think I'll rest for now. Bye!

Sidan collapsed in the barracks, weary from being tossed about by the waves of life, stalked by an invisible enemy, hunted by phantom rifles. He tried to laugh, but his throat just caught. He looked up at the low ceiling, made from iron sheeting that was cold at night and burned in the heat of the day. He was thirsty and wanted to drink one or two sips, but he didn't even have a glass of water. He had nothing except a bedding set donated by the WHO, a few newspapers, a few new books, and a radio.

There was also a Yamaha motorbike he had bought with the money he had earned from selling his video camera. He had been using the camera to make documentary films with his friends from Jakarta, but he had been forced to exchange it for a motorbike, so that at least he could get around in this world of suffering. He no longer had any hope of leaving Aceh ever again, ever leaving the graves of his father and mother and his home and village that had disappeared, folded under the waves. But on that motorbike, he could go out to work, reporting for the local newspaper. That was the only work he could find after his performance-troupe contract was up.

Sidan boiled some water from an irrigation channel dug by German soldiers near a defunct regional military command post. The price of gas had gone up and many of the people in the barracks got their fuel by boiling and straining *jarak* fruit from the castor-oil plant, but because he was impatient, Sidan preferred to buy gas by waiting in a line that was two kilometers long. It was the longest line in the world, but if you wanted to survive here, you had to get everything you needed by lining up. At the crack of dawn you would wait in line for the bathroom, then at midday wait in line for gas at the pump that was far from the barracks. It made your legs cramp.

Every morning upon waking, Sidan still marveled at what kind of world he had been thrown into, especially if he was awoken by one of the earthquakes that came right before dawn, just when he had finally been able to close his eyes out of sheer exhaustion. Sometimes an earthquake high on the Richter scale threw him against the door or flung him under the table. Because he was so tired, he often just kept sleeping wherever he had fallen and was only awakened later by the vibrations of the barracks floor, which shook when the children in the neighboring barracks jumped around, since the floor was made of large continuous planks of wood that connected one building to the next.

Here you never hoped for sweet dreams—if you made it through the night without any nightmares, that was enough to make you smile through the day. But even daylight brought a bizarre reality that was hard to grasp: line up to bathe, line up to do your washing, line up for gasoline, line up to eat breakfast at the food stall, then line up for the bathroom because you are full or sick. Those who were coughing or had malaria would certainly have to line up for treatment at the mobile community health center. Then, the lines were so long that they caused their own unique kind of illness: line fever. Because of the limited medical staff and labor-and-delivery facilities, the mothers who were about to give birth would have to line up in the hall, groaning, so that even new babies had to wait in line to be born. And way at the other end, death also joined the line, laughing heartily and pouncing from behind. *Bam*—you're a goner!

Angel Azrael was exhausted.

Sidan snarled, niggled by a thousand disappointments.

The liars and the traitors are cursed. The trinity of Qarun, Pharaoh, and Baal are cursed. Those who profit off the people's suffering are cursed. Oh, you who ravage everything and suck up our earth's milk until there is nothing left, you are cursed. Cursed! What did we do wrong, Jakarta? What is our sin, oh, you leaders of the Land of a Thousand Intellectuals? On what grounds are we shot, hauled to jail, and slaughtered in the rice fields, in the forest, by the roadside? Are you really that addicted to hearing our agonized death cries echoing in the ravines of the mass graves at Cot Panglima? Don't you realize that we are being treated to a feast of love, that seventy-two virgins dance for each of us in the garden of heaven? But what do you know about us anyway, aside from how to be envious and treacherous, stealing from us and shooting us!

Then Sidan remembered the words of Fikar W. Eda, the Acehnese poet, who in his poem "Rencong" said:

> *Whoever comes*
> *We greet with dancing*
> *And poetry, banquets*

Signs of glory

Whoever comes
We put flowers around their neck
Greet them with ten fingers
And the bow of our head, which makes eleven

Whoever comes
We give them gifts of title
And tributes
Like family

Armed with dagger blades
With sarongs and shiny handles
We don't forget to include
Signs of dignity and grandeur

But how sore are our hearts
From Jakarta, you all stab the points of those daggers
Right in our hearts!
Worse than the Dutch! That's Jakarta!

All the people of Aceh knew this, because they were all historians—the women busy selling their wares at the market, the pedicab drivers, the hotel security guards—they all knew history or at least understood a bit about history, and the teachers, the historians, the professors, and their students knew even more. The Acehnese people were strongly oriented toward the past. To them, Aceh's magnificent ancient history was only yesterday; it was seared into them. They took pride in having been the first region to embrace Islam in the archipelago during the magnificent reign of Sultan Iskandar Muda; he was admittedly authoritarian, but the Acehnese remembered that the people lived in harmony under his rule.

The more the Acehnese people knew about history, the more partisan they became and the deeper they resisted the central government. After thirty years the central government had tried to subdue them with soldiers, and the only outcome was misery. The blood of the people had been spilled and their personal freedom, granted by God, had been stolen.

Sidan: When will Jakarta do more than just make empty promises to Aceh? Sukarno lied because he thought Aceh was just full of Indonesia's prayers and sinners. Aceh didn't know Queen Justice, the Messiah! Just martyrs and dark eschatological dreams!

Firdaus's phone was pending. Ugh! Sidan couldn't wait for her reply. He missed her and he was cranky with nothing here but barracks and lines. He felt like he hated her, but he longed for her. He wanted to be able to actually call Firdaus once in a while, to hear her crisp laughter on the other end of the line. But how could he do that? He had to save his phone credits for text messages and emergencies, and he could not even afford to buy those himself. Firdaus had been buying them for him—not much else could be hoped for in the land of Serambi after the emergency funds stopped coming in.

Above all, though, talking to her was still an outlet for all of his longing and lament. He gave thanks and praise to Allah for granting him Firdaus, a salve for his soul, which was on the verge of madness—indeed, if you were a young Acehnese man in these screwed-up times and you hadn't gone crazy, then you must be dead. Crazy in a refugee tent or dead in a mass grave.

Once, Sidan had seen the tents of Palestinian refugees in Khan Younis Camp and Yarmouk Camp; they were appalling, with narrow alleyways cutting through overcrowded settlements and dreadful slums; with bare trees, dull boulders scattered in the road, and houses that hadn't even been fully built but were already occupied. He never would have imagined that what he had seen in Yarmouk Camp would become his life. But then his house had disappeared. It had been painted ivory, with a spacious and shady front yard full of grass and flowers tended by peaceful and loving hands.

My messy room on the second floor with all the books I collected over the course of my studies, my favorite DVDs and cassettes, my documentary films, my photo albums. Now the only remaining photo I own, besides the ones on my identity card and my passport, is the photo of Firdaus I carry in my wallet. I don't even have any photos of my father, my mother, or my two younger siblings. And I can no longer look at the drawing of the faithful noblemen of the Great Commander Sagoe Bentara Muda that used to hang on my wall. I loved how they carried their sharp rencong *daggers, wearing oversized jackets and dark-brown sarongs with golden embroidery.*

The electricity goes out all the time and water is scarce. Even just one or two dippers full is extraordinary—so don't use any unless you really need it; save it for emergencies. But then again, here everything is always in a state of super emergency. Even though it is no longer a state of military emergency, it's still a civil emergency. It's hard to make a living when you are oppressed by the shadows of the military, separatists, and a lack of work.

Sidan's diploma had been destroyed, carried away by the waves, as if the water had carried away all of his hopes and dreams for a bright future. He was thankful that he had been given an internship at a local newspaper on the consideration of a number of his writings, which were good enough to be published. With that, he no longer had to stress about that lost diploma. Even though the pay was low, he could still write a number of articles or essays with an honorarium that would ensure he could at least afford to eat. But it still wasn't enough to close out his debt at Sulamtaque, not to mention pay for electricity, gasoline, his phone. When his phone credits were used up, he felt too ashamed to tell Firdaus, and he would go to an Internet café on the nights he needed to clear his head. What was important was that he soothed his longing and he could say good night to his beloved.

Sidan: If I stay up late, I like to stay up all the way until dawn, Firda. Night often feels as eerie as a grave of an unknown soldier but all I need is a dance, my body banging out its longing, and my mouth humming the melody, dodaidi . . .

Firdaus: Oh, poor you! You don't have to be a shy kitten with me! Why didn't you tell me your phone credits were used up, you think you're too good to ask for my help? And not sleepy yet either . . . !

Sidan: Maybe if the sun rises, it's just in Aceh. The rubble of houses has to be guarded from looters. I already carved "Papa's House, Do Not Disturb!" onto my door, and I'm not embarrassed that the basic idea behind it is "don't bother me," to preserve my concentration and initiative. That's my creed! Whether there's food to share or not, we still have to eat . . . And no I'm still not sleepy, haha. Did you already drink your warm milk?

Firdaus: Tonight I'm drinking a health tonic! No sweet candy has made it to Yogya. When will the sago flowers bloom? Even the moon is gasping for breath in the Code River.

Sidan: *The moon is swollen with blood, Firda. Every*
night it witnesses insurrection . . . Yogya
spies on the virus in my head. Sago? Sago
fruit may be its namesake. Its skin is rough
and scaly like snake fruit. It's so tasty
mixed with rujak sauce! That's a little
rujak secret from Aceh. It's usually sour on
the tongue, but in Meulaboh they sweeten it
with sugar. Meulaboh is just an old city on
the western coast that is already half gone.
There's no sago left. The occupier's word is
usually delivered from Suak Timah village.
But we'll have to wait three more years
to hear it because then that village sunk,
destroyed in the earthquake, along with
everything else that used to grow there. All
there is left there is kuker, crackers made
from buffalo skin. You want some?

Firdaus: *No! I want you to come to Yogya as fast*
as you can! If you go back on your word,
you'd better watch out! And don't bother
to reply!

Sidan was stunned. He felt his head. It was still there. His hair was matted, not because he wasn't getting enough vitamins but because he had forgotten to comb it. A romantic has no time to groom; that would distract from his search to find himself. Thankfully he'd buttoned his shirt properly. He touched his ears. They were still there. He touched his phone, which he'd placed on the table. He looked to his left and right, at the cubicle walls of the Internet café. He looked at the ceiling and the AC humming away up there. Then he swept his gaze across the entire room. There was no one there except him and the café attendant.

Sidan scratched his head again. He didn't have dandruff. Rain was still drizzling down outside. The clock was showing 2:38 in the morning, Western Indonesian Time. Even three layers weren't enough to warm his body, but the vicious cold was actually coming from the Code River, which was roaring and overflowing. Yogya was losing patience, waiting for the sago palm to bloom. Ah! How could he just stay silent? Did she really mean it, that she didn't want him to reply? Because if he did respond he had one whole volume of the holy book and an encyclopedia of scars at the ready.

Sidan: Listen to me, Firda. No one is going back on their word! I've already climbed so many steps, I even scaled a pyramid that sent me tumbling. But the heaven of Yogyakarta is so high and hard to reach for these injured legs, this soul wounded by so much disaster. But I will not go back on my word! When I am healthy and strong enough to run again, I will surely race up to our heaven once more. Yogyakarta! Please keep my name in your copious prayers. Keep our long prayer rug unfurled, my love! I really mean it about you, about us!

Firdaus: And I am really waiting for you! I'm serious about us! That's enough for now . . . I can't take any more. Go in peace!

Sidan: Okay! I hope you can sleep with a sweet smile, not just a scowl. Ibtasamiy ya hilwaty! Keep

smiling, beautiful! My warmest greetings!
Grazie mille!

Firdaus: *Yup! There's fragrant jasmine near my*
heart. As for the long bridge from
Yogya to Meulaboh, you can measure it
yourself. Bye!

Sidan: *Tomorrow, to be continued, maine pyar pagel*
helized tilmiz, bapa biyung kakang kawah,
mucho gracias, mille la partiza, lun fatih
deniz dinergi kizilay. Sleep! Arigato!

The café attendant had fallen asleep at his table and was snoring rhythmically, not caring if Sidan left without paying however many thousands of rupiah he owed. Unwilling to wake him up, Sidan joined him instead, leaning back on a nearby chair. He wasn't afraid of being intercepted by soldiers on the journey home, nor was he waiting for the rain to stop; he was truly worn out by the fact that he was being defeated by destiny. But he didn't even recognize the word "surrender," and he would get up, strong and tall, once again. On this sad and beautiful night, although his body was exhausted, his spirit was still hopeful and his feelings vacillated between a suffocating longing and a solemn calm.

The two men were awoken by the faint call to prayer from the mosque tower in the middle of a field, spared by the tsunami as a testament to memory and ever more fervent prayers. It was like the field where all souls would gather on Judgment Day, awaiting their fate from God. Dreams and drowsiness were heavy on Sidan's eyelids. Evil spirits debated angels, competing for power in his half-awake heart. The attendant almost rolled off his chair before he jerked up straight and rubbed his eyes, realizing that someone was resting beside him. He smiled when he recognized Sidan.

"Get up, brother. It's dawn."

Sidan's eyes felt sticky and he couldn't open them. The attendant knew he was not a morning person. The rain and wind were picking up momentum, gusting hard, rattling the roof. Then the electricity died. Sidan wrapped his jacket tighter, trying to get warm. He didn't care where he slept and he hoped the attendant would understand. If there had been blankets for rent, he would have certainly ordered a couple. There were two lit candles in the attendant's hand.

"Can I order a glass of something hot?" Sidan asked hopefully.

"You want some coffee? Or ginger tea with milk?"

"The second!"

In fact there were only a couple of bottled and instant drinks for sale there, a few different kinds of cookies, but the attendant gave this extra service to regulars who got there early in the morning, because he himself was cold and needed a hot drink too. As soon as the drinks were served, their chairs suddenly began to vibrate—gently at first, then more violently. The two candles fell and went out. Sidan got up, feeling along the edge of the table, trying to seek shelter underneath it.

Maybe it was a six, he guessed from experience.

He knew this routine by heart. For many months, ever since the ocean overtook the ground, early-morning earthquakes had regularly rattled him. Sidan couldn't stand these dawn attacks, when he was sleepy from guarding the gate of the universe all night long, looking for answers to endless complex matters. At night his thoughts were free to float wherever they wanted. The spirit of an adventurer can't be tamed. Here that was the only privacy that couldn't be violated.

When stillness returned, all that was left was spilled hot ginger tea with milk that smelled of suffering in the weak light of dawn. He groped in his pocket to give something to the café attendant with his melancholy eyes.

"Thank you for your kindness. For the sleep. For the tea."

"No, brother. Just pay for the text messages."

"But you made a glass for me."

"The glass spilled."

"But it wasn't your fault. It was *their* fault."

"Their fault? Whose fault, brother?" asked the attendant, his eyes shining wide with curiosity.

"The forest eaters," Sidan replied casually.

"The forest eaters?"

"Don't tell me this is the first time you've heard about them?"

"I swear. Only just now. Might I know more?"

"Listen up! Neither tsunamis nor earthquakes, flash floods nor tornadoes, ever came to call on us as long as the gorillas were still comfortable in their habitat. Isn't that true?"

"True, true. Yes, it's true, brother. So?"

"After the forests were all chopped down, chewed up by all the National Forest Management, Land Conversion, and Industrial Plantation permit holders from Jakarta, it wasn't just the monkeys, who once hung in the leafy forest, who were lonely. All of us in Aceh became miserable and alone, abandoned by our family members who were taken by the wave that Sunday morning. Isn't that true?"

"True, true. Yes, it's true, brother. So?"

"So there is injustice toward nature. There are those who ravage the environment. There are those who prioritize only their own stomachs and their own families rather than the good of the people as a whole. There are faceless guests stealing from their hosts. Those liars in ties smile with greasy foreheads, riding their Jaguars through the refugee camp uninvited. They suck up the country's milk—petroleum—until it is all gone, leaving nothing behind."

Sidan pounded his fist against empty air.

"Do you want me to make you some more hot ginger tea, brother?"

"Ah yes, you may—thank you!"

The shopkeeper hurried off. Sidan was dazed for a moment, remembering Firdaus's threat. *If you go back on your word, you'd better watch out.*

Oh, Firdaus, how could I ever go back on my word? I can't wait to fly to you, as fast as I can, as soon as I am able. I don't need to wait for an ultimatum. What is there for me to enjoy in these strange days spent in the silence of solitude? Here there is nothing but parched land, damaged roads, debris, and bare trees.

The city is just a wisp of smoke in your eye. The mosque, the barns, the rice fields, the market, the library are all burning with silence. It pierces you to your heart. If I could be reincarnated, I would certainly choose Yogya as the place to be born again. There is nothing left here, Firda. The people don't know what to do. In this dire and terrifying situation, our spirits are muffled in fear. If we leave our houses we are hunted by weapons, if we stay inside our houses we are sought by soldiers. So where can our legs stand firm? Where can our backs find rest? Where can the birds fly home to?

"Excuse me, brother. Please drink this tea so that you can warm up a little bit."

Sidan returned to his senses. His eyes went right toward the ripe and enchanting glass and he didn't let even one second pass before reaching for it. The warmth that flowed through his body gave his mind a little bit of relief, seemed to erase a bit of his misfortune, ease his feelings of futility and dashed hopes. Then a vision of his faithful lover's face danced before his eyes. She came whenever and wherever, when Sidan was sitting quietly or when he was busy working. That face occupied seventy-five percent of his dreams and fantasies.

As soon as the contents of the glass were gone, Sidan realized that a pair of curious eyes was still on him, waiting expectantly.

"So our forests have already been depleted, brother?" asked the attendant.

"Not just depleted and not just our forest. Do you know how big our forests were? More than seventy-four percent of our total land mass! And all of it has been divvied up by nineteen National Forest Management companies from Jakarta, which make a profit of nine hundred billion rupiah every year. Do you know how much money that is? Maybe enough to fill a row of twenty trucks to the brim."

The shopkeeper's eyes bugged out. His entire life, he had never seen even one truck full of money. Maybe he had seen something like it on television, when there was a report about a bank being liquidated—then there had been piles of money, looking almost like stacked ledgers. Maybe a million rupiah in each stack. Once on the news he had seen that Saddam Hussein's son had hijacked three truckloads of money from the bank. The café attendant had thought Saddam's son was the number-one richest man in his country, and he had three truckloads of money. So if the richest person had three trucks, what would you call someone who had twenty trucks?

He shook his head. It was like Qarun come back to life, slinking and skulking around like a thief in the land of Serambi. The ultimate thieves. The supreme burglars. Cautiously, he asked Sidan another question, hoping it wouldn't sound foolish or embarrassing.

"Brother, if I might ask . . . So they are just left to pillage what belongs to us?"

"They have the concessions papers to do it. Despite the fact that, according to local law, this forest belongs to the people of Gayo. Yet it has already been harvested by outsiders, not people from Aceh. We call them 'unsavory elements.' Then there is the hustle and bustle of developing liquefied natural gas projects in Arun. Massive extraction activities carried out hastily, accompanied by excessive emotional business, and every sale, no matter how small, is entrusted to foreign businesses, especially Chinese conglomerates, the bastards."

Now the café attendant was starting to understand the issues a bit. He had heard that natural gas reserves had been discovered in his village of Arun when he was a little baby, thirty-six years ago. From those, Aceh had developed into a large chemical-industry zone, the third richest region in Indonesia. But the strange thing was that despite this, it still had the highest numbers of poor people. Hundreds of trillions were made from Arun gas each year, but not one drop had fallen onto the plates of starving refugees, the real owners of the petro-gas in Serambi.

"How many trucks of money do you think the Arun gas would be worth, brother?"

"Let's say thirty-five containers. Enough to build a road from Meulaboh to the mountains of Geumpang and on to Tutut, all paved with solid gold. Enough to provide luxurious houses to all the refugees, with big yards full of flowers and green grass with satellite dishes on their roofs. Enough to turn this country into an American theme park! To return it to the era of Suleiman or the reign of the great Sultan Iskandar Muda, when Aceh was the strongest state in the archipelago. You wouldn't have to mind an Internet café anymore—instead, all of this would belong to you, even a hundred times this would belong to you. You understand?"

The attendant could not stop shaking his head. Even more intrigued, he hoped that Sidan was still willing to share more knowledge with him, tell him more stories about the hidden treasure trove in the land of Serambi. Unconsciously he drooled, imagining his Internet café growing giant, belonging only to him. In fact, he knew he couldn't even dream of having his own café, because at this point he didn't even have a shack to call his own. Everything had been dragged away by the wave last December 26. His wife and his child had disappeared along with his home.

The Agency for the Rehabilitation and Reconstruction of Aceh had promised to build houses. But all those promises were just empty vessels. Purely hypothetical, just like the reconstruction and rehabilitation funds for Aceh, which came in and immediately vanished—as they said in Acehnese, *bak jein euk u langet*, like spirits rising to heaven, disappearing into the abyss. That was Arun Gas. A row of thirty-five shipping containers full of money every year. And how many years had it been so far? How many containers had been taken, stolen by megalooters, those giant blood-sucking vampires?

Sidan hurried home in his rain jacket. His body and soul needed rest and refreshment. He couldn't stop yawning as he sped his motorbike along damaged streets, covered with the black sludge left by the tsunami, a tangible reminder of grief. Thankfully he didn't come across any military trucks. Only a few vehicles were taking shelter at the security posts or the traffic posts or the barracks posts.

May my heart be steady and my step light, he prayed to himself, feeling Angel Gabriel with him.

When he got home there was still some time left for dawn prayers, but he was too sleepy to recite them properly. If his mother were alive, she certainly would have sprinkled his face with a dipperful of ablution water. That water would chase away the devil dirt that stuck to his face. But he was all alone, and he stretched and fell into a deep sleep. Sidan only regained consciousness at ten o'clock in the morning, awakened by the ring of his phone. Firdaus must have topped up his credits. Ten o'clock? He cried out, remembering his plans to report on the bodies in Lamno.

Firdaus: Hey hey! Get up! If you keep sleeping
        in, when will you get your work done?
        I thought you said you wanted to fly to
        heaven?

Sidan: Sorry! I just got home from heaven. I met
       an angel in the valley of 'Ain. She invited
       me to swim and I almost drowned, and then I
       woke up! So please forgive me . . . Where
       do I have to go?

Firdaus: Oh, beautiful dreamer! Where do you want
        to go? Just ask. Okay, now you're up. I
        have to go to class. Bye, love!

Sidan: Wait, wait . . . sorry, I just got home,
completely drenched from my head to the
tips of my toes. Last night the alabaster
angel came again. For a second I could
barely breathe . . . sorry! She has already
returned to the ocean.

Sidan waited for a long time for a reply, but none came. He wanted
Firdaus to get mad, or jealous, or insult him. Or instead, refill his pro-
verbial glass of hot ginger milk—that would be just the thing for breakfast, so that his spirit would be refreshed and he could quickly bathe
and go to work with his chest blooming with love. Maybe he needed
to send that text again.

Sidan: Wait, wait . . . sorry, I just got home,
completely drenched from my head to the
tips of my toes. Last night the alabaster
angel came again. For a second I could
barely breathe . . . sorry! She has already
returned to the ocean.

Firdaus: Oh, my love. So use an alarm clock. Or set
the alarm on your phone. It's practically
already afternoon! All you dare to do
is dream! If you want me to, I'll come
and get you and take you to the Office
of Religious Affairs to get our marriage
license. If not, just go back to sleep!

Sidan: Agh! I don't have the strength. I have
nothing but a quart of bone marrow left,
I'm not sure that I'll survive. Haha . . .

all I dare to do is dream, but that's allowed, isn't it? The Office of Religious Affairs, when the time comes that'll be easy. Okay, how about I take you to school? Your clothes smell so good!

Firdaus: I used balsam! I had a headache from seeing you just laughing softly to yourself! They say life should be taken seriously, and you're telling me that at this hour you just woke up? Maybe you're just not so jazzed about texting me?

Sidan: I just woke up, seriously! And I'm already up and running, haha, so smile, why don't you! Now that's what I call an angel! Okay then! I want to leave too. Ciao!

Not bad, talking about balsam, the Office of Religious Affairs, sleeping and dreaming again. Sidan headed for the bath line, whistling to himself. This late in the morning the line was already thinning out.

Really, not bad. So look up into the sky of your heart, dwell there in a wide blue universe with your beloved. Isn't this world beautiful? It is important that we seize beauty when it comes so that it always belongs to us.

When it was Sidan's turn in the small bathing box, the splashes of water felt like the torrent of Kakadu Twin Falls in Australia. Sometimes a breeze hit his head, coming off the waves of Suak Timah. He imagined an autumn wind in Canada, shining golden leaves falling through the sky, scattering across the yard and catching in Firdaus's hair, making her look like a bride crowned and bejeweled by nature. To hell with black baked mud and the silent barracks. After washing up, Sidan got ready to speed off down the road. He didn't want to miss the report and be forced to hear the stories from someone else's mouth—because in their work, reporters often just went for sensation, without heart or, what's more, ethics. More newspapers sold when more hearts hardened. Sidan didn't like that.

He traveled along the mountainous road, following the steep slopes of the western coast, going from Suak Timah to Calang to Lamno. The journey took four hours as he sped along in the ravaged muddy road. The coast was unreachable during the early months of the rainy season. Only the people who had stayed behind were left to help one another. Out of two hundred people, only twenty were left in the village. The corpses were gathered on the side of the mountain and buried there together so that they didn't smell. The people conducted a search for the rest of the dead, so that they could be placed into one shivering grave.

Whenever there was a body trapped below the piles of tsunami debris, they usually marked the spot with a flag, which had once been red and white but was now so faded by the rain and the storm of tears that the colors had turned black and brownish yellow, waiting for the arrival of the extraction equipment. But in certain isolated spots, the bodies were still strewn about, left as they were since first they had been pounded by the black wave. Some were impaled on tree branches, sunken under rubble, facedown in the crevice of a boulder, or curled around the edge of a door that had been ripped off its hinges and carried by the water.

Sidan's head throbbed. He couldn't take seeing these devastating scenes everywhere he went. He had tried redirecting his attention, but it seemed as though the entire face of the earth had been turned into a grave, and once again grief tore at his senses. He wanted to text Firdaus, which was the only way he knew how to rise to heaven on earth. But a man who didn't have the balls to face life on his own was a real crybaby. It was just a pile of corpses. Sidan thought of it as not *just* a pile, but *what* a pile. Apocalypse after apocalypse.

Whether before or after the tsunami, this country had an apocalyptic face. Joseph Stalin said one man's death is a tragedy but a million deaths is a statistic. Aceh was no longer a country of tragedy but a country of historical statistics. It was only Sidan who always failed to write of statistics—and when he absolutely had to, he wrote about the tragedy of statistics.

Sidan: Firdaus? How are you doing over there, darling? What are you up to?

Firdaus: Haha, not bad! I'm looking at your melancholy face on television, next to the commander in chief. Are you back from Lamno?

Sidan: Not yet. He came to the city the other day, we were overjoyed. Sometimes the television is so random—why would the face of some reporter be broadcast when meeting the commander in chief? If it was a non-Acehnese reporter, maybe it wouldn't be a problem. But me? We never know when we will die, but we truly understand people who plunder what rightfully belongs to God in a time of peace. I'm euphoric. It's enough that I can smile. If I forget, and start to shout my criticisms, well . . . there are still those who like to make a note of it, Firda.

Firdaus: Now you feel uncomfortable? But you're a journalist. Your job is to look for news. Why would you feel uneasy?

Sidan: Because they are just like the rest of
Bollywood, haha . . . I'm reluctant to be
caught on camera because a lot of ghosts
like to look for a crack to slip through
into our world. But this time, peace isn't
just idle chatter. The orang gunung came
out of hiding because they know the soldiers
of the Republic are under the thumb of
the white man. I'm not worried, but I'm
uncomfortable. If my spirit has to fly, I
will have only one blue widow . . . Right,
my lady?

Firdaus: If you had ten yellow widows, then your
spirit would certainly haunt me! I
couldn't care less!

Sidan: What are you mad for? I'm not done yet,
I'm still unconscious. You're the only one
I worry about. We've already pledged our
lives to one another, right? Or did you
forget? . . . Are you already back from
campus?

Firdaus: Not yet! I'm busy chatting at a café with
a handsome professor I ran into. And he's
paying, haha . . . Bye!

Sidan: Oh really? You're not even widowed yet and
you've already met someone else. So you
are telling me there is a creature on this
earth more handsome than I am?

*Firdaus: Yes! Why should I wait to be made into
a widow? The apocalypse draws near!
I don't have to sit here waiting for
someone who's always late. You snooze,
you lose . . . Bye, hon!*

Even though Sidan knew Firdaus was just trying to get a little revenge, he still couldn't help feeling jealous. In this era where anything was possible, nothing was certain, and if Firdaus suddenly decided to check out other people, he couldn't do anything about it. Sometimes Aceh was as close to Yogyakarta as the blood in his veins, but sometimes it was so far away, like a bridge that couldn't be crossed, that didn't connect. Thinking of that, Sidan grew melancholy. But this time it wasn't because of the corpses—he was afraid of losing Firdaus.

He once again lamented his unlucky fate. He thought of Jakarta and its devious eyes. He thought of Monas and the stolen coffers of gold used to build it. He thought of the potbellies in ties, going through an ornately carved wooden door taken from a beautiful temple in the middle of the Acehnese forest that could only be accessed by a private helicopter. He heard their clinking parties. The bubbling laughter of Draculas who stank of the blood of a thousand Acehnese children. He trembled, unable to speak. He read Firdaus's text message again, and then he wrote back.

*Sidan: It's hard to fence in a woman's charm. Cain
was not wrong to kill Abel . . . it was
fated!*

*Firdaus: Ahaha, Sidan, Sidan! If that's how you
feel, you should try not to always be
late! If you go away, it doesn't have to
be for so long . . . There are lots of
thieves along the road!*

Sidan: Listen, Firda! Listen with your conscience!
       I swear, it's not that I'm not trying! I
       know, as sure as I know anything, that Yogya
       is my heaven and so I will climb to it
       however I can! Wait until the end of the
       month.

Firdaus: Yes, of course I will wait. But if you go
         back on your word, you'd better watch out!
         The expiration date is not guaranteed.

Sidan's heart felt like it was crumbling, confused, and torn. If he had to go back to Yogya, that would mean leaving his parents' graves, shipwrecked and devoured by history. That would mean saying goodbye to Meulaboh and Lingkhe and the barracks and Polem and hustling trying to find work and Sulamtaque. To the children with empty eyes, to the mothers who knit a river of tears from Aceh to heaven, to the fathers who shouldered a ton of life's bitterness, to the anxious uncles looking at the horizon without hope, to friends who guarded their clandestine posts. They who had been aged by the disaster, gone gray in the storm.

You know, Firda, why it's hard for me to leave here? A romantic is like a plot of earth that has been bathed in clear red tears. He also doesn't bathe very often; he loves his body and its intimate smells. Doing laundry is a sin, because it blocks his efforts to find himself, until he no longer recognizes God. We should listen to our natural voice. Even the call to prayer has a musical rhythm. A music of whimpering sobs. Hayya alal falah! *Hurry toward success! But where is success? For decades now we have not found any success! Sometimes a romantic is also narcissistic. Watch out, Firda! He looks at the world how it should be and not how it really is. Black night, white day, red me!*

Okay, I will say bismillah. *A romantic also dies without heaven. He is an eternal wanderer who is forever accompanied by restlessness and longing.*

Sidan: I promise . . . God willing! Let's pray
        together, okay? See you, nite!

Sidan went back home to Meulaboh with chaotic thoughts, torn between piles of corpses and his heart's desire to see his beloved as soon as possible. Centuries of perpetual silence. He couldn't stand it. It seemed as though he hadn't seen a smile as beautiful as hers in decades. Hadn't heard a laugh as crisp as her laughter, hadn't met a woman as pampered as she was in her femininity, one as heated in debate or as full of scorn. He had never met a woman with thoughts as incisive as her pointed analysis.

He let out a husky sigh.

Arriving at his barracks door, he was ready to collapse, typing on his phone in a rush, as if the tsunami were going to hit again.

Sidan: Din! Help me! Come to the barracks this
        afternoon! It's urgent! I'm waiting for
        you! Write back!

Din: Oh sorry, Dan! So tired. Later tonight. How's
      your story coming?

Sidan was frustrated and impatient. He entered the barracks with a wrinkled forehead and a countenance that grew ever more gaunt and dull. He laid his body down to rest, but his thoughts kept racing, rising and falling like the muddy, curving road that followed the western coast from Lamno to Calang to Suak Timah. He wanted to close his eyes, but the more he tried to sleep, the more everything he was trying to hide from became crystal clear, materializing and dancing before his eyes.

He covered his eyes with the palms of his hands, but that just made the giant black ghosts grow even more insistent.

If his brain had been a bowl of noodles, he would have spilled the whole thing out. Then he would be able to sleep peacefully and wake up with a new bowl, with a new menu of food fresh from the stove. He certainly would arrive with a beautiful gift for Firdaus, one full of surprises. He felt guilty that he had left his sweetheart feeling uncertain and anxious for far too long. But before and after the tsunami, all maps and intentions, all plans and wishes had been turned completely upside down.

You must understand that, Firda. But I will come, I will certainly come. And we will be married immediately. Immediately, Firda! What's more urgent in this era if not joy, love, and marriage? Come, let me take your hand and lead you onto a ship of love. I'm already fed up with dreaming, of only holding you in dreams. I'm fed up with washing my hair in the morning with nothing but my own imagination. I want something that's warmer and truly alive. Your popsicle lips and your coconut-sherbet tongue in a time of drought. Mmm! Your eyes like stars above my journey. Your shapely chest makes my heartsick longing explode, oh, future mother of my children. My sadness grows at the fate that keeps us apart. But don't worry, Firda. I will soon fly to you! In a flash! I will leave behind all my past in this village of bitterness for our new village that is full of lush gardens. Paradise!

"So finally you came? But it's already dark!"

"Take a bath! You stink like rotten orange juice!"

"This is how Firdaus likes it. Anyway, it will take too long to bathe. The line is still long."

"Then I'll just go home."

"Wait! I'll go do ablutions in the river that flows for a century. Wait half an hour."

Sidan got up and left Din with a pack of Gudang Garam clove cigarettes. Din was a journalist friend who had helped him out quite a bit during difficult times. Now Sidan needed more help. He wanted to sell everything he owned, everything filling up this miserable barracks of suffering—including the misery, if possible.

"Sell everything? You've lost your mind."

"I'm serious, Din. Help me out. I want to get married."

"What do you mean married? All you have is this chicken coop and you want to get married? Do you want to marry a chicken?"

"You know how handsome I am. What chicken could ever measure up? I want to marry an angel. Help me, Din. I need cash by the end of the month."

"You're serious?"

"In God's name, I swear. I'm serious."

Din thought that Sidan had certainly been driven insane by all the misery he had suffered and witnessed through all his reporting and interviews, all the grief that sliced through his heart, filling him to the brim with pain. He imagined the angel who would want to marry him and carry him up to heaven, rid him of all his suffering.

"Fine. I'll try. But don't get your hopes up. And you should seriously consider all the pros and cons first!"

"I have. I have. I've thought about them too much."

"Alright, then, enjoy your last gypsy days of being single, future groom. May they turn into poetry, a dowry for your bride."

That night, thinking about Yogya and his Firdaus, Sidan could smile a little bit.

Only a moment more, Firda. Not too much longer. The world will no longer be meaningless and there will be no more quiet nights. The time will come for the soft caress of fingers on your cheeks and mussed hair, your neck full of red love bites early in the morning, and your satisfied smile wrapping me in a warm embrace. It will be a dawn without earthquakes. Nothing but the youthful, wriggling enthusiasm of a happy bride and groom. Two breaths completing one another in an eternal harmony.

He felt the need to say good night before going to bed.

Sidan: Today was completely exhausting. But your smile in the middle of the night is like a sliver of bright morning . . . Go in peace!

Firdaus: Good night to you too. Are you tired after the journey home from Lamno? Get plenty of rest and guard your health so that you don't get sick. But I'm not really sleepy yet. It just so happens I'm reading Anthony Reid. Okay, sleep now. Bye!

Sidan: There is no such thing as "it just so happens". . . Good night, baby!

Firdaus: Good night, hon! Now it's time to rest. Sleep when it's time to sleep. And tomorrow wake up healthy as can be. Sweet dreams!

Sidan: This joy in my heart is for you, oh, my life! For you, my love, is this joy in my heart! Sweet dreams! Bye!

Chapter 6:
Land under Water

Sidan: Now here there are four M's: mati lampu, mati motor, muntaber, and molor. Blackouts, dead engines, diarrhea, sleeping in. Maybe after this August there will be one more M: maha merdeka! Independence! For those who have been fasting, please enjoy your feast, but my stomach is still in the shop.

Firdaus: Drink some Oralit, my love! Be careful, don't get dehydrated! I am always praying for you!

Sidan: I already drank down ten packets of Oralit and recited 100 poems. Do you know why the poetry goes with the four M's? It helps you

endure the excruciating pain . . . barf!
Good-bye, future!

Firdaus: *Agh! Are you being serious? Maybe you*
ate something off? Be careful, Sidan,
you should go to the doctor right away!
Where's Polem, or your other friends—
Nangi? Sawang? Leubei?

Sidan: *I'm not doing so bad. I already boiled*
pomegranate leaf for my stomach, I brewed
bitter tea and some sago palm . . .
Luckily, I'm in the village, maybe if I was
traveling I would have to drink some powder
concoction full of chemicals. I must have
been daydreaming about Yogya so much that
I ate something bad—maybe I mistook a rock
for a piece of bread, haha . . . I just
miss you!

What actually happened was Sidan's plans for going back to Yogya had failed, which meant that his plans for marriage had failed and all of his dreams of heaven were dashed. He didn't like to fail, but he had. Firdaus said she understood, but in an annoyed and angry tone, and she threatened to break up with him if he didn't try again before the end of the following month. Firdaus had wanted to get married immediately after graduating college. And now she had already graduated, she was just waiting for the official ceremony in September, but dammit—Sidan had never even been to her parents' house. They had met face-to-face once, and it had gone well. Sidan could charm anyone's parents, and Firdaus's father had been impressed by his good manners and his intellectual demeanor. He praised Sidan as a man with morals and a gracious bearing, an aristocratic carriage. The only thing he didn't like was Sidan's long hair.

"Why doesn't he come here to ask for your hand?" Firdaus's father said.

"He's slow, Pa. He was planning to do it before the tsunami, but ever since then he can't bear to leave Aceh. But he has promised he will keep trying."

"How long will it take? You are about to graduate."

"I've given him a deadline. After that, we'll see. I'll let you know, Pa."

Firdaus sometimes wasn't sure she should keep waiting for Sidan. Even though she loved him to the very marrow of her bones, she was ready for marriage and many other men were interested in her. Even some of Sidan's acquaintances and close friends had put the moves on her, especially after they lost contact with Sidan after the tsunami. Only Firdaus had been talking to him day and night, for weeks on end—for more than seven months now. She was growing tired of waiting.

But it would be too cruel to leave her sweetheart in a sad heap and even worse to celebrate with another man.

So, then what's your problem, Sidan? Why is it that you can't even make a decision to stay or go? What's wrong?

Sometimes Firdaus wanted to join the group of Yogya volunteers bound for Aceh so that she could go and see him. There had been a number of offers. She had also been invited to present a paper at a seminar about the heroism of Aceh in the city of Lhokseumawe.

But above all else, what made Firdaus truly fed up and want to break up with Sidan for good was the fact that he wouldn't give her the address of his barracks. In fact, he wouldn't give Firdaus any real details about his living conditions at all, except for brief glimpses. She wanted his address, not just his e-mail and his cell phone number. She knew that Sidan didn't want any visitors, didn't want to be sent anything besides news. All he needed was a healthy and nutritious spiritual menu that would put him back on his feet so he could fly, gathering up rays of sunlight.

Firdaus: How about if I came to Aceh? If, let's say, there was an event in Lhokseumawe with North Dialogue Forum? If, let's say, I was arriving tomorrow morning?

Sidan: Then I would pick you up in Banda and take you to Karamuhuk Land. That's short for the Acehnese karam-buhuk, which means sunk under water, but there's a good road that goes along the Saree-Tangse-Geumpang-Tutut route, with a view of green mountains. And if, let's say, if it was tomorrow morning, then I wouldn't be dead yet, God willing.

Firdaus: Hey, why are you talking about death? And Negri Karamuhuk, the Land under Water? You wouldn't take me to Lingkhe? Or Tutut? They say Tutut smells the worst?

Sidan: Suharto's daughter named Tutut smells the worst! But wait, I'm touched but I'm afraid I'll die from shock mixed with joy. Could it really be true that we will finally meet in my house? It's such a surprise that an angel from Yogyakarta would grace the Land under Water with a visit, before I even have a chance to prepare anything for her.

Firdaus laughed. Who would really want to visit Aceh, unless they wanted to dodge bullets?

Oh, Sidan! Sometimes you are too naive to lie to. But who is really lying? If only you knew how much I long to go to Serambi. A seminar or volunteer work would just be an excuse—the first and most important reason would be to see you. It is so exotic to imagine your mountainous land, with its beaches and pine trees and its ruined glory. It's just like imagining your eyes, your smile, your sighs, and wild caresses.

Firdaus: Haha . . . who wants to visit Aceh? No! I'm afraid of getting shot! Only my name would make it back home.

Sidan: In the name of my ancestor, Commander Sagoe, I am strong enough to protect you, or at least I think I am—after all, you don't need to be Tarzan to be able to do that! But you don't have to visit now. If you want to, I can take you around next year. Okay?

Firdaus: Hopefully next year the soldiers will have all been pulled out of Aceh. I do want to come. Is it any safer there yet?

Sidan: The soldiers never really leave, they just sneak off to some other place . . . Maybe they only go as far away as Medan, and then when we let down our guard they pounce from behind, just how the Dutch taught them. Leaving nothing but scorched earth, like in East Timor.

Firdaus: And will you evacuate again, to the Land above the Wind?

Sidan: They are staking out all the caves. I don't
want to be far from the center of fire, just
like ants come swarming out of a burning
log on the fire, but then soon return to the
heat and crawl into the hunk of smoldering
wood . . . That's what Solzhenitsyn said.

Now every TV channel was ready to broadcast the Helsinki Memorandum of Understanding. Firdaus spent those thrilling moments in front of the television, just like all Acehnese people, wherever they were, were tensely waiting for the most historic moment, the signing of the peace agreement between Indonesia and Aceh. Students cut class. Workers took the day off. Writers forgot to brainstorm, artists forgot to make art. The people in Aceh thronged to the mosques, which had set up televisions in their halls. Firdaus's friends were also on standby at her place, with their legs stretched out in front of the television.

While snacking on Mayasi peanuts, Firdaus's eyes darted to look at the face of Malik Mahmud onscreen. The leader of the Free Aceh movement, who had been living in exile in Sweden for decades, was cool, steady, and authoritative. His smile was rare and valuable. And his silence was truly golden, like the coffers of stolen Acehnese gold. His lips were like the lips of hundreds of thousands of people in the land of Serambi, locked against all the clamorous thundering of a false world, clamped tightly after suffering all forms of attacks. Firdaus found herself feeling melancholy.

Firdaus: Hi, hon! Where are you at this historic
moment for your country? Get up! Go to
Baiturrahman Mosque!

*Sidan: I can't, I'm in a remote corner of the village,
far from the pomp and circumstance . . .
I'm waiting for peace in a village wagon!
Where are you?*

*Firdaus: Me and all my friends are sitting anxiously
in front of the TV. Watching the people
in the mosque praying for the people who
will soon shake hands in Finland. Come
on! Join us!*

*Sidan: I can't! That's a sin! Prayers of love and
praise are not some farcical drama to be
repeatedly performed for the purposes of
necro-nationalism, like the flag ceremony,
the anthem, or the recitation of the five
principles of the nation. Why is Aceh forced
to carry out those empty gestures while
those in power in Jakarta no longer go to
the palace every August 17 on Independence
Day?*

*Firdaus: Oh, you . . . you never budge, even one
inch!*

*Sidan: No, I don't, my Firda! It's a sin! Read
my poem "Layla Dusk" and you'll know that
gravestones spring up from her alabaster
body. During the peace agreement of 2003
I joined in trembling dawn prayers of
thanksgiving. And then what happened?*

Death and more death! The miserable virus
of holy war against outside occupiers kept
spreading . . .

Firdaus: Yeah, okay, whatever you say!

Sidan: I was actually sent there by the soldiers,
who are heirs to the Dutch. But because I
woke up late, I couldn't go anywhere, so
I brushed my teeth instead! Only now it's
different here, we conduct the flag ceremony
on our way to the barracks bathroom, haha!
Hegemony!

Firdaus: Enough! If you just woke up, then you should
have some burukiek curry for breakfast
first, and then you can start texting.
Over here we are tense and anxious!

Sidan: Fine! But remember he's a vegetarian, so
he rarely gets mad. He only eats burukiek
curry when he is revolting against plants,
and sometimes Turkish bread and Iranian
korma spread that lasts twenty-four hours.
He drinks urine!

The anticipation on the television spread to viewers throughout the country. Firdaus prayed silently, as if she were watching a soccer match between Portugal and Turkey, hoping for a draw. They were all so absorbed, none of them noticed their friend Adib Bahalwan's arrival— even if there had been a sandal thief on the loose, none of them would have cared. They didn't even remember that they had put a pot on the stove, which was now sending its charred, bitter aroma up to the ceiling.

"Fire! Fire!"

Then everyone jumped up, running for the kitchen, which was filled with thick black smoke. Adib became the unexpected hero as he took care of the problem with a pail full of water, extinguishing the flames and slowly cooling everyone down. The remnant of the melted and misshaped pan was like a small monument, a commemoration of the Helsinki peace agreement and those tense moments around the television.

"How strange that suddenly you are here, right at this critical moment," Firdaus said, amazed.

"Nothing is strange if it has been willed. Everything is a coincidence. A coincidence that sets everything right," Adib joked proudly.

"So it turns out it's lucky to have a coincidental friend!"

"But coincidentally, I'm here on serious business!"

"Oh yeah? What's up?"

"I wanted to let you know that tomorrow I'm going to Aceh, along with a group of seven volunteers. So, how about it? Want to come?"

"But . . ."

Firdaus turned pale with shock. All her feelings flared up in a jumble, colorful like a rainbow: sadness, happiness, disappointment, annoyance, love, hate. She was sad because she didn't have the money to buy a ticket. Happy because she imagined seeing Sidan. Terribly disappointed because Sidan didn't want her to visit now, and annoyed when she remembered how Sidan himself had not yet come back to Yogya. Longing ripped through her soul, and she hated Sidan for breaking his promise.

"What's the 'but'? This is a rare opportunity, you know. It won't come twice!"

"You would be paying for it, right?"

"Yes, of course, that's already taken care of. All you need to do is say yes or no. What's your hesitation?"

Firdaus grew more intrigued. The stingy Adib Bahalwan wanted to pay her way? "But where did you get the money?"

"Don't worry about it. I've got the money!"

Adib's job title was officially one of "volunteer," but like so many Javanese volunteers who traveled to Aceh to help with recovery efforts, he was actually being paid a hefty sum by his sponsoring organization.

"The point is," he continued, "do you want to come or not?"

"Yes, I want to! How could I not want to?"

Firdaus gave in. Who cares where the money came from, the important thing was to see Sidan. Aha! She would make him faint from surprise and happiness.

That night she had insomnia. She felt like she had already arrived at the barracks, leaning against the wood walls and the floor with long wooden planks, facing that thin face with its melancholy eyes and faraway look.

"Here are the barracks, Firda. Here is the cracked and destroyed earth. Here there is nothing but quiet, more and more pure love for God, and not limited to just five times a day. What, is he cold medicine?" Sidan was making a joke.

Firdaus grew ever more restless. She only fell asleep right before dawn. She purposefully turned off her phone. She didn't want any contact with Sidan. She had to be in a good condition for tomorrow's journey to the Land under Water.

They were a group of eight people waiting at the airport, volunteers for the most well-known religious organization in the country. Except for Firdaus, they all had three-month contracts, receiving different levels of payment. Firdaus discovered that her round-trip journey from Adisucipto Airport to Cengkareng to Polonia to Blang Bintang didn't cost more than one day's pay for Adib, whose job entailed little more than giving orders and taking meals with the soldiers.

And then, it turned out that Sidan was gone. She didn't know it, but he was already in Simeulue when she arrived.

Firdaus regretted having turned off her phone. Meanwhile, Sidan tried to contact her but couldn't. He assumed his calls weren't going through because of the bad reception in Simeulue. This always happened—every time he went to an isolated village or faraway town.

After five days in Banda she hadn't seen Sidan and felt like she was losing her mind. Firdaus couldn't be in this foreign land any longer without Sidan, without even any contact with him. Her thoughts were chaos. She was afraid that Sidan had met with disaster. Or maybe his phone had been stolen, but then why didn't he contact her on a public phone? Or borrow a friend's phone? Or use the newspaper office phone?

What's going on, Sidan?

"If by tomorrow afternoon he hasn't contacted me, I'm going home immediately, Dib."

"I think it's weird too. Although it's true that he didn't know we were coming."

"I'm just afraid something has happened to him."

"We'll pray. Stay calm, Firda, I'm sure he's alright. Maybe his phone is broken."

"It's never been like this, not for all these months. Neither of us can stand going for too long without contacting each other. It's very odd."

To cheer up Firdaus, Adib invited her to go around Banda, all the way to Syiah Kuala University, on the city's outskirts. There they met up with an acquaintance, a woman who directed a foundation. Firdaus had met her once in a seminar at Hotel Sahid Yogya a while ago when she had been speaking out against the implementation of Sharia law in Aceh from a feminist perspective. Her name was Zakiyah. She was happy to see them and took them on a tour of the Syiah Kuala campus.

"Do all the female students wear *jilbab*?" Firdaus asked.

"It's been like that for a long time. Even without the enforcement of Sharia law, they are used to dressing like that, especially on campus. But in the village or in freer port towns like Sabang, many don't wear it."

"Is there any penalty if they don't?"

"If they go about on the main roads in inappropriate clothing, usually they are stopped by the Sharia police and asked to cover their heads."

"In your opinion, is what those women are wearing appropriate?" Firdaus said, pointing to a group of women standing in front of the economics department building, wearing tight, fashionable clothing that showed off their curves, their necks still visible, and even the tops of their breasts peeking out.

"Sometimes the head covering is just a formality. The *jilbab* is just like a fad. To them, Islam is a simple presence, it's not an obligation. Maybe it's different here than on Yogya campuses."

They moved on, heading toward the Baiturrahman Mosque. It was still morning but the traffic was beginning to grow quite busy, even congested. Sedans, minivans, military trucks, jeeps, motorbikes, and pedestrians all crowded against each other heading for Blang Padang field, where thousands of state employees were scheduled to attend a flag ceremony demonstrating their loyalty to Indonesia. Adib preferred a café across from the mosque, where many people, most of them men, came to read the *Serambi Daily*, chat with their friends, smoke, and drink black coffee. From there Firdaus could see the Aceh River, mosques, and one of the few Catholic churches in Banda.

In the morning *nasi gurih*, rice that had been cooked with coconut milk, was served along with a number of side dishes to choose from, but they didn't have any *bueluekat*, Sidan's favorite, or any Indian-style biryani, which was only served on Fridays in special shops frequented by the upper class. In the afternoon, you could order *mie aceh*, warm and spicy noodles.

"And what's going on with the *inong balee*?" Firdaus asked.

"We are initiating a plan based on the idea that the women fighters of Aceh are one of the important avenues through which the community can achieve peace," Zakiyah replied.

"What do you mean?"

"I mean, widows whose husbands or children died at the hands of the army, the police, or the rebels are all coming together to declare that violence in Aceh must be stopped."

"Has it been effective so far?"

"We are trying our best not to reflect poorly on the *inong balee* from the time of Admiral Keumalahayati four centuries ago, who with complete confidence were able to play a role befitting warriors on the battlefield."

They continued to chat while eating breakfast. Firdaus was fairly interested, but she couldn't stop thinking about Sidan and the fact that he was missing.

"How many of you came from the Sacred Bridge Foundation?" Zakiyah asked Adib.

"For now there are eight of us. We really need more than that, but we are still waiting for others to take their turn."

"Do you have a partnering organization?"

"We are working with UNESCO and inviting children to participate in traditional Acehnese arts activities in order to reinstill them with a sense of self-confidence. We want them to feel empowered, even in the face of all the difficulties that they have experienced thus far."

"That's a wonderful idea," Zakiyah said. "Art can renew the energy to live. I've seen that happen in a number of places. The children become cheerful again, life goes back to normal, the refugees' spirit and solidarity slowly grows."

"In my opinion, reconstruction programs can't only pay attention to physical factors. There has to be a balance between physical needs and spiritual ones, especially when healing from post-tsunami trauma."

"That's right. Sometimes the arts are looked at as trivial, but really they are significant," Firdaus commented, though her thoughts were still wandering.

Where are you, Sidan? What happened to you?

What if Sidan had been captured by soldiers and was being persecuted like in the time of the inquisition in ancient Milan? At first the victims' bodies were ripped apart with pliers. When they reached Largo Carrobbio, their right hands were cut off, and when they arrived at the court of justice, they were stripped naked and their legs, arms, and backs were broken on a wheel. Still hanging on the wheel, their bodies were then hoisted onto a staff, where they were left for six hours, spread-eagled in pain. Then they were decapitated and their corpses were burned.

She had heard a lot of stories like that about the violence that was perpetrated when Aceh was declared a military operational area. Like men who had their legs broken and were then paraded around the village with writing on their backs, THIS IS WHAT AN AGITATOR LOOKS LIKE, then brought to the middle of the forest where their wife and sons were being held captive. These family members would then be stripped and forced to engage in sexual acts with one another while the father, with his legs crippled, would be forced to witness the crazy, hellish scene.

Firdaus rubbed her chest. The delicious fried duck with tomato *sambal* and sweet basil leaves no longer appealed to her, even though it had been her favorite dish when she ate with Sidan at the Bungong Jeumpa food stall in Yogya. Poor Sidan! Where on earth could he possibly be, missing for one hundred and twenty hours? One hundred and twenty *fateful* hours.

Don't you know why I came? Distance and time have tossed me into a sea of confusion, but I have one hundred feet and my wings are strong enough to cross your mysterious sky. I came for you and you suddenly disappeared. You're not hiding from me, are you? I came bringing hope, don't you know that, darling?

But that afternoon was nothing but a heap of clouds. There was no wind bringing news. The phone still said "pending." Firdaus was consumed by worry. She decided that she had to go back to Yogya the following day. Adib gave Firdaus enough money for her journey home, and his heart swelled with a rising hope. He would try every trick in the book to win her, snatch her from Sidan's hands, which were tied by fate.

Wait and see—soon you will know, Sidan, that you are finished. She is now in my arms, which are stronger than a tsunami.

"Take care, Firda! You don't need to worry about Sidan too much. I'll contact you whenever he is ready to be contacted. Okay?"

Adib had accompanied Firdaus to the airport and they were standing on the tarmac as the final passengers boarded the plane.

"Thank you, Dib! You have been so kind to have helped us out, even though the trip was a failure. Now I understand that you are truly Sidan's friend. Really, thank you."

Friend? Adib laughed to himself. Lovely Firdaus was so naive. And she only grew even more beautiful, and sexier, beset by grief in the throes of love.

What beautiful twinkling eyes she has, like morning stars. Black glistering that lights the way of a thirsty wanderer in the wilderness. Your lips, an eddy in the ocean, the focus of my hunger.

"It was nothing. Just being a friend," Adib said. "Hopefully next time we will succeed."

"Well, don't put yourself out too much on our behalf. You have your own business that needs to be taken care of."

"But what are friends for?"

"Okay then, I have to go. Once again, thank you for everything!"

Firdaus then headed for the mobile stairway leading up to the Garuda Airlines plane, while her eyes kept scanning every last inch of what she could still see of the city that had made her spirit tremble with longing and smoldering love. A tear fell, splashing the tip of her nose, then dripping down. Drop after drop spilled. She collapsed into her seat, fastened her seatbelt, and wept while gazing out into the distance, where somewhere Sidan might be missing her too.

She felt a vast quiet. Displaced and stranded, all alone. Sad and shattered.

"Please turn your phone off, miss," the flight attendant ordered sharply, blowing like a gale in the midst of overcast clouds. With a heavy heart Firdaus turned off her phone, as if she were turning off her feelings, still in turmoil.

Without any idea that all of this had happened, a minute later Sidan contacted her from Simeulue:

Sidan: How are you, Light of My Eye? I'm coming home from Simeulue. The reception was terrible, but it's working a bit better here in the airport. Kif halik? How are you?

The message was pending. Sidan jumped. After all these months it was highly unusual—in fact, it almost never happened—that Firdaus's phone was pending. The word "pending" was not in her vocabulary. All her doors were open for Sidan. All the roads were stretched out before him. But now her phone was pending? Really? Sidan didn't believe it. He tried to send the text message again. Failed. He tried again. Failed again. Then he tried to call her. It went right to voicemail.

Sidan thought maybe Firdaus was angry because he had gone to Simeulue without texting good-bye. In fact he had tried to let her know when he was arriving in Simeulue, but it had been too late and his message was stymied by faulty phone reception. For five days Sidan's thoughts had not been truly focused on his duties as a journalist but on Firdaus, because one day without a text message from her was like a day where he wasn't truly alive. He had been dead for five days and now he was trying to live again.

The weather in Firdaus's heart was overcast, moody, and introspective. She spent her layover in Polonia without bothering with her phone or paying any attention to the people passing by. For the flight from Polonia to Cengkareng she was seated between two men with Hindustani faces, dark skinned and with prominent noses. There were many like them scattered around Aceh. Because she knew she was in a sad and sorry state, Firdaus asked for permission to switch places with one of the men so that she could sit by the window.

"Pardon me, but are you coming from Aceh, little sister?" one of the men began.

"Yes."

"Pardon me, but perhaps the region you are from was also affected by the tragedy as well?"

Firdaus was a bit startled. Which region? Did he mean the tsunami? Maybe the sadness in her eyes made people assume that she was a survivor. But that was alright, she just went along with it.

"Yes. Everyone is gone. Only one is left."

"My condolences. If I might ask, where are you from, little sister?"

"Meulaboh," she fibbed.

In unison, both men shook their heads sympathetically.

"So only you survived, little sister?"

"Just me. Now there is no one else," she said, nervous and slightly amused with herself.

"So where do you live now? Who are you staying with?"

"In Yogya, I rent a room. I'm still in school."

"So when it happened, were you in Meulaboh or Yogya, sister?"

"Yogya."

"Oh, so everyone went under? The only one left is the one who was in Yogya? If I may ask, how many did you lose altogether?"

"Just my mother and our house. Not like our neighbors. They lost dozens. And how about yourself?"

"I'm from Takengon but I live in Jakarta. I'm doing research."

"On what subject?"

"History."

"The sons of Aceh still have quite a talent for history. Do you know whether some Acehnese people really have Campa ancestry?"

She'd asked that question because Sidan had said that his mother had Campa blood, which was Indo-Chinese, while his father was Hindustani. So Sidan's Indian face was covered in pale skin even though he was born only two hundred meters from the Malacca Strait. The ocean air had failed to darken his skin.

"If we look at it from a linguistic perspective, judging from the many similarities between the Acehnese and Campa languages, then it is quite possible."

"For example?"

"Acehnese people call birds *cicem*. Campa people say: *cim*. Acehnese people call a smile *khem-khem*. Campa people say: *khim*. Water in Acehnese is *ie*. In Campa it's *ia*. And there are many more similar examples, especially words that are used by coastal Acehnese."

"So how significant is the Indo-Chinese influence, actually?"

"It's not really so dominant anymore, now especially when compared to India or the Middle East."

"Where are the Indian influences most noticeable?"

"There are many. For example, there are dances that closely resemble Acehnese folk dancing. If you look at the Acehnese *saman* or *rampo*, for example, they seem to mimic Indian dance. The moves are quite nimble."

"How about food?"

"Oh yes, from certain aspects of the agricultural system, harvesting equipment, all the way to the prepared dishes. For example, the spices that are often mixed with a concoction of pepper and herbs, and the way of grinding them with a distinctive grinding stone. Clothing and other forms of fashion, especially of the women in the interior, who like to let their hair grow and then shape it into a bun. All these are influenced by Hindu India."

"But is that still true? What are the Hindu influences that still exist?"

"There are not that many from a spiritual perspective. But their culture and civilization have been assimilated into daily life. There are still Hindu influences in the interior—even in houses of worship, like the ancient mosque in Indrapuri."

"Do you agree with people who say the demeanor and behavior of Acehnese people have a lot in common with traditional people—they like to joke around, they are naive, honest, brave, and open, and sometimes so easily fooled?"

The man laughed and said, "Now I'm not so sure that you are really Acehnese, little sister."

"Why not?"

"If you already knew, why would you have to ask?"

"It's not like that. I'm just thinking, as long as I am talking to an expert. What's wrong with asking?"

"I'm not an expert yet. I'm just a researcher. Where do you go to school, little sister?"

Their conversation flowed comfortably, from the origins of the name "Aceh" to its customs and the development of its culture up until recent social changes and the destruction of its civilization and the beginnings of its resurgence. But throughout their talk, Firdaus was daydreaming, thinking of Sidan. When the man, who was named Nizar, said that the destruction of Acehnese civilization happened in nine phases, she bowed her head like a wilting flower, remembering Sidan's sad eyes.

"What is our foundation for happiness, Firda?" he had cried out in a long moan.

Destruction continued without cease. When the central government declared Aceh a "military operational area" in harsh retaliation to the formation of the *orang gunung* and their demand for independence, they violated human rights on an extraordinary scale. This was just the latest iteration of the process of destruction, but Sidan had witnessed and experienced it himself. He had felt it in the roar of his young tainted breath, the curtailed steps of his shackled legs. He suffered pain on top of pain, just like all the young men in Aceh.

Firdaus grew anxious. She was terrified, imagining Sidan being tortured. But she tried as hard as she could to dispel those dark scenes and instead remember all the sweet times the two of them had shared, when the sky was clear and the breeze wrapped the lovers' hearts in a sweet embrace. Because longing had a solemn face. The more she missed Sidan, the more the world became a portrait of her lost lover.

I search for your face in its face. Maybe your eyes are tucked behind the blinking clouds, or you are dancing in the middle of the ocean, underneath the foamy surf, like the tossing green seaweed.

Arriving in Cengkareng after an almost two-hour flight, Firdaus disembarked, carrying sadness in her heart and a story from the Land of Serambi.

"When I come to Yogya, may I stop by and see you?" Nizar asked.

"Yes, get in touch with me. I'll prepare a warm welcome for you," Firdaus flirted spontaneously.

How strange, she thought. *How could those words have just flown out?*

It was as if her thoughts were acting on their own, as if her anger at Sidan suddenly reappeared.

"Oh, I'm nobody special. It will make others jealous."

"For me, all my guests are special. I mean it."

What Firdaus really wanted to say was, *You look so much like Sidan and that makes you special, don't you realize that?* Then they exchanged addresses and phone numbers. Firdaus was saving Nizar's name in her phone when the buzz of Sidan's text message vibrated in her hand. Firdaus jumped.

"What's wrong?" Nizar said.

"Oh, nothing. Just a text from a friend."

"Quite a friend to make you turn pale like that."

"It's really nothing, but please give me a moment to reply."

Sidan: How are you, Light of My Eye? I'm home from Simeulue. The reception was terrible, but it's working a bit better here in the airport. Kif halik? How are you?

Firdaus drew in a long breath and peeked up at Nizar's face, which was still curious. She quickly typed out a reply and sent it.

Firdaus: How are you, Light of My Eye? I'm going home from Banda. The reception was terrible there, but it's better in Cengkareng. Kif halik? What's new?

Sidan: What? Don't joke around, Firda! Isn't it enough that I've been in agony for five days? If you don't believe me, open your e-mail . . . A special bouquet from the land above the coral awaits.

What kind of bouquet? After disappearing for five days, he reappeared with a bouquet? Maybe of ylang-ylang flowers? Even though she was unfathomably happy to hear from Sidan, she was also incredibly annoyed. She had been on a trip to a foreign country, wandering like a nomad in the Sahara for five days. And they had been days of longing and nights of worry. As if in a dream, she had been thrown into the boiling crater of Mount Merapi. All her mixed feelings flared up.

Firdaus: What? Don't joke around, Sidan! Isn't it enough that I've been in agony for five days? If you don't believe me, go see Adib in the Blang Padang barracks. He's waiting for news from you.

A second passed. Five seconds. Sidan was still in Banda, eating two plates of crab noodles at Haji Zul's food stall while reading the Serambi daily paper. He intended to go home to Meulaboh the following day. He was tired of visiting unfamiliar villages and their silent barracks, but he also wanted to start a new journal, which he would call *Culture Journal*, if he could find the funding for it. Sidan read Firdaus's reply. He still wasn't sure what she meant, he didn't understand what she was talking about. With the press of a button, he called her.

"Hello, Firda? Where are you?"

"Haha, in Cengkareng. Three hours ago I was in Banda. Allah the Pure walked my feet to His humble servant."

"You must be joking. I'm in Banda right now."

"If you don't believe me, then come follow me here. Or call the Acehnese guy who is right here next to me."

"Who is he? Why did you come to Aceh without telling me?"

"He's just a friend I met on the flight. I went because I wanted to volunteer, but I didn't do well there. I couldn't get anything accomplished."

"You're a clever liar," Sidan said, laughing. "How can I possibly believe you?"

"Contact Adib in Blang Padang and ask him all about it, or call Nizar, my new Acehnese friend who is sitting here right next to me."

"Nizar? Who is Nizar?"

"Talk to him yourself. He's next to me. Ask him whatever you want to know."

"I'll just contact Adib. Okay then, I hope you are doing well and taking care of yourself, wherever you are. Bye!"

Firdaus was sure that Sidan would contact Adib. He would never believe that his sweetheart had actually reached the Land under Water.

"I'm sorry, but then it's true that you're not from Aceh, little sister?" asked Nizar, who was getting ready to go, having overheard Firdaus's entire conversation.

"My friend who just called is the one from Meulaboh. He's the one who lost everything and has nothing left—maybe the only thing left for him is our friendship. Yesterday I went to visit him, but we didn't get to meet. He is a journalist and was working in Simeulue, and the phone reception gave out."

"You must be so disappointed to have gone all the way from Yogya and not seen him."

"On top of that, he doesn't even believe I was actually there."

Once again, melancholy passed across Firdaus's face. Nizar knew then that her friend was a "friend" in quotation marks. He wanted to inquire further, but Firdaus had become so glum. So he and his companion said good-bye and left Firdaus alone with her thoughts. While waiting for her flight to Yogya, anxious in the terminal, she felt like she wanted to switch her flights around, to head away from Polonia and go back to Banda. How she missed gazing into Sidan's eyes and squeezing his hand until her knuckles were ready to break.

Her eyes were glued to the television screen but her heart was speeding back toward Banda. She tried to read a newspaper but couldn't. She picked up her phone. As soon as she opened it, it rang. The name "Nizar" appeared on the screen.

"*Salamu'alaikum*, little sister!"

"*Wa'alaikum salam*. Call me Firda. How are you, Brother Nizar? Have you already arrived home?"

"Not yet. I'm still in a taxi. My friend just called me. His name is Sidan. Do you know him, little sist—er, Firda?"

"Maybe he's my friend from Meulaboh? His name is also Sidan."

"That's him! We were both members of the Rampagoe artist collective back in Yogyakarta. We used to put on performances featuring Acehnese dance and traditional arts. He asked me whether I was with Firda from Banda? I said yes. I also said that you were still at the airport waiting for your flight to Yogya. Hopefully I wasn't mistaken."

"Thank you, Brother Nizar! Now he will believe me. *Salam*."

Ah! The heavy weight that had been on her shoulders evaporated. A smile decorated her lips.

Now do you realize, Sidan, how serious and how quiet the world becomes when we are not together? What is the meaning of life, floating in a vacuum like this, without gravity, on an unfamiliar planet? This foreign world grows all the more foreign without your face. Like a silent village that has been destroyed by a storm. I can't stand it! So don't say that my journey was pointless. Even the birds know the symphony of my heart. Nothing can be kept from silence. We have to act. We have to look for answers to the questions that pile up, suffocating our hearts; there's no other choice. But I failed.

Firdaus: Do you believe me now? I followed my
         wildest dreams, but I failed! Allah had
         other plans, Sidan!

Sidan: Firda, Firda . . . let me cry these tears.
       This shouldn't have happened, but it's my
       fault. I'm the one who failed. Glory be to
       Allah, He had not yet willed it, Firda!
       Forgive me. I'm devastated!

*Firdaus: Forget about it, don't just get all weepy.
Cry instead because you have not yet
become a martyr. I have to get ready to
fly home to Yogya now. Bye, my love!*

*Sidan: Sometimes, a bad phone connection is just
like hell! What have the lovers done wrong
that they must reap this punishment? This
is a tragedy, Firda!*

*Firdaus: Shh! You don't need to make such a fuss!
I'm going to turn off my phone now . . .
Bye!*

Firdaus's heart melted reading the expressions of bitter regret that burst forth from Sidan's broken heart. That was more than enough to make her spirit feel back in balance. Maybe they really were a well-suited couple. If one grew hot blooded, then the other calmed them down. Because love was understanding. Eyes whose gaze was full of affection. Ears that listened and a heart full of empathy.

Firdaus was sunk in a lake of ash. The cold air conditioning melted in the warm complimentary welcome drink, as she closed her eyes and pictured his face. Oh, she was collapsing, at the very height of longing! Until she lost track of time, floating in a bleak serenity. Until she forgot the Yogya sun and its gleaming luster.

*Firdaus: I've arrived . . . traveling what feels
like centuries from the Land under Water.
So let's say that suffering has also
become a distant memory. Don't hold on to
the remnants of your melancholy! Smile!*

Sidan: Yes. Sounds good! Once again, forgive me, Firda! Do you know how heavy a burden anticipation is? This far-flung land is always unlucky—all the signals are crossed, the reception is always faulty. We work without cease here, the martyrs of the tsunami are on a never-ending voyage toward the source of His Love, but we never quite arrive. A meeting, in any form, often becomes derevolutive energy. Haha, so look for the positive . . . Ibtasamiy ya hilwaty! Smile, my sweetheart!

Firdaus: Allah the Virtuous! Oh Omniscient One! A meeting is an ending. Like the Sufi Rabi'ah, the Mother of the Grandmaster, I'm afraid of the heat of hellfire! Let Him determine what is good and beautiful!

Sidan: Where is there anything as beautiful as the distance between Aceh and Yogyakarta? The daydream of a heavenly garden unfurling just as humankind awakens. Eve is in a frenzy on Mount Arafat, Adam cannot be calm, even for a moment. That's the Araf climax, the legendary meeting of the best lovers in the world who never sleep. They are frozen in time! Time stops for them! I'm scared, yayaya . . .

Firdaus: Oh, you scaredy-cat! Forget fear, I won't

*be afraid of even a thousand meetings!
Meeting time is also the time when
everything begins. What is there to be
afraid of? A new world stretches out
before our eyes. Aren't you ready to be
happy?*

Sidan: *Okay, I'm ready! If me being happy also
means the liberation of all the people in
the land of Serambi, then I will forevermore
refuse to be like Sisyphus, rolling my rock
up the mountain. Even Camus saw that he
could be happy, and so let's go, I will
take you by the hand and lead you to the
Cave of the Absurd!*

Firdaus: *Haha, you don't have to be so dramatic.
Happiness can also be as simple as an
August rain. Happiness is a breeze that
reminds you of your longing. Imagine
life without longing, it would be like
tasteless water!*

Sidan: *Agreed! Now have a rest . . . See you
tonight! Go in peace!*

Chapter 7:
Village of Signals

Having failed to launch *Culture Journal* because he was so distracted, Sidan headed home. But where was home? Was there such a thing as a home with no village?

The road is a timeless expanse, curving across the earth on a long journey of twisting pain. But I am a wanderer, and so how do I scrawl my history into the book of fate? I keep walking in the suspended silence of the interior villages, crawling like a snail through cities that no longer have eyes. The world can busy itself with the business of Antarctica—here we stay up all night, mapping new neighborhoods to be built out of a swamp. Reestablishing our villages, our culture, our civilization.

There was a chain of mountains stretching out like a seatbelt across the belly of the earth as far as the eye could see. Their slopes descended into great patches of wet dirt, with ravines as wide as the world, as if they had been scratched away by a giant prehistoric creature, leaving behind a puddle of black mud and bitterness. A lake of tears kept growing, created by a sunken village. But in the middle there, on a piece of the apocalyptic land, a mosque stood alone, defiantly looking up at the sky, elegant in its misery. An inherited monument from an extinct city.

And my love? Must she also sink, buried by rifles and melancholy, like a stretch of road studded with doom on the western coast of Aceh that has been washed out, swallowed by the tsunami?

He sped along the coast road on his motorbike, carrying the suffering in his heart, stupefied by never-ending questions and the view of nature that never lost its mesmerizing power. Blue sky, green mountains, the sea, and white sand. A field of wet grass newly planned for development as a village in Lam Senia. He turned left in order to visit the encampment.

Sidan: Go to the people. Live with them. Learn from them. Love them. Start with what they know. Build from what they have. But the mark of a good facilitator is when the work is done and all the tasks have been completed, the people say: we did it ourselves.—Lao Tzu

Firdaus: Good people forget the good deeds they did in the past. They are so busy with the work they are doing now that they forget what they have done before. Wise words from China.

Sidan: That's so true! Do you know Lam Senia? I am now at the camp there, where the people are working together to build a village from nothing at the foothills of Blang Ske Mountain. I hope this text goes through.

Firdaus: I've never heard of Lam Senia. But I'm happy to hear that. I hope your days are full of Lao Tzu's wisdom. Do you like it there?

Sidan: Ah! Don't ask. A large open field will be transformed into a village. Most of the people here were widowed, but they have been united by fate, and have coupled up once again. Love has given them the spirit to build a better life.

Firdaus: That's wonderful! But I hope you are just being a good facilitator, and not being like most of the people there, haha. Why don't you go home to your village?

Sidan: Right now my village is the business of those with technical expertise in carving out a hard life along the coast of the Malacca Strait. I'm on a sort of pilgrimage, thrown out of my motherland into uncharted territory. Maybe it's the Country of Love . . .

Firdaus: But when is the Country of Love ever mapped out?

Sidan: Maybe it is in the clear lake of the soul. The goddess Aphrodite resides in the green banks of the heart. But often too, love is just strawberry-flavored goat shit. Are you

ready for eternal madness? Learn from the
tiny baby, how he loves his doll without
expecting anything in return. Aha!

Firdaus: Oh, my dear, since when do you dig a grave
in the Lord's cemetery? I'm drinking
maple-flavored strawberry juice. The tiny
one loves strawberries.

Sidan: That's one thing and don't force it, if
at some point he starts to vomit. The
most important thing is to liberate and
fortify yourself and be humble. Not to
enslave lovers. Nobody is the ideal. Life
is immanent love, haha!

Firdaus: Life is immanent love, not immanent goat
shit, haha.

Sidan: Oh, that's a side effect when the hand of
a man touches the hand of a woman. When
Abraham's sword is on Ishmael's veins,
rationality disappears, logic hits a
dead end. It is the lunatic who achieves
enlightenment. It's not really love if you
haven't eaten steak yet!

Firdaus: Have you eaten steak, Sidan?

Sidan: I'm eating steak right now, under an apple
tree, and suddenly the third fruit of
eternity falls, a poem from Firda of the

*dagger eyes! Do you want to come to Aceh
again? I'll pick you up tomorrow!*

Firdaus: *Haha, phooey, no thanks! You should be the
one to come down from your mountain . . .
why would I wait for a ridiculous death?
I want to live for a thousand more years!*

Sidan: *Tomorrow I'll take you around Darussalam,
so you'll know how much more colonial
Jakarta is than the Netherlands. Here bad
dreams stand so tall and firm they turn into
monuments. I'm sure that whoever comes here
doesn't know how crazy it is in Aceh, how
history repeats itself and we die again,
evacuate again. They're so naive!*

Firdaus: *Yeah. What's even more naive is that it's
already dusk and I haven't taken a bath
yet. Bye, hon!*

Sidan: *Okay! Have fun splashing about, free inside
your cool and quiet and fragrant bathroom. A
pure spa. The sweet smell of your body wafts
all the way to the barrack of suffering! I'm
going to spy on you, silently drink in that
beautiful view to my heart's content with no
one to stop me!*

Firdaus: *You better not spy on me! Usually it's
the single guys who have been praying
unsuccessfully to find their soul mate who*

join the CIA so they can become Peeping Toms.

Sidan: Praying to find a soul mate? Are there any of those prayers like that I sent you that you have saved? It seems to me that it's no good to keep them stashed away in a cupboard. Send the freshest verse back to me, and I won't have to be a CIA spy anymore!

Firdaus: Allahumma inni as-aluka hubbaka wahubba man yuhibbuka wal amalalladzi yuballighuni hubbaka. Repeat that over and over until you are in an altered state, and I guarantee you'll be paired up with a fiancée in heaven.

Sidan: Haha, thanks! Allahumma . . . breathe! Allahumma . . . take a breath! Allahumma . . . but hey, who has arrived in your front yard? Some crazy foreigner whose prayers have been accepted? Haha, thanks, but I'm still going to sleep alone. See you!

Firdaus: Nobody has arrived in my yard . . . No one's come down from heaven, it's just a fleeting image of God's flickering dance. Sleep as deeply as you can, enjoy the single guy's rest! Go in peace!

Sidan: Oh, the single men get inspiration from the sky, but the moon goes into its chamber and

bathes in a harem pool, with its gilded
body and tapering fingers. My warm greetings
to you! You're not going to wash up after
all, my lady?

Firdaus: Humph . . . I'll bathe my alabaster body
like Cleopatra splashing in Niagara Falls,
like a gliding white swan, glowing with
the fragrance of heavenly jasmine. And
you're not invited, hahaha . . .

Sidan: CKCKCKCKGHAGHAGHPSTPSTPST oooSSTSSTSSTC
KCKCKCKEHMEHMEHMCKCKCKCKBSTBSTBST
oooCKCKCKCKCKooo, that's a mantra to tame
desire, my lady. My head is spinning!

Firdaus's crisp laughter soared across the sky. Let him feel it. In front of the tent in the Lam Senia dusk, Sidan could only scratch his head, imagining her alabaster body splashing in an eternal heavenly pool. Silence twisted his soul and longing gnawed at his back. Then the world seemed to disappear, taking everything with it. Or maybe it was the door to his wounded heart giving in to defeat.

He got his guitar and created a new world in poetry, a world that was sweeter and more welcoming than this one. A world where he was a prince and Firdaus was Cinderella. Not this present, discordant world. Then the villagers came, by twos and by fours. Gathering, bringing their fragments of hope and maps drawn up on crumpled old pieces of paper. All eyes wanted to see him. All hands reached out for him. Then Sidan joined in like family, to begin to rebuild the mosque with crumbling walls.

A map was unrolled and a village began to materialize, like a group of pilgrims in Medina. After one day of devoted labor, the mosque was gleaming again. The call to prayer echoed harmoniously throughout the quietly budding Lam Senia like a chime at the front door calling for the master of the house. Announcing that a life of promise had arrived, like a heart that was in love or a blooming rose. Then the plans drawn out on the map began to materialize further. There were days of bright sunshine. Without clouds hanging above, they faced the morning sun.

But Sidan was a true wanderer. Always flowing, always moving, according to his own time. There were dozens, hundreds, thousands upon thousands of loose pebbles, there was moss where he tripped, slamming against coral and steep cliffs. Without a home. All he had was temporary shelter, an ephemeral world, as night and day he searched for permanence. He smiled to see the view of tents stretching out as far as the eye could see.

I'm not alone!

Look, Firda. Silence enfolds the troops in the desert silence. Desolate and deserted. Let me draw your eyes in the blue sky of my longing, which is unbroken, without end. Your faithful smile blooms in every flower and every blade of grass, green from the sky's rain. Where is the cave where I can hide from your fragrance? There is none. The memory of you is fragrance itself. This intoxication never dies.

Sidan was supposed to continue on to Takengon, but he remembered that Adib had promised to come visit. Maybe his old friend from Yogyakarta could help ease his longing for that old city, with the aroma of stewed jackfruit and its beautiful young women. He hurried, and, impatient to hear the latest news of his idol, he lost track of the difference between the real path and the path of his imagination. He was too eager. He had been fasting for too long. He wanted to gulp down refreshment from those stories, but he was too hasty. He didn't realize how slippery the western beach road was, and it swallowed him, taking him into sorrow's throat. As if spurred by a demon, Sidan was thrown from his motorbike, flung down onto the ancient white sand with a crash. Left black and blue, slammed by his own enthusiasm.

Oh, Firda. It's not yet clear when Eid al-Fitr *will be, but loving you is like having a line of bleating sacrificial goats stretching out before me, all my days. Look over here, there is fragrant blood trickling out of my temple because I was too eager to hear stories of you, my angel. And then, look at this chest, its heart beating out a rhapsodic verse. But this country has no heart to share, it refuses to help along the love story of one of its children.*

Sidan: Dib! I've been thrown by fate! Please come
       to a white tent at the foot of Blang Ske
       Mountain. Lam Senia. It's the only thing
       standing, along with a mosque.—Sidan

He had to be carried back to the white tent by a handful of soldiers who happened to be passing by. He was seeing stars—maybe he had bumped his head on the rocky sand. A little raw patch on his arm was no big deal. He was thankful he hadn't broken any bones or gotten a black eye. Even though the soldiers had laughed at his battered guitar, calling him a bohemian busker, it was better this way. In such a sorry state, every one of its strings inherited the discordant notes of time.

Later you'll see for yourself, you damned crew cuts!

"We thought you were in trouble, arriving with them?"

"No, no. This time it was purely an accident. I'm sorry, but I may have to stay here a little longer."

"We would prefer it if you stayed. It's just that we know you have a lot of work to do as a reporter. But don't worry. We'll take care of you."

"Please don't go to any trouble. Maybe there is something else we still need to talk about, and so He sent me back here."

They came, one after the other. Every tongue brought its own story. Sidan felt he had become much richer than he had been before, and the riches that came with those stories—whether they were cheerful or tragic—were effective, healing medicine that brightened his heart. When the heart is harmonious, it builds a path that cuts through physical pain and illness. There were tears, there was restless talk and witty humor and even terror, and it all was the blooming rose of love. He saturated his white tent with the quiet breath of the eternal wanderer.

Then Adib arrived with a number of his friends. Sidan had only wanted to see Adib, but to the group, volunteering in Serambi was like going on a camping trip, full of recreation and singing. They only worked every once in a while and then were given their salary, folded in an envelope. As soon as he approached them, Sidan could already smell the aroma of horseshit. It wasn't the white tents they were interested in visiting, but the captivating white sand and the grandeur of the blue sea. A beauty that was not diminished by tears.

"Adib!" Sidan cried.

"Sidan! Praise God! How are you?"

"I am how I look. It's nothing. I'm just a little dizzy. I was thrown by love, Dib."

Adib chuckled before saying, "The commander of Serambi knows no injury. You just went rolling through the sand, and now you are even more beautiful. So be patient, you don't have to rush. Everything in its own time. Yes or no?"

"Yes. Tell me, what did you bring from lovely Yogya?"

"You're sure nothing happened to your head?"

"I'm just a little dizzy. My eyes are seeing stars. If she were here, my heaving longing could be delicately massaged . . . Is she still as fresh and lovely as always? Come on, tell me. I can't wait, Dib."

"Patience, Dan. Allah favors the patient."

"Say that she is even more like Layla in her anxiety."

"Exactly as you imagine. She is more beautiful in her anxiety. Women are even sexier when they are in torment. The more threatened, the more in pain, the more lonely, oh my God, their beauty has no comparison."

"That's the logic of a rapist. I prefer to appreciate how they endure a trial. Women have strong endurance. Megawattage. Look at

Sri Mulyani, Indonesia's finance minister during the economic crisis in 2007. She is now the managing director of the World Bank. Or Khofifah Indar, the minister of women's affairs. They are cool and collected, even when declaring martial law."

"You think that is also the case with Firdaus?"

"Exactly! I'm sure she was braver to come here than I was to go there. She has a thousand ways to achieve her dreams. The Acehnese heroine Cut Nyak Dhien never surrendered until death cut her down. That's just like Firda."

Adib silently rejoiced to find Sidan in such a pitiful state.

Don't you know that I'm the one who brought Firdaus here? It was thanks to my kindness that she flew all this way, only to find failure and disappointment. Do you know, Sidan? She had already inscribed the first gray notes in her journal, and that was before the dark notes that came later. So be careful. If one day a black front line comes galloping, those are the special forces that will demolish you and send you to hell, erasing your history from her memory.

"Your strong woman is really lonely, Dan. Yogya is a lonely place for her without you. Why are you so slow in making her dreams come true? Or maybe all your dreams are already dead? I hope you are healthy and well."

"I'm so healthy that I can endure anything, Dib. I am just part of a generation that has been ripped up by our roots. This country leaves us nothing, not even a sliver of hope."

"You don't have to worry, Dan. I think your angel lives with almost perfect loyalty and faithfulness. The distance between you two just makes her longing for you all the more alive. Honestly, all she needs is some certainty."

"In your opinion, is it possible for certainty to be born from uncertainty?"

Sidan plunged even deeper into feelings of alienation. He was an orphan. Then pain centered in his heart as memory after memory stabbed him like a capable needle, making him collapse, drenched in red. Who knows how long he had been an empty shell—maybe ever since he was born onto this blue planet. Alone, befriended by an alienation that was growing ever more alienating. Then vertigo hit. The road studded with pebbles that stretched out before him was still long, overhung with coils of fog as wide as the horizon.

"Be honest, Dan. Do you still long for Yogya or do you want to live in this land of suffering?"

"Whatever it is, this is the land where I was born. It raised me, just like a mother who has nursed her child. I can't turn away from its suffering face. That suffering actually unites us even more. But Yogya is the village of my love. What does life mean without love? Can we survive without its breath?"

Sidan couldn't bear to think about his future because his future didn't exist. It had collapsed before it had bloomed—none of the pistils ever had a chance to meet any of the seeds in the process of fertilization, none of the potential offspring ever came into existence because of the parched earth. Because there was no fertilizer. All that was left was junk and sheer waste. It was better to sleep and never wake up, or stay a child forever. Don't ever grow up and become fully aware. Knowing too much was an eternal torture.

Adib encouraged Sidan to take work as a volunteer, like him, suggesting that he would get a pretty good honorarium that might help him prepare for a future with Firdaus. Sidan was intrigued for a moment, but not after he heard what he would have to do. He had survived in the journalistic and documentary-film worlds because both of those were ways to bear witness to a brutal, shallow, and materialistic era, to a river of tears and an encampment of great suffering. He quickly realized that his path and that of his friend had intersected, but were already diverging.

It was better to focus on the film that he had been working on. Lam Senia had everything that he wanted to capture: Wind, the flickering of generator lights, tents, frogs, the rustlings of a pair of newlyweds as they created new life, the buzzing of beach mosquitoes, rolling waves, and a sliver of golden moon high above. And an even more intimate sense of longing, which was his companion day and night. Piercing to his core.

"Let me focus on my own world, Dib. I'm not interested now. Maybe some other time."

"You don't want to join her as soon as you can?"

"I want to do it in my own way."

So sure of himself, thought Adib. *How could Firdaus stand waiting for this slow snail who was creeping along around the earth in a thousand years of uncertainty? Aha! You are either pretending to be stupid or you really are a jackass!*

Secretly but enthusiastically, Adib sent Firdaus a text about Sidan's condition:

Adib: You shouldn't be too shocked, Firda, to hear that Sidan truly no longer has the courage for life. He has surrendered before the fight!

Firdaus: What do you mean, Dib? The word surrender isn't in his dictionary. And I should know, I'm the historian who has recorded his entire life's journey. Sidan is the prototypical Acehnese man. A real Acehnese man!

Adib: What do you know about Acehnese masculinity? He has already ruined it with his pessimism. I tried to lift him up, but he prefers to wallow in an ocean of death. What else can I do, Firda?

Adib's words rocked Firdaus. She didn't believe them, but they were not unbelievable. With all of the problems and misfortunes that Sidan had been hit with, maybe he had lost the strength to fight back. Because they kept coming, one after the other. There was no time for him to breathe. Maybe Adib was right—and it was so hard to cross the distance between Yogyakarta and Aceh to find the truth for herself.

Firdaus: Hon! Tell me why you rejected Adib's kindness? Is your Acehnese courage to challenge the waves already spent?

Sidan: What do you want from me, Firda? I have my own world. I develop from the things I am doing, things that I like to do. I don't need to join in the zombie feast. I'm human. A real man. You don't need to doubt that!

Firdaus: Zombie feast?

Sidan: Do you know Father Kun? Kuntoro Mangkusubroto. He's the former minister of mining activity who was appointed to head the rehabilitation and reconstruction of Aceh. He has it so easy, but he says his men work hard. They have no knowledge of Aceh but still they flock here, party for a while, and then go home filthy rich. We are stunned, standing dumbfounded in front of our barracks doors . . . That's the Dutch East Indies!

Firdaus was happy to read that. It reassured her that Sidan was still human. He didn't want to become a vampire.

Firdaus: Well, I'm glad you still can endure being human, haha. Do whatever you think is best and enjoy it. I'm still by your side. Get back on your feet as fast as you can and lift up our boat to cross the sea of love! My greetings.

That's what's hard, Firda. Oh, Firda! If I say, "What does material wealth have to do with love, with this life?"—well, certainly everything has meaning. If I say, "There are spiritual riches that are more valuable," well, where is that meaning to be found? Maybe we already own a part of it. Including the spirit that you breathe out all the time that inspires me to get up again, darling. Even though they've already stolen everything. Even though they have sucked it all up, leaving nothing but a parched future.

Sidan: I'm trying, Firda! And I'm not weary or fed up, I beg for your prayers and understanding about all the dire circumstances that assail me, my darling!

Firdaus: Don't worry about it. It's enough for me that there are still stories from the battlefield. I'm waiting for your return, my hero!

Sidan: Adam fought just to be able to greet Eve on the Arafat plain. Did you know that, darling? Okay, maybe tomorrow I will leave for Jakarta. You sleep first. Rest up so *tomorrow you can work hard! Sweet dreams!*

Firdaus: What's your business in Jakarta? But whatever it is, Jakarta is only 45 minutes from Yogya, haha. I want to see you afterward.

Sidan: I'm just finishing the film Suak Timah at Universal Pictures. Our funds are limited because the film doesn't have a willing investor yet, so be patient, yeah? I feel the Arafat plain is getting close. Wait and sometime I will come from Aceh to get you . . . saleum ateuh jeumala.

Firdaus: Agh! I just want to see you for a moment. Think of this as my last request before I die! What the heck is saleum ateuh jeumala? Are you speaking in Acehnese?

Sidan: Kapaloe dikei kupemate ate sinyak gob. Teunang saboh wate teuma kujak tueng ba u Atjeh . . . may you be happy, so may the seedlings bloom into flowers . . . welcome their presence, full of prosperity. Okay. Bye-bye!

Firdaus was practically drowning in dreams when a telephone call from Adib woke her. Dammit! In the middle of the night like this? Even Sidan was always considerate about respecting her health and rest. Why didn't Adib mind his manners?

What news could be so important that I have to hear it in the middle of the night like this?

It was only her curiosity that moved Firdaus's hand to accept his call.

"Sorry, Firda. I guess it's already the middle of the night. I was just sitting here, getting carried away by thoughts of your predicament."

"Why are you putting yourself out about our business, Dib? We're doing just fine. It's enough—let us take care of our own problems. Thank you for your attention, but I'm sorry, I'm still sleepy."

"Wait a minute, Firda. Maybe you can convince Sidan to return to Yogya with me the day after tomorrow after I've finished my business. I think he just feels too embarrassed to accept my offer."

"I'll think about it tomorrow. Sorry, but I'm really tired. *Salamu'alaikum.*"

Damn you with all your offers! I certainly don't know where you get your money. Do you know that you will be responsible for each bill and coin on Judgment Day? Maybe you all would laugh and think it funny that in this fast-paced era, people are actually competing for the chance to sample the fires of hell? Or that at a time when most people are wearing themselves out trying to beat one another to the illusory peak of success that there might still be a few who waste their time remembering the Exalted One?

Don't pretend you don't know, Dib! Hundreds of thousands are lying on their backs in agony in the quiet barracks with empty plates, empty gazes, and empty futures. There is nothing covering them except silence wrapped in an even more-encompassing silence. Meanwhile you all dance in celebration and fill your plates with their blood. Do you still think of yourselves as do-gooders? Aren't you embarrassed by the clear-eyed children scavenging for a drop of warmth at your feet, which are cozy inside in your leather shoes?

Look at the widows mending their clothes thread by thread, sewing up wounds that never end. Fetid days in a cardboard box full of holes for giant spying eyes. There is no privacy. There is no independence, not even in dreams or in a coma. But you all laugh loudly, as if you owned the universe. Imagine if those widows were your mother, and those young women were your younger sisters. Those orphans your children. They are the clandestine youth, the youthful energy whose breath is cut short.

Thinking about all of this, Firdaus was no longer sleepy. She would have contacted Sidan, but she remembered he had to guard his health and get plenty of rest for the next day's journey to Jakarta. She tried one more time to consider Adib's offer. But didn't all the coffers in Father Kun's padlocked warehouse actually belong to the victims of the tsunami? They were the only ones who had a right to it. Meaning that Sidan's hands were clean enough to hold at least some of that fortune. Wasn't that how it was?

But what if that fortune trickled down? What if it first went into the hands of some other faction, and then could indirectly arrive in Sidan's hands in a pure fashion?

Firdaus was anxious the whole night, going over every potential opportunity for Sidan. If she had power like the queen of Sheba, she would order a minister: "Like Archangel Michael, smile on all my people who are weeping because of the tsunami. And you'd better not try to embezzle their money, not one cent." If she were the sun, she would meticulously record the scene, barracks by barracks, teardrop by teardrop, until nothing escaped her. Then she would arrive at the white tent at the foot of Blang Ske Mountain and there she would find a lonely young man racked by hunger. She would be lost all night, in supplications to the sky:

"Ya Allah! If I had been born as the Raja Suleiman, I would have moved the tsunami so that it swallowed Jakarta. Monas would be violently shaken and rattled, not coddled and cradled, right, Lord? Imagine! The earth would split and out would come mud, sulfur, and black sludge. The State Palace, that old center of Dutch colonialism, would collapse. *Poof!* Because there is no one who loves us as sincerely as death, right, Lord? Armed with memories, we form a guerilla family and head toward a martyr's death in Karbala. One! We are One! The prose of death is poetic, romantic, and delicate."

But what of that friendless long-haired young man in his white tent? Now he longs for death? That is poetic and romantic? How strange are the colors of this country's heart. My minister fishes around in the coffers, without a middleman, borrowing directly from the source. He imagines Archangel Michael smiling down on him. At first he thinks this is the only way to prevent leaks, when the pipe is longer than the water coming in. He counts what's in the coffers while estimating how long it will take to get it all.

He laughs, realizing how inefficient his method is. He could work until Judgment Day and still not be finished. He quickly changes his strategy, because my minister is always dynamic and proactive about progress. He chooses one thousand men who are free from records of corruption, collusion, and nepotism, and then puts them to work, but it isn't enough! Now he hires ten thousand ma'had graduates, Islamic scholars known for their inner and outer purity, who remember and truly understand the meaning of the hadith arrosyi wal murtasyi finnar: *those who bribe and those who take bribes are experts at hell—er, or is it hellish experts? And then those damned parasites who bribe and take bribes are included too.*

Because they really know their prayers, the white-clad religious students fly with weightless steps, like fragrant balls of cotton perching on the roofs of the silent barracks, carrying coffers on their heads, as Michael smiles. In only a couple of months, darkness has been erased in the land of suffering. It is fitting that my minister pats his chest. Then comes the report: "A lonely young man reported to the Lord that he has a lover who imagined she became the queen of Sheba, the wife of King Solomon, the raja with long curly hair. And all the stories are a collusive concoction made from the fruit of her thoughts." That means . . .

She's a rebel!

Subversive!

Firdaus gasped.

Collusion? Even just fantasizing about becoming queen, this country had already become a magician. Abracadabra! Black became white, doves became vultures. Crows caw like hawks. Deconstruction, you say? Oh that, your head in your ass and your genitals sprouting out of your brain. So let's walk with our hands on the ground and our legs pointing up to the sky. Look at the clouds from a different angle, then you will see they resemble a burial shroud. Another Noah's flood might come like a thief in a night without stars.

Exhausted from imagining all the possibilities, Firdaus floated up into space, wrapped in a beautiful verse—In Your name, Lord, I live, and in Your name I die. Amen. Slowly she moved toward the edge of a mountain, maybe the foot of Blang Ske, and she saw Sidan way up high calling her name. Firdaus! Firdaus! She tried to climb. The call pierced her heart. One, two, her feet climbed and kept climbing, trembling, afraid of the gaping abyss below.

She foundered again and again, gasping for breath, but she didn't want to lose track of the voice that was calling from the summit. She kept trying and kept climbing. Crawling inch by inch, faithfully measuring the distance with her soft fingers and her sobs filling the strange silence. Where are you, Sidan? Why don't you reach out your hand to me? Firdaus climbed, clutching a safety rope that was taut and stretching up into the sky, unscalable.

All that is left is half a breath and your shadow passing by.

Then, *craaack!*

The rope broke. There was nothing to stop her fall. Only red earth spewing angry lava below.

Go away, I don't know you!

Firdaus slid head over heels, tumbling down to the bottom of the ravine at the foot of Blang Ske Mountain. The entire contents of her brains celebrated her graduation: her history was finished. And so the book of life closed. All she had to do was wait for the angel interrogator.

But hold on! How strange! *Why does the angel look exactly like Sidan? Are there really long-haired angels? And how many angels use a video camera, like Sidan when he is making a film? Does he really want to shoot my grave?*

"Name?"

"What?" Firdaus gasped.

"Say your name."

"Firdaus."

"Your full name?"

"Firdausidan."

"Don't mock me."

"Who's mocking who, Mr. Angel?"

"What do you mean, angel? I'm the director of *Layla-Majnun.* Don't tell me you forgot? Read the script. Memorize it. Let's go, start again!"

"Sir, may I make a suggestion? What if the film's title was changed to *Firdaus-Sidan?*"

"What for?"

"Well first, their conflict is more tragic, eternal and second, their story is more realistic."

"What is their story like?" asked the angel director, who had Sidan's face, glowering but intrigued.

Then I told our story to him.

Firdaus woke up, trying to guess what the dream meant, trying to figure out whether there might be an encouraging interpretation. But Joseph, the interpreter, was long dead. All that was left were ghosts roaming uncertainly in the streets. Only her intuition and an attachment to the stories behind the dream became a kind of key to understanding a little bit of the secret. Then she pictured the unraveled knot. Aha!

For how many hours had she been taken on an adventure through that magical, awesome realm of the unconscious? She awoke on the horizon of another consciousness that whispered bursting flames of enlightenment. She had to go home to her village to look for some reassurance from her parents. She wanted to hear their thoughts at times like this, when she was stuck, absolutely at the end of her rope.

They who are seasoned by experience and me, who is still raw and new.

Wondering about the meaning of "home" and still seeing the images from her dream, Firdaus daydreamed the whole journey to her parents' house. She began to wonder what had really prevented Sidan from coming to Yogya? So he didn't have any money; some could be found. He couldn't bear to leave his village? That could be taken care of. What was it about the future that Sidan feared? Images from the past? Maybe. But they could live in Yogya, or Jakarta, or many other cities, if he wanted.

Dusk had almost fallen when Firdaus got out of the shared van. She was used to taking a carpool home; it was practical and comfortable. But it would still take a few more minutes for her to reach her house. She preferred to ride a pedicab rather than one of the motorcycle taxis that crowded at the intersection. Firdaus rarely went home, and in a pedicab she could enjoy the view of pristine nature along the way. White fields of sugarcane flowers and green rice paddies stretched out in neat square fields, as far as the eye could see. Hummingbird flowers and paddy oat trees.

A row of cotton shade trees sheltered pedestrians on both sides of the road for miles, like a row of straight and still green soldiers, ushering in the breeze from the clear flowing rivers, full of crabs and crawfish that crept in between the water spinach nodding under the damp dusk breeze. On its banks a pink mimosa opened and closed, enjoying the time of day.

Ten years ago, this road was still rough, full of pebbles and potholes that were hard for two-wheeled vehicles to navigate. Trucks hauling sugarcane made it worse, and year after year it had become more ruined and broken down. The local official who won the election promised to have it paved with smooth asphalt, but that was just hot air. It never happened until a very accomplished kid from the village, who had become a religious expert and wowed the nation, on his own initiative convinced an investor from Jakarta that he had to smooth the road for the religious students who were seeking heaven in the afterlife. Because the religious man was naturally more intelligent than the investor, the investor followed along as instructed and paved the religious man's road, smoothing over every curve, evening out every dip and bump.

The pedicab kept going, and the pedicab driver started breathing louder, competing with the wind. The sky was orange on the western horizon, radiating magnificent color, the beauty of a peaceful sunset. The birds flew in a line, cutting across the horizon in rows, going home after a day of enjoying the pleasures of nature. As far as the eye could see on either side of the road, there was only a wide expanse of green, then the school building elegantly guarding the gate into the village. There was a soccer field next to it, and Firdaus sighed.

"We've arrived, sir."

"Which house, miss? If I'm not mistaken, it's in front of the mosque?"

"You still remember!"

"I just forget which side of the mosque."

"The eastern one belongs to Mr. Ahmad; the western one is my house, sir."

The village was continuously improving. After the road from the city was paved with smooth asphalt, many visitors—diligent religious students and performers from the capital alike—arrived to participate in the large prayer recitation and religious study every full moon. Then came the booksellers, merchants selling religious items, others selling toys, all kinds of food, assorted local goods, imported perfume, and even traditional medicine. There were also all different kinds of cars, from knock-off brands to Jaguars and BMWs. Sometimes there was a limousine. All of them passed along this paved road. Then tourists would study prayer recitation straight from the religious man's mouth or just enjoy getting lost in the crowd.

In the middle of every month of Qamariah, when the full moon appeared high in the heavens, this small village carved out a new history for itself as the crowds arrived, one after the other, their eyes shining. They were thirsty for knowledge, hungry for wisdom, and some just longed to reap good fortune and change their luck. Verses were recited, echoing throughout an atmosphere that was hoarse and exhausted at first, and slowly began to nurture and soothe the cold in the people's hearts and minds. In the sultry night air, under the light of the full moon shining in between the caressing palm trees, thousands of people held a dialogue of kinship. The religious man, now known as a preacher, shared an intimacy with the hopeful religious students through the melodic verse.

Students from Australia, Canada, Holland, and Japan, whose grandfathers had been incalculably cruel, were busy with their questions and their cameras. Because the preacher spoke with supple language and wise discussion. Because politics, economics, literature, music, and protests were also the stuff of life. The fabric of brotherhood had to be woven in order to strengthen it.

A microphone was passed around in between the crowd of faces, until someone took it. He spoke with a voice that trembled, perhaps because it was overcome with emotion.

"It's like this, preacher. This country has just been deluged with Noah's flood in Aceh. What can be interpreted from that event?"

For a few moments, the preacher was taken aback by that simple question, which wasn't really that simple. He straightened his flat-topped black *peci* hat and stroked his hair that was down to his shoulders—the people often criticized him for it, but the preacher always teased in response that even the Prophets had long curly locks, so certainly their cleric should be permitted to.

"The tsunami came to Aceh," said the preacher, "in order to offer awareness, an opportunity for momentum so that the people of Aceh could reestablish all the aspects and dimensions of their Acehneseness. Its identity as Serambi Makkah, the port of Mecca, the character of its culture, negotiations of its future, consolidation between all of its factions, contemplative prayer recitation, and all kinds of spiritual and intellectual exchange and conversation will determine what they will become at this point in history." The preacher took a breath before continuing. "The world's heart pounds in anticipation, waiting for Aceh to rise again and exceed our expectations in the fields of politics, culture, and even humanitarianism."

Then he read the poem "Tears for Aceh" by Emha Ainun Najib:

Tears for Aceh
Were yesterday
Today comes the epiphany
Morning comes with darkness and destruction
Midday is nervous and confused
Afternoon is still sadness and suffering
But when the night arrives
Aceh prostrates itself in meditation
The days of Aceh are constantly changing
Days of frustration become days full of gratitude
Days of trauma become days of power
Days of despair
Become days of renewal
Aceh's days are not the days of tsunami
Aceh's days are post-tsunami days
It could even be that Aceh's days
Are days of tsunami wisdom
Aceh's days are days blessed by the tsunami
Aceh moves suffering

From its shoulders to the dirt
Buries it with pride
In the name of the martyrs in God's heaven
Aceh looks far into the future
The look in its eyes is
The brightness of a vision of history
In its right hand is held Aceh's authority
In its left hand, the shield of their protector
From all subjugation, enslavement and deception

Aceh is Allah's underdog
With the might of the tsunami
That other nations
Would never be able to bear

Aceh is no longer afraid
Of death
Because the tsunami was more powerful
Than all death

Aceh is not afraid of anything anymore
It will become the Port of Mecca
Not the Port of Washington
And not the Port of Jerusalem . . .

A pensive night. All eyes and all ears were opened and the full moon on high glowed even brighter, blazing in their hearts. The bit of enlightenment that had just been blown by the wind gently entered the inner crevices of their hearts, sighing out a rhythm of struggle in a life increasingly lived in unison on earth. Sympathy and love bloomed for their brothers and sisters far away in Aceh, and that longing for those faraway brethren became the glue that unified their souls. We are one people!

This was the full moon in Sepoi village, far away beyond the bends and curves and dips and bumps in the road, made crystal clear by the shower of light emanating from the Quranic verses that echoed throughout the assembled religious scholars, the brothers, and sons. From their studies and prayer recitation, this country was not just billowing foam, but glittering pearls nestled in the mussel shell of civilization. The religious men, the philosophers, the comedian *kyais*, the original clowns, each of them had beautified this country and were ready to greet the proclamation of civilization.

Firdaus folded her arms, quiet in the midst of thousands of thundering souls. She was in the middle of an ocean of people, but her spirit was carried away by the preacher's poem. Her house was only one hundred meters away from the courtyard where the prayer recitation was being held. This event had been going on for a long time, but it was new to Firdaus, who only came home once a year. It was her destiny that even after she'd arrived home to her village, the air that entered her ears was still echoing Aceh.

In bed that night she went over the conversation she'd had with her parents.

"If you are ready to suffer and struggle, go to Serambi Makkah, stand face-to-face with your hero," Mother said. "Because life is a struggle."

"But remember," Father warned, "the Aceh of today is an Aceh whose future is still somewhat uncertain. I'm not sure about it, because everything there is still in the process of getting ready . . . Unless Sidan wants to move to Yogya or somewhere else, that's another matter."

"We want to stay in Yogya. It's just difficult for Sidan."

"What's difficult about it, my child?"

"It's too hard for him to leave his village because his mother and father's graves are there. But . . ."

"There is no but," Father insisted. "Uncertainty will never be a good foundation for building calm, peace, or, what's more, happiness. There people go out looking for calm and see what happens. Your only option is to try to endure. Maybe he will become a hero, but not for you. You know?"

Firdaus knew. There had to be a certainty in her demeanor in order to convince her father. But how could she be certain if everything was still up in the air? She sometimes wasn't even sure that Sidan would really come to get her as his fiancée, but thought instead he might just come to ensure her destruction—or maybe he wouldn't come at all. All of a sudden she shuddered. It was too hard to imagine Sidan breaking his promise. It was truly bitter to think about it.

She lay there, paralyzed on the edge of her bed, tired and frustrated. Their faces flashed by one by one: Hussein, long-haired Jayeng, Adib Bahalwan, Mas Candra. Ugh! They passed by as if they were ready to be chosen, like cakes at a banquet. But none of them stood out. Because she was craving her ideal food, the one that had been her favorite from the beginning of her life and would be until the end of time. What was the point of eating those other cakes, even if they were brought from another country or even from another galaxy—the more they were pushed on her, the more nauseated she felt. Because there was only one she imagined in her mind. There was only one seared into her heart.

But what does my struggle toward you really mean? You don't go anywhere. You don't hasten to look for the Arafat plain. You stay still, right in the place you fell from heaven while constantly imagining the heaven you just left. Sometimes you are so resigned. Maybe you've given up? No! It's not the Acehnese way to give up. Falling from heaven doesn't mean you won't find the river of paradise. It's still there, a valley waiting at the end of your search.

Her irritation overflowed. All her feelings overflowed. She wanted to contact Sidan. Send him a text. But no, she had turned off her phone on purpose. She needed to mull things over. Contemplate. For a week. Two weeks. She needed to confide in nature, to the morning breeze in the shady coconut orchard. Every morning while back in her village, Firdaus went jogging with Farah, her little sister who was in middle school, three times around the sugarcane field. *Mens sana in corpore sano!*

When she arrived back home, she would pick lime and starfruit, make juice, and drink it. That was her mother's favorite elixir for staying young and slim. For breakfast she ate only a small plate of fried rice with an over-easy egg. She chewed it slowly while enjoying the melodious songs of Hafez, who was a well-known singer from Egypt, the country where the people had prominent noses and round eyes like fairies, the country whose people had fought in the Crusades. Her father had brought the cassette home when he'd returned from his schooling there.

Father said there was no other voice in the world as melodious as that of the nomadic Sulubba people of the Arabian desert, with their white skin, round blue eyes, and blond hair, who spoke Arabic and lived in the valleys near Hejaz in western Saudi Arabia. Primitive and mythical wails, fused from two beautiful peoples, the Philistines and the Greeks. He liked to speak of how now the best place to hear their crisp verse and soft abiding symphony was in a pub on the outskirts of Damascus.

Firdaus laughed. She remembered how much Sidan disliked these songs, especially those by Sabah from Lebanon. She was one of the stars of the east, and she sang like a dove sings from the top of a palm tree. *Derkuk-kuk! Derkuk-kuk!* Charming the universe. Sighing out a galloping trill as she pronounced the lyrics *Gani tulabis-samakh* . . . the suspect begs for mercy.

Sidan had said, "Oh, you, who sings in the leaves of the swaying palm trees, your beauty is agrarian and domestic, not maritime or cosmopolitan."

But an educated man like Sidan was ultimately subdued by the agrarian eyes of Aphrodite, the Javanese goddess of rice, Queen Firdaus from the great Majapahit Kingdom. Because love knows nothing about geography. It doesn't care about politics. It doesn't care whether war is raging or subsiding. Love hacks away at village boundaries. Religion and nation. Love runs from the empty froth of words. Love has its own country of beauty. Firdaus and Sidan are only two of its many billion inhabitants. The Land of Love.

Firdaus would spend hours communing with nature in the lush, silent orchard while pretending to fish in the pond with Farah, digging fingernails of longing into bunches of golden bananas. She cried and was angry. Yearning and irritated. Sometimes she felt there was a thick wall keeping her from Sidan. She knew these were modern times, when distance or even family disapproval could not keep two lovers apart. It wasn't like in old novels. She could fly to Aceh in a couple of hours, just as Sidan could come to her. But that wall kept following her like a labyrinth, winding endlessly around her.

"You're daydreaming—be careful you don't get struck by a *dhemit* spirit!" Farah cried from the end of the pond.

"What *dhemit*? Any kind of supernatural being is welcome to my body. Lift up my body if you are in fact strong enough, spirits. Fly me all the way to Banda Aceh!"

"Banda Aceh or Meulaboh?"

"Either one. Serambi Makkah!"

"But where is Sidan?"

"In a crevice of Blang Ske Mountain!"

"Is he one of the people being persecuted?"

"He is always persecuted, despite the fact that he's not a separatist, not a thief or a corruptor. He's always seen as dangerous because of his passionate intellect and historical knowledge. He's part of the youth that is truly dangerous to those in power."

"Why would you want to have a lover who is a dangerous man?"

"It's because he's so valuable that he's seen as dangerous, Farah."

"I don't understand."

"We are under the umbrella of a super secular theater state. None of those in power are pious, they are all like crazy Brutus, unwilling to take responsibility for their actions . . . so people who have hopes and dreams and are awake to the truth are very dangerous to them, little sister."

"So what are Sidan's hopes and dreams? What makes him seem so dangerous?"

"He has a dream of being an independent person in Serambi Makkah. And that's dangerous. Even though the proclamation of independence has resounded for decades."

"That seems strange, doesn't it?"

"Wherever you go, when the state is good, then even the smallest, most remote villages will be well. But if the state is absurd, it becomes a nightmare for everyone, until they have infiltrated every aspect of our private lives. Do you understand?"

"Sort of."

"The distance between fact and fiction is as wide as a fraction of a strand of hair—that's Serambi Makkah. Because its bilious history is so incredible, it almost sounds like a fairy tale."

"But hasn't the crazy state regime collapsed?"

"The military regime is gone, but the Pinocchios still reign with impunity. After the territorial dispute over Ambalat, all that's left of the Dutch East Indies is Jakarta. And the separatists have been around since 1945. The region has been completely exploited. The important thing is that even a country as big as the USA is a federation, not an iron fist. Where is the Indies socialism, the Indies democracy?"

Even though she didn't understand her fully, Farah was happy to be talking to her big sister about important matters.

Then she ventured, "Father said you picked the wrong future husband, sister. A man who loves death more than anything is not a good choice for a husband."

"And when in this world can we refuse death? We can't make it budge even one inch, Farah. But Brother Sidan loves life. I don't feel like I have made the wrong choice."

"And you are ready to take the necessary risk?"

"Very ready."

"Can I tell Father that?"

"Tell him that I have decided with certainty that I choose Sidan. And I will certainly be able to bear the responsibility for any risk I take!"

Farah could see how earnest Firdaus was. But for a moment she was still unsure. She imagined that if her older sister married an Acehnese man, then she would come home even more rarely than she already did. Plus, Farah had heard that to be a beautiful woman in Aceh was very risky. Many thieves in sheep's clothing would kidnap pretty women with all different methods and tactics. Even if she had a husband, he might not have the balls to face vicious kidnappers. They often worked in gangs.

"You are brave enough to face the thieves who steal women, sister?"

"In Aceh, you mean? No, I'm not. That's why Sidan has to leave Aceh, and we will live in Yogya."

"Oh, well, if that's how it will be, that's great! I'll tell Father."

After Mother and now Farah supported those plans, all Firdaus's father could do was try to think positively. He was fairly democratic in giving her freedom. She was already mature enough to make the important decisions about her life. Neither of Firdaus's parents had a problem with Sidan's professional prospects—it was his character that was the most important to them. It was enough that the couple was of the same faith, had the same level of education, and shared the same dreams. They were emblematic of their generation, who would build their own futures. Mother and Father realized that, because they themselves were well educated.

So when she returned to Yogya, Firdaus could smile with the ticket to her wedding in her pocket. She carried a blue butterfly that was ready to take flight in her heart, beating its wings under a bright sun and full moon that were ripening in their orbits.

Good morning, Yogyakarta!

Chapter 8:
A Bride without a Crown

It took three days to finish editing the *Suak Timah* film. Sidan couldn't stand to stay too long in the defiled city that stunk of the bad breath of corruptors and was claustrophobic with materialism. In Jakarta, the rainy months were plagued with electrical outages. They could only use the Universal Picture Studios facilities at night. The AC was freezing and the room was silent, and he was left alone with nothing but his phone and some chewing gum as company. On his first rainy afternoon in Jakarta, he received a little bit of warmth sent from Yogya, in the form of a text from Firdaus, but then she went mute. She didn't contact him and he couldn't contact her—her phone kept saying "pending." Then the electricity died and didn't come back on until two in the morning.

Usually, the moments when the lights went off were when they had their best chats, from about eleven at night until two in the morning. When the world was fast asleep, rocked by dreams, they were wide awake, playing and having fun, riding the waves of reception, humming, and dancing the Layla-Majnun dance. But now the flame of love that usually illuminated the nighttime had been extinguished. Sidan wondered what had happened. He kept on trying to contact Firdaus through his friends in Yogya and the host mother who supervised the house where Firdaus lived, but to no avail. Nobody knew where Firdaus had disappeared to.

Sidan's urge to go to Yogya right away grew more urgent. So what was he waiting for? He was sure Firdaus was playing hard to get, trying to lure him to her as soon as possible. He longed to grow wings and fly to meet his beloved. He didn't have enough money for a hotel, but he still had a few friends left in Yogyakarta who were taking even longer than he had to graduate. He could spend the night with one of them, and he didn't need to worry about how he would get home yet. If he had to walk back to Aceh from Yogya on foot, he would do it. Adam and Eve did it, long ago—and that was how Arafat became so blue.

Sidan: Sin, please pick me up at the airport at 9.

Husin: Okay! If I'm a little late, don't worry. The twists and turns of these old city roads are like my own flesh and blood, now that I have learned them, I never lose my way. I'll be there!

Sidan: I'm not worried about that, but don't be too late! My legs are already falling asleep!

Husin: Haha! That's normal, friend. Plane flights always do that to you! I bet you're worried you'll get a cramp too before you land. Take care!

Sin was Husin Assegaf, an eternal student who had been in Sidan's class, an activist born in Maluku. He yawned—even the late morning was too early for him, in a city with lulling breezes that meandered through the plazas and apartment complexes. But his phone had been on, so he had been forced to answer. Plus, it would be a pity for a friend to come from so far away and be left stranded, and to him, Sidan was more than just a friend. He was a rival who always spurred Husin's courage to get up again—inspired him to rise higher and higher, even though in fact he often fell short.

Husin left and raced toward his friend and rival.

Welcome back to the city of horse-drawn carriages, friend. Look, now townhouses are cropping up everywhere. Medical centers and traditional medicine peddlers stand side by side. Vendors hawk their wares right in front of the sleek Carrefour department store. Here there is truly nobility in the heart of the people. They meet each other in complimentary greeting. They haven't yet become "you and me"; there is still only "us." Isn't that beautiful?

The friends hugged each other warmly, one still smelling fresh, the other stinking from a day's journey.

"Your eyes are shining even brighter than ever, my friend!"

"The tsunami opened my eyes. There is no suffering. There is no panic. There is only Firdaus! How is she?" Sidan asked eagerly.

"You mean you don't even want to ask how *I'm* doing?"

Sidan clapped his friend on the shoulder, laughing, and said, "I can see how you're doing, you're right in front of me, and that dingy blanket you carry around with you everywhere is giving off its same old smell. I bet you still procrastinate with your prayers, don't you?"

"All of us here have to put off our prayers because we are so busy dealing with the urgent matters that are lined up like a row of beggars stretching from Jakarta to New York," Husin said. "You haven't forgotten what that's like, have you?"

Husin and Sidan sped along. The Yogya wind caressed Sidan's body, like gentle fingers, massaging his soul. The warm morning sun only further enticed him to gaze into the eyes of his beloved.

What are you doing, darling? Look, I've come! Finally I've come. I did not go back on my word, Firda. I did not have the strength to leave my heaven behind. In your eyes, my life begins.

Even though Husin knew that Firdaus's house was closer to the airport than his place, he didn't know whether Sidan wanted to rest or freshen up before seeing her.

"If I know you, you must want to go right to see her."

"Yes of course! I can't stand it."

"Don't be like that, friend. Rest and take a breath, freshen up and put on your makeup first, like they do in films. And speaking of films, how is your latest?"

"It's doing alright! So far, there's nothing like it. The only thing that comes close is *Coming Home* by Zhang Yimou, and as for him? Let's just say he's still a rebel like always."

"The rebel meets the dissident . . . You're crazy, Dan! You want to recruit more separatists, don't you?"

"Yeah, using Marxist law from the Hegelian tradition, plus Johan Galtung's structural pyramid of violence, the dialectic of eternal resistance, Arendt's rebel Sisyphus, and Julia Kristeva. Cool, right?"

"How is it cool to only turn left? I thought you said you wanted to spread love and compassion?"

"But left is sexy. It is the ultimate love and compassion."

Husin could only laugh and shake his head. He understood. Sidan couldn't wait to turn on his phone. He was still full from the fried noodles he had eaten on the plane. Still, he said good-bye to Husin and refused a ride to Firdaus's place, because this was his private business. He wanted to be alone when he offered her, his soul mate, a bouquet of all the surprises, all the poetry and longing, all the declarations of love and flowers he had saved in the chambers of his troubled heart.

"*Salamu'alaikum!*"

There were four friends hanging out at the house where Firdaus rented a room. A knock on the door in the morning was unusual, so two of them, Ima and Muna, looked at each other questioningly.

"*Alaikum salam.* Who is it?"

"Sidan!"

Hearing the name Sidan, Ima and Muna stared at him in shock. They let him in and, along with Firdaus's other roommates, crowded around him, full of genuine regret and sympathy due to the information that they had to give: Firdaus wasn't there. She had gone back to her village a number of days ago and they weren't sure when she would return. Her phone appeared to be turned off.

"Why did she go back to her village?"

"We're sorry, but she didn't say anything about it. All we know is that in the days before she left, she seemed quite upset and then she decided to go home."

"What do you mean, the days before she left?"

"When she came back from Aceh but before she went back to her village."

Sidan looked at the floor, melancholy and heartsick.

"Does anyone know the number of her home telephone?"

Ima and the rest looked at each other and shook their heads. Sidan grew weak, pining. Now he felt the disappointment Firdaus must have felt when she was in Banda for a week without any contact, without even a brief meeting.

Whose fault on earth could this possibly be? Maybe fate?

He didn't want to go back to Husin's house, but instead went to the theater group he had built on campus back when he was in school. There were three friends, all with long and curly hair. Their names were

Pa'o, Mbojing, and Iqbal. Once Sidan arrived that made four long-haired friends.

They swarmed around him, welcoming him back with uproarious cries. Boisterous laughter broke out and then fell silent. Then his story came bursting forth from his melancholy heart.

"But it seems like only a week ago she was on campus," one long-hair said.

"That's just this campus. But she's always on Brother Sidan's campus; she never leaves or goes anywhere without telling him about it, isn't that right, brother?"

"I'm serious. I really want to see her. Help me out. Who has any tips?"

A barrage of suggestions came flooding: call her relative Mr. Emha because he lives here in Yogyakarta; call her neighbor; it would be better if you went right to her house to propose to her parents as a surprise and fix the date of the wedding and the honeymoon in Kaliurang. But all this was easier said than done.

Sidan weighed his options. If he went to see Mr. Emha, then he certainly would get an answer. So he quickly left, heading for the house with a tall iron fence and a guard ready to question him.

"Do you have an appointment?" asked the white-and-blue uniform.

"Yes," Sidan lied, knowing that was the only kind of answer that the uniform would accept.

He was allowed to enter the yard, with its lush plants and meandering path up to the door. He pressed the bell for a long time, but there was no response. He stood there until he was fed up, but right as he was about to leave, the door opened. There stood a young proletarian man, who apparently had just finished bathing. His body emitted the smell of an unfamiliar soap.

"Who are you looking for, sir?"

"Brother Emha. Is he in?"

"Oh no. He and his whole family went back to the village for the monthly prayer meeting. He might be there for a while because he's also going to celebrate his younger brother's wedding. What do you need?"

"So you are looking after the house? Do you know his address back in the village? Or his telephone number?"

"I'm one of his employees at the press. I don't know his address or telephone number. But I've been to his house. I know which way to go once you've gotten to town."

"Are you from the same village, brother?"

"No. I'm from Mandar, in Sulawesi."

That meant he really only knew the general direction toward the village from the center of town, not precise directions. Plus, there was no way Sidan would go to Firdaus's house and meet her parents in his current condition, especially with his limited finances. In truth he really wanted to see Firdaus in order to explain the whole situation and look for the best solution for moving forward. Because he felt that he had grown old before his time amidst the storms of life. But he hadn't died. Heaven was still waiting, faraway in the distance.

Sidan asked himself, *How long should I wait, with vague information and rapidly emptying pockets, for Firdaus to return?* He had known that the journey back to Yogya would be a gamble, but he hadn't been able to deny his desire. Now he had to once again consider his dwindling finances, or he would be stranded and forced to become a vagrant, selling plants like back when he was in school, or peddling books from door to door, waiting for his money to run out.

He only had enough to fly back to Jakarta—where would he find the money to cover the rest of the journey home, from Jakarta to Medan to Banda? He was too embarrassed to go to the houses of the few successful men and women he knew who were also from Meulaboh. Nor was there any way he would bother his other friends about it. After all, they were also far from home, just trying to make ends meet. But what about Jakarta? He had many friends there. It made more sense to couch-surf in the metropolitan capital, with many friends, than in this overly polite city filled with horse-drawn carriages.

"I failed, Sin. Fate had other plans. Let me try my luck in Jakarta. Thanks for everything."

"Don't give up so fast, my friend. Wait a little bit. Who knows, maybe the silent anticipation will make the surprise even better?"

"Don't make me even more unsure about this. I'm already stressed out enough as it is."

"What's the problem, my friend?"

"I have just enough money to get back to Jakarta, and I'll still have to beg at the National Monument."

"If that's the only problem, then let's try this first: you stay calm and eat at my house. Okay?"

"Until when?"

"Until the yellow light goes on."

What was there to be afraid of? It wasn't right to refuse the kindness of a friend. Sidan tried to hold out for six days, and then a week. Then two weeks cleaned out his pockets. Still no Firdaus. There was no sign of her at all, just a deepening silence. Sidan had already surrendered to the situation, ready to wander around homeless in the city. Then he texted Adib Bahalwan explaining his situation, and the immediate response made his heart pound once again.

Adib: Hahaha, Sidan! I've always said we're friends! Don't tell me you've already forgotten the days when we would stay up all night, preparing for huge demonstrations in front of the mayor's office. We'll always be friends. How much do you need? If it's just enough to go home, I can transfer that amount right away. And then it'll be taken care of, right?

Sidan: I don't have even one cent in my pocket, and
       I need to go home, Dib!

Adib: Text me your bank account number as soon as
      you can. I'll be waiting.

It was crazy—Adib transferred Sidan five million rupiah, just for his journey home.

Sidan: Why so much? I just need the bare minimum.
       It will take me years to pay you back this
       much.

Adib: Hahaha, Dan . . . Sidan! You are always
      so naive. This isn't a loan but a gift to
      you from a friend. Let's not talk about it
      any more, just use it and enjoy your time
      with her.

Sidan: Wow, Dib! You are too kind! Yeah, okay then,
       if you are sure then, thank you. Thank you
       very much! Until we meet again in Banda,
       take care.

After sending the final message Sidan said to Husin, "That's how rich he is now. He has only been scraping around in Aceh for a little while and he's already so well off. This world is insane!"

"And you thanked him?"

"What do you mean? Of course I did."

"That's really your money, isn't it? Your survival rations that they stole. Why would you thank them? It's *them* who should be thanking *you*, kissing your feet!"

"Hey, I'm just thankful that he wants to give me back my ration."

"Just a portion of it. There are still billions missing."

"Well, maybe later that'll be the concern of the Archangel Michael, or Munkar and Nakir, the Denied and Denier, when they test the faith of all souls in their graves because the earthly law collapses in a bankrupt state."

With all of the strangeness of fate, Sidan finally flew back to Aceh. Adib picked him up at the airport, which was close to his office.

"So it's all taken care of, right? When will you two be married?" Adib asked.

Sidan stayed silent and seemed to wilt. Adib grew even more curious.

"Well, if it's not taken care of yet, that's alright. Just relax, my friend. The world is still turning. The apocalypse is still a long way off. Just keep calm, everything will happen in good time."

"Time just mocks me, Dib."

"Why? What's the word?"

"The words aren't clear, but they make up black verses whose meaning will be revealed in time. I'm exhausted, I'm sorry."

Adib's curiosity was heightened even further. He could tell from his friend's spent and defeated eyes that clearly something was wrong beyond Sidan just being short on work and needing money. But Adib didn't say anything. He took Sidan back to the tent encampment, which had grown so large that it now took practically a century to cross. Sidan had returned to the silence that was mighty and incomprehensible but sometimes also a familiar friend. Because aren't we all born from silence? We are born from silence to move through silence toward the eternal silence. Silence was great. Silence wore the crown of stillness like glittering gold.

Sidan sat in contemplation in front of his white tent, holding a guitar that a Frenchman had given him. He looked up at the clusters of clouds moving high above. The wind breathed a symphony while the ocean waves stirred his worry.

Oh reigning silence
There is no meeting place
You hide behind the clouds
Your scarf is fragrant in my embrace
This is the tragedy of Sidan and Firdaus . . .

He kept on humming and singing his heart out. He forgot his duties and his exhaustion. He forgot how he had been away from work for two weeks without sending word of his whereabouts, so his news had become news for the reporters who jumped on every development in the life of dying souls. Hour by hour, second by second, time piled up as he sang song after song. After he would finish one song, he would try to contact Firdaus, but her phone kept saying "pending." He tried again and again. He really could not believe such a distance could be created by nothing but faulty cell phone signals. Ah! How powerful signals were.

The reception has killed me with lonely quiet. Majnun is truly alone in the vault of the sky. Without Layla, the world is just a great confusion.

Sidan was being driven insane. He floundered in a gnawing emptiness, slammed by longing. He had never been this lonely, never felt so desolate and meaningless.

You steal all my peace
Lock me in a cage of enchantment
And you torment my spirit with longing
A decade of longing
That never ends . . .

He clutched his phone and punched in Firdaus's number and as it rang he shouted angrily, "Come on, pick up, Firdaus! Pick up!"

He looked down at the screen. He opened Firdaus's texts and reread the words that by this point he had memorized, because he read them over and over, every time he had spare time. It was his favorite activity—if this life could be arranged according to his wishes, he would choose to text Firdaus for as long as he lived. The minutes spent texting were radiant for him, as if for a moment the world was in the grasp of his ten fingers. He could fly for miles, leaving the mocking reality of life down below.

The world of words would always be vast. It brought tenderness in times of absence. Nights full of flame, warmth, and passion.

Being cast out of your embrace for two weeks feels more like two decades.

Then the telephone rang.

"*Salamu'alaikum*, Dan. You're doing well, right? What are your plans for tonight?"

"Ah! Dib," Sidan said, reluctant to be disturbed. "I'm trying to be fine and okay. Even though they keep on attacking me, I'm still a man."

"Who said you were a woman?" Adib said. "Can I come to the barracks?"

"You don't need to come right now, Dib. You're still here for a while, right? Let me rest a little first. I need plenty of rest."

"Yeah, okay, when you have some free time contact me. Enjoy your rest. You don't have to have so much on your mind. Just relax. *Salam.*"

But actually Adib wanted to see Sidan when he was powerless and laid low. He sped along the road toward the white tent at the foot of Blang Ske Mountain. He hadn't been able to contact Firdaus either, so he was alert and intrigued. He found hollow eyes staring out from a body collapsed in a heap. Sidan looked neither angry nor pleased at Adib's arrival. He just needed to be understood. The backpack he had been using during his two weeks away was still lying there, unpacked, untouched.

"Dib, I already told you I wasn't ready to greet you. Or do you want to take a nap in my palace? Be my guest."

"I'm sorry, Dan. Your tone of voice made me nervous. I can see that you are not doing well—you don't look any better than you did before. Wouldn't you like to take a bath so that you feel a little fresher?"

"Who has the time to take a bath? I already washed my face and did my ablutions."

What did Sidan mean suggesting he didn't have enough time? Adib was even more curious. What was Sidan really doing, to the point that time was so precious that he couldn't even bathe or brush his teeth? What was keeping him so busy—work or his daydreams?

"So you're too busy, it seems?"

"I'm really busy. You know me, right? I've always been a busy man. I'm even working in my sleep, Dib. Don't tell me you've forgotten?"

"You're still working in your sleep? At least you still have the energy for jokes."

"Jokes? What are those? I don't have time. I'm very serious in my life. Because I want to be like the famous poet Chairil Anwar—*'sekali berarti, sudah itu mati,'* remember? I want to do something useful before I die."

Then Adib felt satisfied, coming to his own conclusions. Sidan was in a bad way. He was in a raving delirium. His eyes were drifting, reflecting what was in his heart, but meanwhile he couldn't clearly see the person right in front of his face. Adib resigned himself to share Sidan's fate for the evening. He lay down next to his friend. Sidan awoke and sat up again, pouring out the suffering and worry that was still raging inside him.

"I've lost, Dib. Suddenly I feel like I've failed."

"Oh dear, friend, you're not making any sense."

Sidan starting singing in a loud voice. He thought that Firdaus's feelings were hurt and that she was trying to shut him out by turning off her phone—something that had never happened before, except by accident. His gamble of going to Yogya had been nothing but a meaningless show of love. A gust of wind passed. But no, that trip had in fact meant everything! Firdaus had asked him to come and he had fulfilled her request.

"Maybe her phone is broken or she isn't getting any reception, like what happened to you when she came here."

"She's gone home to her village before and her reception has never given out. And if there *was* some sort of problem with her phone, then I'm sure she would call me immediately from a pay phone."

Adib decided that Firdaus must indeed be in some sort of trouble, but he invited Sidan to forget his crisis for a moment by going out and eating in a nice biryani restaurant. He was still quite curious about Sidan's ability to keep Firdaus all this time, and he felt he himself deserved a little credit for it, because he had been the one to open Firdaus's eyes to that cold figure who was blind to the world—despite the fact he himself fancied her.

"There's plenty of time, Dan. She will return to you. You're sure of that, right?"

"But for how long? I've read the defeat in her eyes. Or maybe I'm the one who has given up? She has threatened to break up with me so many times, even though she's done it in a gentle way."

"And your reaction?"

"We've made a commitment to be faithful to one another. You know how I feel, Dib. She's the only thing that I have left in my life. I've got nothing else. But this is my situation. Fate is not yet on my side."

For a moment Adib was compassionate and felt guilty for having wanted to steal Firdaus from Sidan. He himself still had a lot, everything that a person could wish for in this life: a family that loved him, money and peace, work and the opportunity to travel for pleasure, to enjoy the beauty of the world. Maybe the only thing he didn't have yet was a sweetheart. Adib was a tenacious worker who believed that time was money. And if he sent Sidan five million, that was one way to buy him out, like a capitalist buys out his competitor in order to destroy him.

But Sidan thought differently. He looked at Adib with pure intentions, like nothing more than a loyal friend. Sidan, who was so gullible to the world's deceit, was comfortable in his own skin even with all the enemies that surrounded him—in fact, he felt that he didn't have any enemies. He guarded the meaning of friendship and he received kindness easily. He felt that all you needed was to be thankful for the good fortune that came from God; you didn't need to deify the middleman too much. Because the only real god was Allah.

Adib felt he had planted something good and useful in Sidan, something that would certainly grow and develop, and he believed the profit should only go to him, not to be shared with others. The cold white tent was now filled with two warring breaths, and could barely contain their trembling vibration, almost exploding, full of fire and flame.

"She's at the age where she's ready to marry, surrounded by many beetles chirping in her ear. I have seen her getting close with Jayeng."

"Jayeng? What was she doing with that ugly longhair?"

"Nothing. He's just deeply in love."

"You mean he's in love with Firdaus?"

"Ask all the eyes that have looked into your sweetheart's round eyes. Are there any who aren't in love with her? But only a select few can become heroes, strong enough to return her fierce gaze."

"Jayeng is not a hero. And if he was, he would maybe only be a hero to others. To Firda, there is only one hero. Remember that."

"You're quite sure of yourself. Good! That means you haven't surrendered yet."

"In a season like this, love is like faith to me. It undulates, rising and falling, but it never surrenders."

Damn, thought Adib. *He is still philosophizing about love. Look, Sidan, I will knock you down some other way. You have faith but nothing else, and your faith will crash on the rocks. You don't have a pair of strong wings that can carry you all the way to the foundation of a new life. Your wings are broken, only one still works, and it too will grow shaky with the onslaught of time.*

"So why don't you marry her? At a time like this, many couples find that marriage is a blessing."

"Yes. Marriage gives new life to those who are weak. But we are still strong enough to think things over and weigh our options a little bit more."

"Too much consideration will only make things more complicated, Dan. Just be flexible. Do what's practical and real."

"The problem is, this isn't a matter of getting something simple, like buying a bicycle or hailing a pedicab, Dib. We are preparing a round-trip rocket ship heading for another planet. It's not as simple as it seems."

What, like Sputnik? Sidan really has gone crazy! He's basically homeless but talks of rocket ships. Instead of collapsing, he's rising even higher, towering unexpectedly. Really, from where does he draw that extra breath so that he can thunder like this, full of magma and ready to unleash a mighty explosion in the atmosphere? Neither of us has experience plucking the flower of love, but his passion is still greater than mine. How is that possible?

"Agreed."

"Cool, right? Let me stay poor, so that I'll stay cool." Sidan laughed.

Adib was dumbfounded. Sidan was coming in and out of a muddled consciousness. He was laughing uproariously at a fate that he wanted to reject. Or was that laughter itself the most perfect language of rejection? If it wasn't, then why was he laughing like that? He must be in the middle of some kind of performance. Speaking his own private language.

And those eyes . . . It was as if Sidan no longer saw the world he was living in, as if he had taken up residence on another planet. Who knew where he was wandering to, in the deepest recesses of his soul, that faraway and mysterious place?

Maybe he's meeting Firdaus and forcing her to say that she is still willing to be patient and is still holding on to their commitment. Maybe he's talking to her about the meaning of being faithful or mapping out a village of love, the place where they will live. Maybe he's imagining their days full of swan songs, his days spent chatting happily with his pure angel.

Every time a smile passed across Sidan's lips, Adib's heart beat faster with jealousy, and every time his eyes narrowed and his forehead wrinkled, Adib exulted, quickly switching his perspective to enjoy the feeling of victory. Then Sidan began to scratch at his dandruff. He wondered where it came from—maybe his own mocking and frustrated heart.

Sidan sighed and then mumbled, "No, maybe only now I have just lost. But a person doesn't die when he is defeated, he dies when he stops trying, isn't that right, Firda?"

"What? What are you saying, Dan?"

Sidan was somewhere far away in the clouds and just glanced at Adib for a moment, lost in his own world. Adib could not believe that Sidan could be so oblivious to his surroundings.

It was the middle of the night. It was freezing. The pounding of the waves grew wilder. It felt like the entire world was nothing but a specter of unending darkness, jet black and hissing like a giant cobra. Then silence came creeping slowly and surely, ambushing and swallowing everything.

On a night like this you are strangled by time, trapped in an airless tunnel of the past. You twitch, powerless to consider your options or try to seek safety, because it annihilates everything. You collapse as if beaten, stranded thousands of miles away from consciousness.

Oh, Firda! I guarded our nights of shining blue flame. I perfected them with love poetry. I planted them full of blooms of religious devotion. And now where does the wind blow to, leaving behind an eternal silence like this?

Sidan stared thoughtfully at the ground. Wet, bare, anguished earth. They had gone out looking for a river and returned with a new river in their hearts as the frozen night was melted by fate.

"The cold is so strange tonight," Adib said.

"Not just tonight. All the weather here is supernatural," Sidan said.

"How can we get warm?"

"You don't have to worry about that!"

Sidan went into the tent, trying to exercise his frail memory, searching for the hot drink mix. It wasn't on the small table. It wasn't in his
backpack. Then he remembered his backpack and what was inside.
Then he forgot Adib and his hot drink as he grew distracted, fiddling
with his digital camera and the film that he had just finished. Aha! He
would screen the film in the new village of Lam Senia next Saturday
night. It would certainly entertain the villagers. Many of his young
filmmaker friends in Jakarta liked documentary film.

"It turns out they like my film, Dib!"

"What film? I thought you were going to get me a warm drink."

"Let's put this on and you can see my work."

As soon as they turned it on they were startled by a loud clap
of thunder. Then lightning flashed—all the electricity went out. They
could add tonight onto the never-ending chain of dark black nights.
The rain pounded chaotically, tossed about by the howling wind. The
two men huddled in a frigid jail cell of night. Without light, without a
fire. The darkness of the jungle was complete, like a blind man in a cave
of ghosts. Monsters danced naked, with red flame eyes and a thousand
smoldering snorts of revenge, their fingers dangling.

"I can't breathe!" Adib yelled.

"What, you're going to freak out just from this? We've gone for
months like this here. Even more than this, for years."

"In this land of natural gas reserves?"

"Yes. It's like the gas never really affected us, because all of it was
stolen by the regime and taken to Jakarta to pay off the national debt.
For a long time Aceh donated charity to the Republic, so why are the
people in our land poor? Oh! It appears they have been robbed by the
sons of the asshole kings!"

"Yes, you're right. To become a king in this country you have to be
a thief and a robber. Greedy, ruthless, cruel—and paranoid."

"Exactly! The trinity of Qarun, Pharaoh, and Baal! And that's how
his minions are too, his troops and cronies. From the center to the

margins. From the asshole kings to the goat-class rulers, all with just one field of expertise: stealing."

"They are 'wanted' in the afterlife."

"The strange thing is they are the most calm and comfortable, as if they were the king of *tuyul*, those spirits sent to do your mischief and steal other people's money for you. What judge can capture a *tuyul* if all the judges have already been made into *tuyul* themselves?"

"I think you and the entire young generation of Aceh should go into law. Then you all can become judges and put the *tuyul* back in their place. Force them to return the stolen treasure or, if not, punish them with strong justice, make an example of them."

"Why do we have to become judges? Every person has a sense of justice and goodness. It doesn't matter whether they are from Aceh, Papua, Maluku, Java, or Kalimantan, everyone can become a fair judge if they really want to."

"That's easier said than done."

"There is nothing easy in life. Everything has to be fought for. But that is alright, as long as we keep our ethics and guard our morals. As long as at some point someone takes responsibility! Above the judges there is a judge. Behind eyes there are spies. There are two angels with eagle eyes always watching Father Kun. That's all!"

Adib was startled to hear Sidan mention Kun—Kuntoro Mangkusubroto—or more precisely, mock him.

Sidan must have really wanted to say that there are also a pair of keen eagle eyes next to me because I work for Father Kun, and since I am getting paid by the rehabilitation and reconstruction of Aceh program that he heads, I sip from the river of money that flows down from the top of Kun Mountain. But hey, I'm a good guy—I even helped Sidan regain his balance when he had stumbled so that he could face his future with courage. It's appropriate that I would get paid. If I get a large honorarium, it's because I'm a manager who has done a lot of good for my men. I'm not wrong, am I?

What's more, I took care of your sweetheart's trip here, and I gave you millions of rupiah too. My status as a volunteer is intact. Ha! A volunteer who gets paid? I guess that is strange, isn't it? Real workers who drip sweat and blood are only paid with a bag of rice and sometimes even then that comes late and is soon gone, finished in one day. But people like me, we get paid thousands of times more. What kind of policy is this?

"What's important is that we have good intentions. Intentions, Dan. Intentions . . ."

"Good intentions aren't enough, brother. Even tangible and concrete things can be manipulated, let alone something as abstract as intentions. Ah . . . let's just go back to sleep."

"The blanket, Dan."

"Tomorrow I'll ask the WHO for one. Now, make do with what we've got. Soak in Aceh, just for tonight."

"But how will we sleep, shivering and our teeth chattering like this?"

"Every day we shiver at the height of fever, Adib! Our days are spent in a coma, and time doesn't pass here anymore. We want to speak but our teeth chatter so badly that our jaws can't form the words. We are on the verge of death with only seconds left to live. The poverty is deep and intense. The theft is so flagrant, so oppressive. Like in Lhokseumawe— next to the billion-dollar gas fields and the luxurious gated communities, there were huts, standing in a silent but telling contrast. And then the army burned down the huts.

"Or are you forcing me to give up my only warmth?"

"We can share it between the two of us."

What was this, one blanket for two people? They weren't Layla and Majnun. *If you were Layla, I would have already wrapped you up tight, without having to compete for warmth, because the purest definition of warmth is when Majnun and Layla are singing together in one rhythm under their blanket. To me, this definition is patented, it cannot be violated. So don't try to change the standardized formula.*

Adib's teeth chattered harder. The rain was pouring down from the trough of the sky in a rhythm that pounded in his chest. The longer it went on, the more regular it became. Only their location, in the plains high on the slope, saved them from a flood. They were lucky there were no landslides. But the universe was still pitch dark. Adib gave up, cursing. Sidan relented for the sake of friendship. He threw the blanket to Adib, who was pensive and frozen.

I'm already used to this. Maybe Adib needs it more than I do.

Like a pangolin curling its body up in a storm, Adib snuggled up under the warm blanket next to Sidan, who was now the one whose teeth were chattering. He went and got all his clothes, shirts, jackets, and sarongs, and he burrowed under them, falling headfirst into the darkness.

"What are you going to use to get warm?" asked Adib.

"I'm going to imagine her. Just relax. If you're still cold, you can sleep in your car or go back to your tent!"

"There's no way I would leave my friend to shiver alone here."

"Don't act like you're such a good friend. You stole my warmth tonight."

"I won't do it again, but I really can't take it this time."

"You will never be able to take any of this. No one can bear it, except us. Yes, only us."

"Don't be like that, Dan. Tomorrow we can buy two blankets."

Sidan laughed. Blankets?

Yogya has one chamber in my heart. Aceh's chamber was taken by my mother. So there are no more blankets here. Just shivering and starving vagrants. This cold is eternal. Cold is heat's enemy. We freeze like crystal in the prayers of a cold heart, no longer bothering with whatever you burn as you set the universe on fire. We have already turned to snow and ice.

"You don't need to add to a pointless list. This country is already crammed with profit-seekers. Just take my blanket and let's go to sleep."

"You can sleep without a blanket in weather like this?"

"The difference between sleep and wakefulness is mere semantics. It's really more a matter of feeling, just like rain and drought. Hot and cold. I can sleep when I'm awake and vice versa."

"You are so bizarre, Dan."

"Am I really the bizarre one? Ever since I was born, I have sensed all kinds of strangeness in my house. Their stares, their every move, the sound that comes out of their throats. Everything in this land is bizarre and absurd, and they seem even more absurd the longer these eyes wander through its absurd villages and cities. We live in an absurd cave, whose way in and out is nailed shut. This is us, this century is a cave of bears. It's bizarre, right?"

Adib, who had just started feeling warm and sleepy under the blanket stolen off the body of his lonely friend, suddenly jumped up—there was something urging him awake. It wasn't hard to find Sidan in the dark. He was just lying there facedown right next to him, delirious. But his delirium was so heartrending, coming out from a fragmented heart stuck in a far corner of time. A cold wind whistled high and strange in his subconscious.

"I think it's time for you to come out of that stuffy, absurd cave. What's wrong with moving to Yogya? You can begin anew there. You have so much talent that doesn't need to be stuck in an endless labyrinth for no good reason. What's more, there is an angel who is still waiting for you to add a new verse to her song."

"Oh Benevolent Allah. What happened to you, Firda?"

Adib gasped at the sound of Sidan's heart-wrenching lament. The surging moan momentarily drove out the hubris and greed that drove him to want to steal the lover of this agonized idol.

Look how easily Sidan gave his blanket to me. The only warmth he needs is the image of Firdaus. How disgusting I am. Bah! I should quickly repent before Sidan's moan shakes the heavens to bury me alive.

"Let me take care of Firdaus," Adib said. "I'll let you know when things are settled."

I mean, I'll let you know that you have truly failed to capture her. But if you are finally ready to move to Yogya, then I will let all my greedy intentions die.

"What are you going to do?"

"Something. Wait until the time is right. You will receive the most valuable offering from your friend here. Now let's sleep."

"You sleep. I'll guard the night so that the dawn doesn't escape."

"You don't want to sleep too?"

"I'm listening to Him. He asks, *Am I not your Lord and God?* And I reply, *Yes, You are our Lord, and we are Your witness.* I'm asking our Lord to tell me, is this disaster?"

For the third time, Adib was dumbfounded.

Oh, you, torn apart by suffering, you definitely can't sleep. Instead, your nights are filled with questions and intense dialogue between you and the Ultimate. And you grow even more intimate with Him, more completely enlightened. Face-to-face, all secrets revealed to you. Are You our Lord, and are we Your witness? If you are finally able to find the answer to that question, you will have a better death than I, maybe even dying many levels above me. How is it possible?

You know I am terribly jealous. No! You may not come face-to-face with God, nor even with anyone who might help you reach that higher level. We must be the same, equal. If need be, you lower than me. You are just a bare copper palm tree trunk hovering at the edge of the abyss, Sidan. While I am an olive tree, standing tall for a thousand years. I'm the strong one. Am I a symbol of peace between you and my Firdaus? No. Just an inconsistent equivocator, who changes with the weather and gusts of wind.

"Did you hear my answer?"

"Yes. They who are left behind are chosen, while those who go are the chosen of the chosen."

Dammit! You only think positively. Your enthusiasm is quite optimistic. I can't stop wondering how you can breathe such a bright fire of life. After everything has disappeared, you keep burning. But you are also arrogant, Sidan! Do you really think you are part of a chosen people?

"Have you heard how many corpses were found still intact after so much time had passed?"

"Why are you asking that? They are people who were 'witnessed.' The martyrs, the chosen ones. Not even termites could touch King Solomon."

"Meaning there are those who are martyrs and those who are not."

"Why do we need to discuss this? They are martyrs," Sidan insisted.

How do you know? Why are you so certain, with your most prestigious honorific degree? What would happen if it turned out that among them there were liars, thieves, provocateurs, drug dealers, witches, and small-time pharaohs? What would happen if it turned out there were two enemies who were both destroyed by the black wave and died together and then were buried together? Can two mortal enemies be martyrs, if in fact they are waiting for their duel to continue in the afterlife?

What do I care about dreams, which are just as absurd as the weather in this country. But maybe it's good to cherish a dream as beautiful as that. Martyrs.

"Fine, you win. Good night!"

With those words, they went through the door to the cave of black night. Sidan to the west, Adib maybe to the east or south. Clearly Sidan had a stick that was trained to lead him in the dark, as black as the face of death. He was accustomed to traveling through a jungle of what he thought of as Stone Order mammals—people who had lived under the New Order, a regime so repressive and primitive it had taken them back to the Stone Age. So he was comfortable and breathed deeply—like Yusuf in the well, who, with the gift of prophecy, knows a caravan from the kingdom of Ngayogyakarta Hadiningrat will pass by and take him as a foster child to meet the virgin Zulaikha, Potiphar's wife, Firdaus the daughter of Abdussalam al Hajj.

Meanwhile Adib, who stumbled along carrying the burden of bad weather, advanced and retreated between dreams and wakefulness the whole night long, entering and exiting the mouth of a crocodile and the enraged clutch of savage claws. He awoke with a curse, thinking he had fallen from the tenth floor of a hotel, with armed guards who laughed at him, pressing the butts of their cold rifles against his neck. His blood vessels almost snapped. He gasped for breath. His legs were paralyzed, his blood was frozen and couldn't flow. It turned out he had pulled the blanket up too high, hiding his frightened and suffering face.

Dawn came, bringing the realization that a tornado had ripped up tents and knocked over whatever had been standing tall, flattening everything. Adib shouted in panic along with the villagers who were running back and forth, topsy-turvy. But underneath it all, an even deeper silence flowed. There was a gathering point that remained unmoved—it had been slammed by the tornado but was still firmly rooted: the mosque. It was only a few steps from Sidan's tent. Even though his body was weak with fatigue and cold, Sidan still had enough strength to calm the people. They gathered in the mosque and prayed, seeking strength in togetherness.

Nature had a black face. The electricity had not yet come back on. Azrael's breath had whispered in their ears. Then they moaned supplications, tears falling as if from a grieving sky.

Sidan looked up and whispered to the universe, "Allah, don't abandon me."

Sunrise unfurled itself like a drunken snail. Faces withered by thunder began cleaning up again, because life had not stopped and would not stop. The new village that had just started to grow was forced back to a crawl, overcoming bitterness after bitterness. But they could not give up and they were ready to work—they would tackle any task, as long as they weren't sitting quietly with their hands in their laps. Catching fish, opening a shop, teaching, doing construction for government rehabilitation and reconstruction projects, or working for a foreign humanitarian organization.

Sidan looked for his digital camera, the only treasure that could bear witness to the fact that he had ever lived enthusiastically in this world. He found it, but it was wrecked. He dug through jumbled piles, souvenirs of the tornado, looking for a copy of his film *Suak Timah*, the film that he was so proud of. He found one but it was covered with mud. And his wallet, holding all that was left of his life and all that he would need to secure his future—the photo of Firdaus, his passport, and his identity card—where on earth could it be? He still had it with him. It was safe, stored in the pocket of the jeans he was wearing. He breathed a sigh of relief. Thanks be to God. All was not lost yet.

"Sorry, Dan, I might go crazy if I stay here too long. Come on, get all of your things and let's go."

"Where are we going to run to? Is there any hiding place that can shield us from this beautiful insanity? You go alone and let me stay here and appreciate it."

"Why are you so stubborn? Isn't someone still waiting for you?"

"That's none of your business."

"If you stay here too long, you will soon be finished."

"Screw you! You're not God. Fortune tellers aren't wanted here."

"So what next?"

"It's true that it's dark here. But in the dark we can see the light swirling around our hearts."

"You don't need to philosophize. Think about your future."

For a moment Sidan looked at the face of his old friend. Of course *he* was thinking of the future, shining with success and happiness. Who could be comfortable when their heads were being dashed against the rocks again and again?

But I am the son of this land. It is my home that is being torn apart, and that is not a good enough reason to leave it behind—in fact it's the opposite. I can't bear to be far from it. After being repeatedly slammed, this is me, tough and weather resistant. Life is just a ceremony of greeting.

"I am thinking about it. And that is why I am staying. Now go, and thank you for your kind visit."

Adib couldn't take any of it. The shattered village, Sidan's eyes shining, as if he had just uncovered a secret hidden treasure. He returned to Banda with a thousand questions. His body was tight and sore and his thoughts piled up on top of one another. He stepped into a food stall called Haji Karim, which could be considered somewhat elite, with its special menu of Indian biryani rice served on Fridays. It was crowded with patrons this morning and Adib looked at the Arabic faces, so much like his own, enjoying their meal.

He ate and thought of Sidan. Then there was a soft trill. A text message. Maybe Sidan? Firdaus?

Firdaus: Hello, Dib! How are things in Aceh? Don't tell me your friend is leaving his phone off for a whole century? Tell him to get up if he's still asleep! I hope you and your fellow workers are all healthy.

Adib tried to contact Sidan. It didn't go through. He tried again and nothing. This was the chance he had been waiting for. While filling his stomach he thought, *What would be the harm in saying that Sidan had completely failed? With no hope of leaving Aceh, growing ever more downtrodden, he still needed a companion to share his fate. And so he chose a woman from his village, Firda. One who lived close to his barracks. So forget him, and begin again with someone new. Your future is brighter without him.*

He needed a place with a comfortable and calm atmosphere to call Firdaus. Adib hurried away from the food stall and went north. Maybe it would be quieter next to the mosque. He tried to contact Sidan one more time to make sure that his friend was still not reachable. Safe! Praying, his heart pounding, and trying to adjust the volume of his voice to the most pleasant tone, he called Firdaus.

"Hello, Firda . . . *salamu'alaikum* . . ."

"Hi, Dib! *Alaikum salam.* How are you?"

"How am I or how is he?"

"Both. You both are well, safe and sound, right? Please wake him up if he's still sleeping. I want to talk to him, Dib."

"So impatient? And who is he? I'm here alone. It's just me and an angel. Where have you been, Firda? Don't you know that he went to Yogya and didn't see you? He was cranky and swearing."

"Swearing?"

Firdaus's voice sounded quite worried.

"Yes, swearing that he would get married this month or he would never marry."

"You promise, Dib? Do you know what date it is? You're being ridiculous."

"I promise! But I forget the date that he mentioned. Only his swears reached my ears. You're ready, aren't you?"

"Ready how? There's only three days left, brother! If he wants to get married, he'll have to marry the moon above his grave. Wake him up quick, Dib! Let me talk to him!"

"I don't know where he is, Firda. His phone is constantly turned off. Maybe he's preparing for his wedding celebration. A little while ago I was told to order a special shirt for the prince. Do you want to be carried off wearing traditional Javanese or Acehnese clothes?"

"My tradition is Muslim, don't you know?"

"Now I do. If that's how it is, then . . . hopefully there isn't a bride."

"What do you mean, bride?"

"Um . . . yeah, a bride."

"Hey, asshole! Speak clearly!"

"Firm and spicy? Are you ready?"

"Even if it's as bitter as tinospora leaf, I'm ready. Spit it out."

Adib hesitated at Firdaus challenging him. Sometimes she was like a lioness that was seeing red, about to attack her prey.

It would be unimaginable if she found out I was lying. She would tear my heart to bits. But do I have to retreat now? After the way looked clear? No! This opportunity won't come a second time.

"Yeah, hopefully there isn't some other bride who will be by his side."

"What do you mean? He's preparing to marry some other woman?"

"You have to realize, Firda, Aceh is increasingly in disarray. Don't dream of heaven here. And I know there is no way Sidan could bear to see you upset."

"There's no way. He can still be straight with me. Come on, connect me to him, Dib. Look for him in the barracks. Please!"

"It's pointless. Wait a little bit and you'll see the news on television. Prepare yourself, and don't be shocked."

"What do you mean?"

"Sidan is no longer in any barracks. He's been taken."

"Don't give me a heart attack—who took him? Where?"

"I'm sorry. To paradise, the bride and groom. I'm sorry . . . *salamu'alaikum.*"

"Wait! Are you playing with me? Who was with him?"

"A magnificent entourage. I saw the look in his eyes, like a glowing prince."

Firdaus couldn't breathe. She was gasping, powerless, lifeless.

She screamed in her suffering! Between sure and not. Anything could happen in this absurd time. But Sidan? She hung up the phone.

He is an honest and faithful man; how could he betray me? No matter how bitter or difficult, we promised to be faithful to one another. What happened to you, darling?

She steeled herself not to believe. Meanwhile she knew that marriages did often happen in the barracks as one way to survive prolonged suffering.

*Are you like the weak, Sidan? Not strong enough to face the onslaught
of silence? But why with another? You still have eternity with me. No! Adib
must be lying. But hasn't he been a faithful supporter of our relationship?*
Firdaus remembered how he had paid for her journey to Aceh.

Firdaus: I believe you and I don't. But help, Dib!
         I want to contact him, no matter where
         he is, and whatever condition he is in.
         Please! Find him for me!

All Adib had to do now was simply convince her of the lie. He was
just worried that Firdaus might contact another friend, especially one in
Aceh who might go see Sidan. So he contacted Sidan himself and made
sure—yes, he was still unreachable. Maybe his cell phone was broken
or had been washed away in the tornado. Now was Adib's moment.

Adib: I'm going to try, Firda. But don't get your
      hopes up. It may not be a big deal, but I
      think he changed his number. Maybe he wants
      to enjoy his days in private. I'm sorry, but
      I will try. Be steadfast! Salam!

Steadfast? Firdaus was knocked over by the word, limp and weak.
She couldn't stop thinking about this crazy change. Her chest was boiling lava, ready to erupt, but there was no way for it to get out. All the
doors were closed. All the cracks were clogged. There was no stream to
accommodate the flow of a broken heart. She looked up at a thousand
lights that seemed to mock her. It's still morning, miss, they said. But
to Firdaus, night was falling.

*Oh Allah the Merciful! Don't throw my soul into a dark dungeon
without light. Extend Your affection and embrace this heart with the caress
of Your love, oh Lord! You know my eyes are blind to all others. These ears*

225

*only want to hear his chirping poetry of longing. He is not strong enough to
pass twelve hours without news from me. And I am not able to rise above
this grief, Lord. Don't let these two burning flames be extinguished by the
weather.*

She thought of her father, her mother, and their hopes. She also
remembered Jayeng, who also had pursued her. But her memories of
Sidan returned even clearer, like a mirror. She saw this blind man, who
only awoke for news of war and the battlefield, with his young spirit,
full of burning embers in his chest. A cheerful traveler, a mountain
climber whose ropes never tangled. A long-haired ascetic romantic.
Firdaus's soul trembled, swimming in an ocean of memory. To her,
Sidan was the epitome of an inner and outer beauty that pulled her
into its undertow.

So even in the afterlife, she would never be willing to give him up.

That afternoon Adib went back to check on Sidan in Lam Senia,
making sure that his friend was really in a trance and would not get
up again to welcome Firdaus. It was true. His phone wasn't working.
Sidan proclaimed the sky had fallen and its rubble had struck the dark
corners of his heart. He was getting ready to go on a trip to Suak Timah,
following the earthquake damage along the western coast, from Banda
to Lamno to Calang until Meulaboh. He said he wanted to know the
condition and the stories along the road. He would set his own wounds
aside.

"So you still don't want to move back to Yogya?"

"Yogya is still a village that is far in the distance. Not yet. Someday."

Someday? To Adib, someday was still far away. Good! He didn't
need to hurry—he would settle the matter of Firdaus in good time.

*Be calm, Firda! You will be taken care of before Sidan's sun shines
again.*

While helping his friend prepare for his journey, he secretly contacted her.

Adib: I've been looking for him all day and I've failed, Firda. His tent is silent, his office is abandoned. His friends and acquaintances don't seem to care that much because here people leave and they never come back, it happens all the time. They go to the land of twilight.

Firdaus: Thank you, Dib! I wasn't able to contact any of his Acehnese acquaintances either. It's like he's vanished off the face of the earth. It's enough for now, let me put this matter aside for the moment. Let me know whenever you come across him. Salam.

Everything is safe and under control, he thought, relieved.

"Are you ready to go with such a gloomy face? That's dangerous, brother," he said, looking over at Sidan.

"The journey always makes me happy because it's a process. That's not why I'm gloomy."

"So?"

"I'm thinking. It seems as though the Agency for the Rehabilitation and Reconstruction of Aceh is confused about how to use up two trillion rupiah per month, to the point that they throw parties where they invite performers from Jakarta, despite the fact that it costs billions. The profit earned by the sweat of martyrs disappears into the pockets of outsiders in the course of one night. Meanwhile in the distant villages, our babies aren't getting enough nutrition and the earth is dry. The people's hearts are as quiet as if they were in a cave."

"Maybe they are thinking that amidst all the waiting, the people need some refreshment. That's not wrong, is it? And the performers are selected specifically to be a good fit with the local culture. Of course the babies need to get their nutrition, but it's almost like there are too many problems, and it is too overwhelming to try to fix them all. But if that's how you feel, you should help admonish them. Don't just keep traveling around all over the place. You'll get sick, man."

"A real man must marry nature, mountains, and water. You should join us sometime, going to Meulaboh via the coastal road and then coming home through the mountains. It's great, Dib."

"Which is better, the coastal road or the mountain road?"

"I like them both. When you go along the coast you can enjoy the softness of the air and get splashed with little ripples of enthusiasm. When you go hiking in the mountains, you are filled with an energy that makes your sweat gleam."

"After the enthusiasm makes your sweat gleam . . . then what?"

"Then you reach the summit, feeling a mix of exhaustion and happiness. Nature indeed sucks you in."

"And hikers indeed like to be sucked," Adib said with a wicked grin.

"You and your dirty mind."

Adib got up to leave his friend, whose eyes had started to brighten. He couldn't stand to spend another whole night in the barracks. All the daily schedules and the work agendas for his staff were already neatly conceptualized. There was nothing more he needed to think about or review—all he had left to do was instruct and oversee. What he needed now was to have some fun, to cope with the boredom. But here the earth still just had a sorrowful face. In the daytime he could go to Lhoknga Beach or eat with the soldiers, some of whom had been members of the student regiment on campus back when he was in college, like Syamsul.

"I like it here, Syam," said Adib.

"It's a sacrifice, brother!"

"How much longer do you have left?"

"Just one month."

"What's your most memorable moment out of these five months?"

"I almost was a goner when they opened fire on us during an invasion of our guard post in Tiro."

"What happened?"

"It happened at night, after *isha* prayers, a week after I arrived. They attacked us from three sides. The battle lasted from nine until eleven-thirty. The attackers were using a grenade launcher and they hurled twenty grenades at the post. But only three exploded."

"Did they explode near you?"

"Yes, one of them was right at my feet! One of them exploded near the gate, another one in the school building."

"And then?"

"We calculated. We weren't afraid, but we couldn't just play at exchanging gunfire, *pow, boom, bang*! And I didn't have my Kenwood walkie-talkie. I usually talked to them through the radio. I would insult them to make them talk."

"Who was their leader at that time?"

"That attack was led by one of their well-known figures who goes by the name of Ahmad Provost."

"How did you feel when you counterattacked?"

Syamsul suddenly fell silent. He drew in a deep breath and clutched at his chest. Looking around, he replied, "In my opinion, this war shouldn't have happened. We are brothers. Look at the color of our skin."

"But it *has* happened."

"That's the thing! There's no smoke without fire, brother. Did we just randomly come to Aceh for no good reason and then cause the disaster ourselves? No."

"Any other experiences?"

Syamsul wrinkled his forehead, then laughed to himself.

"Well, don't say anything, but it turns out the Acehnese people are bullshitters."

"Oh really? Come on, tell me," Adib said, perking up, hoping that this story could help dull Sidan's luster in Firdaus's eyes.

"We had finished eating dinner in one village. This man came holding out a cigarette. It was special, he said. I took it and smoked it. After just one drag, suddenly I collapsed and couldn't get up until the next morning."

"Was it ganja?"

"It was a rolled-up leaf sprinkled with sugar, and oh, how it tasted! I've been to the Philippines, Cambodia, Thailand. Nothing was as delicious as that. Then, early in the morning, I mumbled, 'I'm supposed to report for duty this morning, but I can't get up . . . Help me!' That man laughed long and hard. He left and came back with a jugful of water. He held out the jug for me. I drank and was immediately sober. It was so weird."

"It was just a jug of water?"

"It was boiled cannabis root, an antidote to intoxication. I said, that's forbidden. He left, laughing and singing, 'It's just water in a jug, just water in a jug.'"

"He tricked you."

"He tricked himself, because then I knew that they were making alcohol from cannabis sap and storing it in jugs. They also poured liquor from bottles into those jugs and then would sing, 'It's just water in a jug, just water in a jug.'"

"So where did the leaf roll come from?"

"They pluck a stalk in the foothills and then plant it next to their houses. Every morning the women chop it up and mix it in with their food. They've been doing it for a long time."

Adib was growing bored and antsy because he was still thinking about Firdaus and his schemes to capture her. He said good-bye and moved off to the side to contact Yogya. When Firdaus saw Adib's name appear on her phone, she didn't feel like talking. She just let its shrill ring pierce the night, so that Adib would think she had already fallen asleep—or, hopefully, realize that she was sick of the world. Firdaus wanted to be completely alone.

She was soul-searching, whispering to her Lord, "It is You who moved this spirit toward Your light, oh Brilliant One. With Your love, this heart knew love. A heart that once was dull and dead grew blazing with its flame, even though this was mixed with misery. I know, Lord, You don't want to test my power, which is weak. What is the world for after Adam has gone? Eve must certainly try to encompass all hope. But I am not Iqlima who is ready to hold hands with Cain, the killer of her Abel."

I am Eve, who waits for Adam on the Arafat plain!

Now a text appeared:

Adib: Are you alright, Firda? Can you pick up the phone for a second?

Adib wasn't giving up. He had to speak to her tonight. Because the time for his secret plan to work was running out.

Once Sidan gets home from Suak Timah, there is no way he will stay silent. He will certainly decide to buy a new cell phone, and then all my dreams could crumble.

He quickly sent the text again and her phone rang out like a crazy person raving in the pitch-black night. That was unusual, and Firdaus felt something wasn't right. Maybe Adib had found Sidan? What other important news could he have at this hour? But if she picked up all of a sudden, what was the most appropriate excuse for why she hadn't picked up before?

"Dib, I'm so sorry, I was just praying . . . but it seems like it's important. Did you find him?"

"Thank heavens you're alright, Firda. Sorry for disturbing your prayers. But this *is* important. Someone told me they met Sidan in Lamno, and he was with his blue-eyed fiancée—she must have Portuguese blood. But he didn't give me the address. I'll try to get better information tomorrow."

Firdaus was unable to speak after hearing the word "fiancée." Her heart pounded violently. So all of it was true? She still was determined not to believe it, but Adib was her only source of news. She wondered how Sidan could have made such a crazy decision so fast. Or maybe he had truly lost his mind after being attacked left and right by the never-ending trials of life? Sidan was the face of Aceh, which was swollen, sad, black and blue. Maybe he had lost his strength and had decided to submerge himself in a foreign well in order to satisfy his thirst?

But as far as Firdaus knew, Sidan was not the type of man to take a shortcut. He was a pure wanderer who loved the process. Who knows, maybe a flash of lightning had turned him into a rabbit. Firdaus could not understand. She tried to calm her heart with prayers that overflowed in moans, rolling through the dead of night until she fell asleep. Sidan appeared to her above a coffin, his face full of scars and blood. His teeth chipped, his skin blistered, half his body scorched. There was no smile on that ghost's face. Firdaus was transfixed, forced into this upside-down world.

Awakened in fright, she wiped away the sweat dripping from her temples. *Subhanallah!* Thankfully it was only a dream. But she kept on falling asleep only to be startled back awake until morning. For five days she couldn't go anywhere. Her body was sick with fever and her soul was flying. Time after time she ignored Adib's calls. Her hands were paralyzed and her mouth was a mute knot.

She purposefully wanted to suffer alone. Let this body and soul move through the transition. She could let herself cry in the first week, but not in the following season. Full moon after full moon passed, bringing a lasting peace of mind. Because Firdaus only believed in what she already understood. She rejected all other possibilities, just like she rejected the suitors who lined up on her front porch in vain. Now her daily calendar rotated around Sidan's shadow, alone in the gloom.

Sidan, who was enfolded in clouds!

Chapter 9:
Port of Departure

The passing seconds roar louder and louder, like an airplane that has just taken off. A new world in the sky. Firdaus soars in a busy daily vortex of lectures and conferences. She is a woman who has taken it to heart that fifteen thousand women per year become targets of violence in a country where men have failed to be true leaders. She speaks loudly, exposing the latent sickness in the body of the family, which is the basis of any nation's culture. Various institutions, campuses, and organizations invite her to speak. Now she is like a bird that chirps and whistles all day long with a silent inner melody.

But the world's charm has evaporated. Firdaus flies, swimming across a sky that is not completely new, with the enthusiasm of a hunter prowling the horizon of longing. Sidan has become a shadow in the opaque mirror of her memory. She doesn't care. This doe bounds through the days, gilding her wound so that it becomes an everlasting treasure. Forget Sidan. Forget all defeat and look at the world through new glasses that are blue.

I'm still young. Even though defeat is in my left hand, victory is in my right. Let life be in balance.

But Sidan is a full moon that fills her gaze wherever she turns, making her blink, blinding her to the flicker of faraway stars. Her heart is snowed in. Firdaus remains unmoved by Adib's advances, along with those from all the rest of them, the mustaches who waste their time trying to capture her heart.

"Let my time be only for those who have been pushed aside by the sweeping arm of history."

She keeps speaking and responds to worldly questions. To address those questions that cannot yet be answered, she raids the library with a burning heart. Because the world is a place where questions and answers can become friends with each other. If a problem isolates itself behind an iron fence, it won't live very long. Firdaus is now absorbed in a question-and-answer dance about the angels, women, who make up the majority of the universe.

"All women are angels. But scaling the heavens takes incredible energy. Many are lost, but there are also many who are saved."

So she reads, writes, and speaks. She reads leaves, flowers, twigs. Mountains become books. The ocean and the sand become encyclopedias. The streets and plazas are lush forests of wisdom. Firdaus is wistful on prayerful nights. Tears and flame both fight for a place in her soul. In silence she thunders. On dark nights with a thousand full moons she reads the signs, interprets a vocabulary of secrets.

"The angel who is gentle and pretty becomes an object of dispute, fought over by middlemen and pimps. Middlemen in *kopiah* skullcaps and pimps wearing ties. They are both the same, profiting off the sweat of the crippled."

Reading the book of the world sucks up her daily energy. Firdaus is sweating with love for her neighbor, making sense of life with her love, which has a million different flavors. Days turn into weeks. Weeks turn into months. Months turn into years.

Four years have passed.

This week she has to go to Aceh, not for Sidan but for them, the *inong balee*, the women warriors who are victims of the suits who carry loaded guns. She doesn't have to worry about the cost, her trip has been paid for by the organization in Banda that has invited her. There is a strange, brief shiver when she reads the word: "Banda." It's the same whenever she reads the words "Aceh," "Serambi Makkah," "Meulaboh," or anything about that land at the end of the archipelago, because they are all synonymous with one stark face: Sidan.

The memory of that face intrudes on her consciousness again. But it doesn't last long. It draws further and further away with the passage of time and the hardening of her scars. Everything has been surrendered, preserved in a crevice of time. Sidan is now a memory, a memory so beautiful that Firdaus only wants one like it forever. He occupies a throne in her heart, no one can move him or even try to detract from his glory. He is her eternal prince! Buried in eternal silence.

But because she still feels nervous alone in a crowd, she has to contact Adib to see if he is willing to pick her up at the airport. Unable to hide his surprise, Adib erupts in a joy that is tempered by caution and nerves. Certainly there's no way that Firdaus realizes he lied to her? Hopefully she hasn't discovered the truth—and if his secret is still safe, he can launch another attack to win her love.

"Firda! How long will you be in Aceh?"

"Only two days this time. But maybe at some point I will need to do a survey for my writing and I will stay longer. I've been so busy recently, Dib. Don't forget when I land."

She speaks so casually, evenly, and plainly; she doesn't even mention Sidan. Maybe Firdaus has truly forgotten him. Adib himself doesn't want to mention Sidan and bring back the past. He feels that the timing is right and his heart flashes with happiness and victory. He prepares gifts and surprises, but decides that since he only has the short time of two days, he will just try to get the conversation going. At the most, he will take her to a few local ethnic restaurants.

I will quench your thirst for Aceh, Firdaus! Don't worry. Sidan is not your only source of happiness here. There is me and many other delights that you must sample. Prepare your heart for a coming change. I will welcome your arrival with a carriage fit for a queen.

He grows more excited with each passing moment, but for some reason he also feels sick to his stomach, inflamed with restless anticipation.

He imagines Firdaus. Her beautiful round eyes, twinkling like falling stars over Lhoknga Beach. Her pair of thirsty lips, the peak of glorious beauty.

But a real man doesn't lose his head over that. But your eyebrows, your warm, plump cheeks like hamburgers on a platter. And your body.

That's why men suffer convulsive dreams when they are single. Inhaling the fragrant aromatherapy of a mermaid's body in their fantasies.

The minutes crawl by like a snail. Why is time moving so slowly? He wants to make the clock move as fast as his heart, which is bucking and running wild. It feels like he has been waiting for eight years. He's dripping with cold sweat. He needs to give himself another spray of Charles Jordan cologne on his wrists and hands, which will extend to greet the angel, and also his neck, in case Firdaus is willing to accept his embrace. Hopefully there won't be any Sharia police to spot them.

Adib: Where are you now, Firda?

Ah, her phone is still off. She must still be in the air.

The trip from Polonia to Banda only takes forty-five minutes. Firdaus is enjoying her complimentary snack while talking to the older woman sitting next to her. From her appearance, Firdaus knows she is a high-class woman, maybe the wife of a high-ranking official in Aceh.

All the brands she is wearing on her body are international. Indeed, Aceh is a global village.

"So you are just going to Aceh for an *arisan*, ma'am?"

Firdaus is amazed the woman would fly all this way for a monthly meeting among friends, a social gathering sweetened by a pot of money that everyone contributed to and would go to a different woman each month.

With an embarrassed whisper, the woman elaborates into Firdaus's ear. "Shh! Also to sample the young blood there and whatever else can be enjoyed in that city full of destruction, little sister! I like staying there. Only one of our children is living in the family home, to keep his father company."

Firdaus takes a closer look at the woman beside her, from the top of her head to the bottom of her heels, which are propped up on pumps as high as Tengkorak Hill. She looks to be a little over fifty, but she is still in good shape and all of the wrinkles in her face have been cleared away by some potent cream. Her eyes are wide, like a doe atop Seulawah Mountain. She is still full of vitality, which she aims at young men. She can arrange it with her phone, she says, then they can rendezvous at the same fancy restaurants where the wives of the high-ranking officials gather for their monthly *arisan*, cheerfully spending all their money on a good time.

Their husbands are busy with conferences, gatherings, urgent meetings night and day, because the funds from the regional government budget have to be used within the year—if they aren't, they lose what they haven't spent. The budget to buy a governor's car alone is probably in the billions, and that isn't even counting the cost of taking care of the car, household expenses, household items, health care, and official travel and services, which are also in the billions. And on top of that there is the maintenance of the officials' homes, the care of the household, operational support, vehicle repair, and gas.

"How long will you stay in Aceh, ma'am?"

"One week at the most. But we don't like to go far from Banda. You have to understand that we have to be thrifty with our fuel. Our funds are limited," she pouts. "For gas and oil we only get about one hundred and fifty million, for vehicle maintenance five hundred million, batteries and tires one hundred and fifty million."

Firdaus winces, startled. One hundred and fifty million for gas and oil? Maybe that is how much one of those women could get from winning their *arisan,* so she thinks it is very little. Maybe she has never gone to the refugee barracks, where the women had only received a survival ration of ninety-three thousand rupiah a month—and that had been in the early months after the tsunami before the aid stopped coming.

But just the high-heeled shoes alone that this woman is wearing probably cost at least seven hundred thousand. Her bag, six hundred thousand. Her dress, made from silk and lace, has to be two million. That is not counting the white-gold jewelry on her fingers, her arms, and her chest, which could total hundreds of millions.

And if you turn your head in her direction, you will smell the aroma of expensive perfume wafting off her body, as expensive as BLV, the price of Giorgio Armani. Don't ask about the credit and ATM cards in her wallet. In total she is walking around carrying thousands of gallons of tears of the women in the refugee camp.

In disbelief, Firdaus asks another question. "So are you or your husband from Aceh?"

"Both of us are. My husband is from Nagan Raya. I was born in Lamno. But a lot of our family lives in Jakarta. And for now two of our children are in college in Jakarta, so I am staying with them. We're renting an apartment in Taman Rasuna for the moment."

Lamno? Firdaus looks for a trace of blue in the woman's eyes but she can't find any, which means she is the descendent of Acehnese natives, not Portuguese. And Taman Rasuna? That's a luxury apartment complex for celebrities, whose yearly rental probably cost as much as it would to buy an entire house in Yogya. Maybe one of this woman's children was working as a film star while finishing up school, so that it wouldn't be difficult to afford to rent such an apartment.

"Wow! Taman Rasuna is expensive, though, isn't it, ma'am?"

"It sure is. But there's no other choice, little sister. Even though we only get a household budget of a little over one billion, we have to make do. We have to be frugal and save," she says, shaking her head and pouting again.

Firdaus is no longer having a heart attack hearing all these fantastical numbers. She begins to understand this woman from another perspective. Luckily, the woman shows absolutely no desire to ask anything about Firdaus, so Firdaus grows even more comfortable interviewing her. It will be good for comparative material in tomorrow's seminar.

She imagines the eyes of the *inong balee,* with bowed heads and stiff and swollen legs, not knowing where the world was headed. Then Admiral Keumalahayati, the first female admiral in the world, appears to open their solemn eyes to the blazing flame of jihad. Let's move! Advance, and look at the world with the eyes of justice! Let's chase out the thieves who steal life's treasures. Make a fist with your gentle hands, oh *inong balee*! Don't stay silent like angels who have lost their wings. Let's keep breathing the fierce breaths of our martyred husbands!

"Where do you live, little sister?"

Firdaus is startled back into the present.

"Umm . . . Lam Senia," she replies, just making up something.

Luckily, the plane is beginning its descent. Firdaus pretends to busy herself, looking through her bag. But as soon as she sees the airport and remembers that she will soon be walking on Acehnese ground, she grows antsy. No matter how, with all her might, she has tried to forget Sidan, the harder she tries, the more clearly she sees him in her mind's eye. Who on earth stole my sweetheart? Was it a woman like this one who stole him away? Giving him splendor with hot money from her husband?

No! Sidan is involved in something, but not with one of them. He is involved with life, with his revolutionary thoughts. Maybe he has found a secret volume whose pages have never been opened or seen by the eyes of the world, and he is reading it chapter by chapter to the audience, just like he used to recite tales in the Sunan Kalijaga auditorium. Maybe he needs to be alone. Maybe he is writing in a diary, sitting in a white tent at the foot of Blang Ske Mountain.

"Is someone picking you up, little sister?" asks the woman, who has walked with Firdaus from the gate.

"I have a friend coming. And you?"

"Probably our driver. My husband's always busy. Is that your friend?" she says, pointing at someone who is looking in their direction.

Firdaus looks where she was pointing. Adib isn't there, but she sees someone approaching, emerging from between the crowd of people waiting to pick up passengers. The sight of someone with long hair and Che Guevara eyes pierces her heart.

"Sidan!" she cries out in disbelief.

Then a noisy crowd descends. A figure, suddenly there among them, is sought and surrounded by journalists and their equipment. Cameras. The lights from their flashes swarm like fireflies around an arriving delegation. Apparently someone important has just arrived from Jakarta. The journalists are busy taking turns interviewing him. Surging, rising, and falling. Sidan is lost in the swirling waves and Firdaus cannot reach him.

She is stunned, rooted in place, frozen where she stands. Her eyes dart about, searching. Where has Sidan's shadow gone to? She forgets about the woman at her side, who is looking at Sidan and drooling, the blood of her second puberty rushing up to her scalp. She wants Firdaus to introduce her. But Firdaus is too distracted to notice. She doesn't even know if Sidan has seen her, or if it was really him that she saw. Maybe she should push through the crowd to find him?

But reticent with embarrassment, Firdaus doesn't move, hanging back until the time is right. All the while, her eyes don't stray for an instant from the rolling waves before her. Her heart blooms and rustles, buffeted by a wind of longing. She doesn't realize that there is someone standing behind her whose heart is also hissing, buffeted by a wind of jealousy and misfortune. He is looking at his friend there, that friend he wants to destroy, dancing with a deadly beauty in Firdaus's eyes. Who else but Adib Bahalwan?

He falters as he realizes what is going on. How could Sidan suddenly be here? Right when Firdaus arrived? Had they planned it? Or was it just a coincidence?

A coincidence that will make things worse for me. Firdaus must be waiting for Sidan forever; she doesn't care that I'm waiting for her. The fact is, her eyes have never moved an inch from Sidan, and I saw how Sidan was looking at her. He knew. They both knew. They must be waiting for each other. Damn!

Hurriedly Adib leaves, before everything becomes even more embarrassing for him. He just hopes Firdaus doesn't know the truth, that his lie has not been exposed. He decides to sneak away, to get far away from all the potential terrible outcomes. He doesn't realize the woman from the plane is drawn to his stricken face.

Bursting with curiosity, she says, "That man was strange, wasn't he? Like a spy from a phantom realm. Do you know him, little sister?"

"Who, ma'am? Which man?"

"The one who was lurking behind you. He was just here, but now he's over there."

Firdaus quickly turns her head, startled. She just sees a man's back, hurrying away. She has a vague sense, between recognizing and not, between remembering and forgetting. Her eyes sweep the entire space and she realizes she is still at the airport. Her brain starts to work again, the gears of her memory begin to turn. She remembers that Adib had promised to pick her up. Whose back was that, hurrying away?

"Adib! Wait!" she yells frantically.

But her voice only echoes in the cavern of her heart. She wants to run after him.

"He's already far away. So you know him, little sister?"

"He's my friend. He said he would pick me up."

"So then why did he leave you all in a hurry? I thought it was the one over there who was here to pick you up."

The one over there? Oh, did she mean Sidan? Firdaus remembers Sidan again and her eyes search for him. *Where did you go, Sidan? Where are you? Where is the crowd now?* There is no more crowd, no more waves. There is no Sidan, there is no important figure, there are no cameras with their flaring flashes. There is nothing but the glowing embers of longing and an orange silence. A longing that evokes shadows and dreams. *If only you were here to come get me with some poetry.*

"I'm here to pick you up, Firda."

"Sidan?"

"Yes, love. Come on, let's go."

"Where to?"

Yes. Where are we going, Sidan? Where will you take me? To the village where you were born? Where is it? I want to go to your house. Birds who sing their songs of longing fly home to their nest. Fish dance merrily while looking for a safe resting place. Ships dock at port. Planes land at the airport. Where can lovers stop to rest?

"We're going home. To the palace of my heart."

Firdaus is frantic.

The palace of your heart? Don't joke around, darling. I'm tired of playing with time. Tell me where we are going. Where is your house?

"Where?" Firdaus asks impatiently.

"It's not far from here, miss. About five kilometers," a voice replies, a woman with a name tag on her chest.

The name tag of a seminar organizer. Firdaus returns to her senses and blinks a few times, her heart pounding. She feels embarrassed and strange. She looks around again. There is nobody there to greet her and bring her out of the airport except the two organizers. Firdaus doesn't believe anything she has just seen.

But I'm not dreaming. They were just here. I felt their presence, I saw them with my own eyes.

She looks over her shoulder again and again, checking to see whether Sidan's aroma is still floating in the air, sending rain to quench the drought in her soul.

Meanwhile, at the far end of the airport parking lot, Sidan has idly opened his handicam and is smoking while flipping through the faces that show up on the screen. Suddenly, he chokes. Staring, stunned. It feels like his heart stops when his eyes stop on a face. Those beautiful, searching eyes—yearning and sad, as if they have been waiting restlessly for centuries.

"Firdaus?" he exclaims without understanding.

Was it real or only his imagination?

He checks the image's time stamp and is astonished.

Today, this hour? Meaning that Firdaus was at the airport, that she arrived with that group of officials? Meaning I just filmed her and I didn't even realize it? And I thought I was already crazy enough.

Helter-skelter, he runs back to the arrivals terminal. Searching desperately, darting, and struggling.

Where are you, Firdaus? Don't play hide and seek with me again, darling. I am too exhausted from all these games, I'm frazzled and weary. Come on, show me your face, angel. There's nothing else we have to wait for. You've come and I am here to greet you. With some blue poetry.

He checks the whole space, peering left and right. Grasping at all possibility and dreams. Scrutinizing everything. But there is nobody. He doesn't find anyone to greet him. Sidan is stunned. He collapses weakly into a chair, pounded by silence. Alone. Not understanding what game fate is playing. Shivering, solitary under the sun. Then his cell phone chirps.

Unknown: `birds return to their nests / marmots look`
`for their field / but where can lovers go`
`home to?`

At first he feels as if he is being taunted. But who else could that strange number belong to, contacting him without a word of greeting, if not Firdaus, daughter of Abdussalam?

Sidan jumps up, happy but unsure, practically convulsing.

I will chase you and I will shoot you! Oh no, no. I know you don't care for weapons. The truth is this: I will chase you and we will make love. Until death and doomsday, Firda! Where can lovers go home to?

Sidan almost faints.

True travelers in a world without shelter!

Indeed it is said that the rhythm of life is made up of arrivals and departures, not just in the airport, but everywhere. It's like the changing of the seasons. And yet, wherever they end up, lovers always find a way to meet and speak their heart to one another.

About the Author

 Abidah El Khalieqy was born in 1965 in Jombang, East Java. She graduated from an all-girls Persatuan Islam boarding school in Pasuruan and Sunan Kalijaga State Islamic University in Yogyakarta. She began to write in her youth and has had a productive career, publishing nine novels, most recently *Mimpi Anak Pulau* (*An Island Child's Dream*, 2013); two short story collections; and the poetry collection *Ibuku Laut Berkobar* (*My Mother Is the Shining Sea*, 1997). Her 2001 novel *Perempuan Berkalung Sorban* (*The Woman in the Turban*) was adapted for the screen and won several awards. *Geni Jora* (*Light of the Morning Star*, 2003) was judged Best Novel by the Jakarta Arts Council in 2003.

El Khalieqy's work gives a voice to women, including victims of polygamy and domestic violence, whom she feels are still often marginalized in Indonesia. Her work has been widely anthologized and has received numerous awards.

About the Translator

Photo © 2013 Sandra Angeline

Annie Tucker translates Indonesian fiction, prose, and poetry. Her work has been recognized by the PEN/ Heim Translation Fund and published in *The White Review*, *New York Times Magazine*, and *Words Without Borders*, among others. Her translation of Eka Kurniawan's novel *Beauty Is a Wound* was included on numerous "Books of the Year 2015" lists, received critical praise from *The Guardian*, the *Financial Times*, *The New Yorker*, and others, and was a *New York Times* Notable Book of 2015. She lives in Los Angeles.